Other books by Pat Estelle

The Stigma of Growing Old in America
The Challenge of Being a Woman
The Confessions of a Southerner

Angels
PLAY PIANOS

PAT ESTELLE

ISBN: 978-1-4834-3133-8 (sc)
ISBN: 978-1-4834-3132-1 (e)

Lulu Publishing Services rev. date: 05/14/2015

♪♫ *Chapter One*

Jimmy was small for his age, fourteen and just a little more than five feet tall. He weighed about ninety-five, maybe a hundred pounds. But small stature certainly didn't detract from his good looks. He had dark brown hair, an olive complexion and gray-green eyes; beautiful eyes, about the color of moss. There was a dimple in his chin, and almost always a smile on his face. Although his hands were small, what was more prominent and eye-catching were his perfectly shaped, long, slender fingers. Our mother told him when he was three years old that his long fingers meant he would be able to play a piano, and that turned out to be true. I can almost see him now, sitting there on that old piano stool, playing his little heart out.

That smile and those eyes were the first things that got your attention when you looked at Jimmy. And if he was talking to you it was hard to look away. His eyes could see into the very core of your being. At least that's what I thought; I was sure they could see into mine.

Jimmy was my brother, my sweet, lovable older brother. He was only two years older, but everybody said that he had qualities of a person who had lived a long time: wisdom, insight, good judgment and a big, big heart. Jimmy had other qualities as well, or gifts I should say, that weren't mentioned out loud for fear that people would brand him some kind of freak. And he certainly was not a freak. He was smarter than any person around, and that included the grown-ups. Jimmy knew more in his fourteen years than a lot of people would know in a lifetime.

That may sound silly, but it's the truth. He could sit on an old log down by the creek, holding his fishing pole and waiting for a fish to bite, and tell me all kinds of fascinating things as I sat there with him and listened intently. He would gaze into that water and tell me about every creature that lived there, and the ones that lived in the surrounding trees, as well. He knew what and who lived beyond that water and those trees. Jimmy could talk about people I'd never heard of, people who lived long ago in far away places. He learned a lot of those things from books, but some of it he just knew, and I don't know how he knew.

When our mother told him at age three that he would be able to play a piano, Jimmy said he'd wondered aloud how could he if he had no piano. But she assured him that he would get one, somehow, some way. And he did; it seemed like a miracle on his fifth birthday when our great-aunt Naomi gave Jimmy her old piano. He never had a single lesson, but learned to play practically any song he ever heard, by ear. I thought that was absolutely amazing. And he could sing, too; as our aunt would say, "prettier than a mockingbird."

And then there was me, Becca, the only other child of Elizabeth and Edward Johnson. As my daddy would say, just a prissy little girl, and I had no musical talent whatsoever. Frankly, I didn't think that I had any kind of talent at all, in spite of Jimmy's assurance that that was not true.

But Jimmy was gone now, and I could imagine his soul flying – no, it would be *soaring*. He would be singing too; his singing and piano playing would really be something to hear, and the piano would be a brand new one. He used to say that someday he would get a new Baby Grand.

Oh, how I was going to miss Jimmy! More than anyone could possibly know.

I just couldn't stop crying; I wanted to, and not because of my daddy's icy glare. I used to freeze in my tracks when he stared at me that way; now I didn't care, but I could tell that he was getting real mad at me. You see, he never liked to hear me or Jimmy cry. If he spanked us and we cried, then he'd spank us even harder until we stopped. The only way I could stop crying was to hold my breath while I ran to my room, about the only place where I could cry all I wanted to.

Jimmy never did cry much, but I remember one time when he was about eight or nine, he fell out of a tree and broke his arm. He really cried that day, and Daddy just acted awful, taunting Jimmy, "Oh, you little sissy! Smart boys like you aren't supposed to cry like thumb-sucking babies. Why can't you act like other boys, huh? You been mollycoddled too long by your mama, that's why!"

But my brother never seemed to be bothered by name-calling or criticism; if he was, he never did let on. In any case, criticism was not something usually directed toward Jimmy, except for that which seemed to spew so easily from the mouth of Edward Johnson. In fact, Jimmy was more often praised, commended, admired. And he deserved all of it; Jimmy was very special.

And now here I was returning from his funeral with Daddy, who never cared anything about Jimmy, or me either. At least that's how it seemed. He'd stopped by the hospital for a few minutes the day before Jimmy died. That was the first time I'd laid eyes on him in a long time. And then yesterday he called and said he'd be by to take me to the funeral. I wanted to tell him *no, that I wasn't going anywhere with him*, but Big Mama said maybe I better not do that. I've been staying with her and Papa while Mommy's in the hospital.

I made no bones about the fact that I didn't want to see Daddy. What I really wanted to do, since I was forced to go with him to the funeral, was to scream at him, hit and kick him until he was bloody and bruised. I wanted to tell him that it was his fault Jimmy was gone. But I didn't do any of those things. I kept my mouth shut, and my fists and my feet to myself, which was probably a good thing.

Why he had always been so mean to Jimmy, so critical of everything he said and did, is anyone's guess. I think, though, that being around Jimmy forced him to acknowledge his own weaknesses and flaws. And his ignorance; I figured out long ago that he wasn't very smart. I believe that he resented Jimmy for being everything he was not, for having so many of the qualities he lacked. Edward Johnson was a disagreeable man with a terrible temper, and didn't seem to have a bit of kindness or compassion for anyone. I don't think he should have been allowed to have the title of "Daddy." He had never behaved the way I thought one should; he was like a mean stranger who happened to live with us. Maybe I should have stopped calling him daddy a long time ago, and just called him plain ol' Edward instead. He wouldn't have liked that one little bit, not then and not now. But so what! He no longer has authority over me. His days of beating Jimmy are over, and I think they're over for me, too. I was bragging to myself, thinking that he better not try anything with me these days. Would I actually stand up to him? Well, you can be sure that I would've made a real effort.

If you knew him, you might understand why I felt that he never fulfilled his role as our daddy. And if you knew Jimmy, you would have an even harder time understanding how Edward Johnson could be *his* daddy. I didn't understand that myself!

Don't misunderstand me; I know where Jimmy came from, I just don't know why. You see, I think that he's much too smart, much too gifted, too kind, too caring and generous to be a part of Edward Johnson. Maybe he was some kind of miracle birth. So my question would be why it appears that some kids have been given the wrong parents here on earth? I think that God must have a good reason for doing those things, but it's a reason I'm quite sure I'll never know; it's a big mystery.

I was so happy to get back to Big Mama's house. Daddy didn't even get out of the truck, and all he said to me was, "Be good, Becca." I hadn't smelled whiskey on him, so I'm sure he was anxious to get a drink. That's probably why he was in such a hurry to leave, and I bet he had a bottle of whiskey or some beer hidden in the truck. He probably would start drinking before he got back home.

Big Mama and Papa, having just returned from the funeral, were sitting on the sofa, still in their good Sunday clothes. All of a sudden I began crying again, so hard that I was almost losing my breath. I ran to Big Mama, and she just held me close and sang a song about angels. When she finished the song, and my sobs had become mere whimpering and sniveling, she said, "Sweetheart, just let me go change my clothes and I'll be back in here and we can talk, we can sing, we can do whatever you want to do." She gently pushed me from her lap onto the sofa, where I sat until she returned.

It wasn't long before she was back in the living room, still looking sad, but putting on a brave smile as she said to me, "Now my sweet beautiful Becca, it's time for me to tell you a story. It's a true story about a wonderful family, their joys and sorrows, laughter and tears. But there were far more joys than sorrows, and more laughter than tears. Maybe we should call it the wonders of an angel named Jimmy.

"Although Jimmy's life was short, it was filled with excitement, adventure and mystery, the kind of things most people only dream about. He was brilliant and gifted with extraordinary abilities, some beyond our understanding. Compassion, kindness and generosity were only a few of his attributes. Jimmy will never be forgotten, not by his family, not by the hundreds of other people whose lives he touched. He brought us a kind of knowledge and insight that we never could have received from any other source. Surely Jimmy was a gift from God, on temporary loan just long enough for us to realize what we would've missed without him.

"But you, my darling Becca, are still here with us, a blessing for which we're all thankful. And I want you to know that I love you so very much. Now, maybe it's time for you to hear the story." Big Mama's voice was a little shaky and there were tears in her eyes, those big beautiful eyes, the color of blue that's hard to describe, maybe like the sky on one of its brightest and prettiest days.

"No, no, Big Mama, I can't listen to anything about Jimmy right now. Please, let's not talk about Jimmy, it just makes me too sad," I told her.

Her next words were spoken so softly that I could hardly hear them. She said, "My sweet, sweet Becca, it will be a long time before that sadness goes away, maybe never. But Jimmy would want us to keep smiling, to try to overcome sadness by remembering all the happy times we shared. So let's pretend that he's here with us, listening to the story. I believe that his spirit is here, and that somewhere he's watching and smiling. If we think of that, maybe we can smile just a little bit, too."

At first, I thought it was silly to pretend that Jimmy was here with us, but decided to go along with the idea. I wasn't smiling, though, not even a little bit. Then, in the blink of an eye, I was crying again. Only it wasn't just crying; I was bawling, worse than a baby. I couldn't even speak.

As she held me in her arms, trying to comfort me, Big Mama said in a trembling voice, because now she was crying too, "Oh, my precious little girl, we've lost the one who delighted us, enchanted us, regaled us with joy and laughter; he was a rare, unique treasure. Now there seems to be gloom and darkness. But we'll pray that it becomes easier one day. And it will; how would we manage, how would we survive if it didn't get easier? And we will survive, Becca!"

At last, while wishing with all my heart that Jimmy really was here, and trying my best to picture him sitting beside me, I managed to say, "Okay, Big Mama, we'll pretend that he's here, but I know I'll cry the whole time you're telling me the story – I don't think I can help it."

"You cry all you need to, Becca. But you must try to remember that even though you can't actually see your big brother, he'll be by your side if you need him or if you want to talk to him. You'll feel Jimmy's presence, I know you will."

Big Mama hugged me close to her for a minute. Then, with her heart breaking, she gave me her best smile, even as tears streamed down her cheeks. With my hand held tightly in hers, we slowly made our way out to the screened-in back porch and lay down on a big old fluffy featherbed.

❄ ❄ ❄ ❄ ❄

♩ *Chapter Two*

Elizabeth Bolin Johnson said that Friday, February 2, 1945, was cloudy, windy and bleak, and it was Groundhog Day. It was unlikely that a groundhog had seen his shadow on such a gloomy day. 'Course if you believed that those little creatures could predict the weather, then you would expect spring to be coming soon.

Elizabeth knew from the minute she woke up that morning that her baby would be born sometime during that day or that night. Naturally, she didn't know if it would be a boy or a girl, but had a few names ready for either one. Her husband had told her that the name made no difference to him, and expressed no desire to have a boy-child named after him. Her mother's suggestion for a girl was Norma Jean or Ruth Ann, and if it was a boy either James Ronald or David Alan would be good.

So on that cloudy and bleak Groundhog Day in 1945, James Ronald Johnson was born. He would forever after be called Jimmy, or Jimbo.

Elizabeth was only seventeen years old, and had been married to her husband, Edward Johnson, for almost a year when Jimmy was born. She had never given marriage much thought until her parents, Troy and Annette Bolin, had encouraged her to marry Edward after he'd asked them for "her hand in marriage." He did that before he'd even talked to Elizabeth about it. Her parents thought he was a good catch, saying he seemed like such a nice boy. Edward's family had a big farm, harvesting mostly cotton and soy beans. Supposedly they were well-thought-of out in the rural area where they lived, in a big, pretty house. The house had running water and electricity too, a luxury only a few people out in the country enjoyed. Very "well-off," according to Troy Bolin, Elizabeth's daddy.

Before getting married, Elizabeth and Edward hadn't really dated. Edward had come over to the house several times, and they had sat around and played checkers with Elizabeth's mother and daddy. One time Edward ate supper with them. But they had never even been alone together, except for a few minutes in the living room when everybody else was in the kitchen or some other part of the house. Actually, it was hard to be alone in Elizabeth's house. She had a younger sister, Amy, and two younger brothers, John and Tommy. They always seemed to be around interrupting whoever was talking, or interfering with whatever was going on.

Maybe that was one of the reasons Elizabeth had agreed to marry Edward at age sixteen; she was tired of being around all those people in a small, crowded house. She had no privacy, no time to herself, just worked around the house and on the farm. Her parents had had no objections when, at fifteen just after finishing the tenth grade, she told them she no longer wanted to go to school. She was hoping to get a job at McLaughlin's Dry Goods, the larger of only two department stores in Garden City. That was the closest town, about fourteen miles from their farm.

A few people living out there in the country worked at the shirt factory in Garden City, but Elizabeth didn't want to do that. She'd been told that it was really hard work, and that the building they worked in got hotter than Hades in the summer time. She didn't know how she'd get back and forth if she did get a job in town, but somehow she'd figure out a way if ever that became a reality.

Elizabeth didn't get the chance to apply for a job; the year she quit school she had to help with harvesting the crops. Their farm was very small compared to a farm like Edward's parents had.

But they usually did manage to gather a few bales of cotton, some soybeans and corn, making at least enough money to pay off a few bills and buy Elizabeth and the other kids a new pair of shoes, and a few clothes for school.

After she said yes to Edward's marriage proposal, Elizabeth started thinking that marriage would be a lot better than working in a department store, or working on the farm. She began to think of it as an adventure, a new and exciting life. She expected they would go on trips, go to county fairs, amusement parks, and maybe the circus. They'd go fishing, sit on the bank of the river and eat the picnic lunch she would have so carefully prepared. In the back of her mind she even imagined that some day Edward might buy her a horse of her very own; she loved horses.

On Sunday, March 12, 1944, Elizabeth had become Mrs. Edward Johnson. If she thought her life was bad before marriage, it didn't take too long for her to realize just how good she had had it; marriage was certainly no adventure. Or maybe it was, but a risky and hazardous one. She longed to be back with her mother and daddy, her sister and brothers. As a matter of fact, not too long after being married to Edward she began to think that life was about as bad as it could get. Edward Marcus Johnson was a big, big disappointment.

She had never for a minute believed that she was "in love" with Edward, but she did like him. He had been nice to her, and could sometimes say things that made her laugh. He was twenty-two years old, and nice-looking, too. Elizabeth considered herself a pretty good judge of who was nice-looking. Edward was about six feet tall, sort of skinny, had a lot of dark brown curly hair, and big blue eyes. She liked the fact that he always had his finger nails trimmed evenly and they were nice and clean. She was really pleased, had to smile to herself, when she saw him in dress pants and dress shoes, and he wasn't wearing white socks. She and her friends had laughed at the school principal for doing that.

Anxious to leave her boring life, she had thought, *what could be better than being married to a nice, handsome, hard-working man?* It hadn't occurred to Elizabeth that he might be a slobbering drunk, a real s.o.b. She had known Edward for a mere three months when they got married. By the time three months of marriage had passed, she was thinking, *what have I done, and will I ever be able to get out of this?*

Chapter Three

The first few weeks of marriage weren't bad. Edward was somewhat considerate of Elizabeth's lack of knowledge and experience about sex. She had been scared to death on the first night of what they called their honeymoon, and was pleased when Edward showed a gentleness that she would see only a few times in their life together. Although at the time she was thinking that their life together would be a "bed of roses" until "death do us part."

Even though she had known little or nothing about sexual intercourse, and for her it certainly was not the most favorite part of the honeymoon, she knew that was one of her duties as a wife. One little bit of a disappointment had been that Edward didn't carry her over the threshold into the hotel room in Garden City, where they stayed for two days and nights. It was Elizabeth's first time to stay in a hotel and she liked it. They ate meals in a café except for a time or two when Edward brought peanuts, candy bars and coca colas back to their room. Other than trips to the café, a few walks around town and going to a picture show, that room was where they spent their time.

After those two days at the hotel, Edward helped Elizabeth move her things into his parents' house. But that was only temporary. Three weeks later they moved out to a rural area that was about twelve miles from the town of Gillette. The house they moved into was owned by Edward's father. He told them they could live there rent-free if they would take care of the place. But it was quite a distance from his parents' home and that would be hard for Edward. He loved his mama and daddy and would really miss them. Still, Elizabeth had been optimistic and excited about the move, the new life.

Elizabeth didn't have much experience with cooking, but made every effort to learn the foods her husband liked to eat, and eventually did a pretty good job of preparing some of them. There were often many attempts before she was successful, but she believed in the old adage, *if at first you don't succeed, try, try again.* And oh, how she tried! Not only in cooking; she tried, tried, and kept trying over the years to please her husband, to make him happy.

Early on in the marriage, Edward was not too critical of Elizabeth's bungling in the kitchen, told her that it took a while to learn how to cook and that her cooking skills would improve. He encouraged her to ask his mother and her own mother questions when she needed help. But she didn't know how she was supposed to do that since she didn't have a telephone to call them, and they lived miles and miles away.

She'd seen his parents once and her mother only twice after three months of marriage. Didn't he realize that? Of course, she had no plans to bring it to his attention. She wanted to be as agreeable as possible and avoid any kind of conflict. She had quickly learned that Edward didn't want to hear any back-talk from her. He would fly off the handle over nothing. And he couldn't seem to tell when she was just joking or teasing; he'd get so angry, so teasing him was a habit she needed to break.

Elizabeth knew that she was sorely lacking when it came to domestic skills, but wasn't sure she was interested in learning more than what was absolutely necessary. Her mother had, on a few occasions, tried to teach her about cooking, sewing, even knitting and crocheting. When Elizabeth showed little interest, it was decided that she shouldn't be forced to do things she cared nothing about. Of course she and her siblings had chores to do around the house and farm, but when given a choice, she did outdoor work rather than the household duties. She had milked the cow, fed the chickens and pigs, and sometimes mowed the yard. Mowing was a hard job; pushing that old mower around the huge yard took hours.

What Elizabeth had liked most was to be playing softball or riding one of their horses; she could spend hours riding. The family had two that they used on the farm and they were real tame and gentle, perfect for the kids to ride. Now that she was married, Elizabeth had to give up horses, unless her dream of Edward some day buying her a horse came true, and that didn't seem likely. She guessed she'd have to give up softball, too.

It was a big disappointment for Elizabeth to learn her husband's true colors, because they were certainly not good. Edward wasted no time in wielding his control; he told Elizabeth what to do, how and when to do it. He was surly when her family visited, and Elizabeth guessed that he was sociable only with his beer-drinking buddies. Truth of the matter was that he just didn't seem to like people very much. Elizabeth might have been able to ignore those things, but couldn't ignore Edward's belligerent attitude, his explosive temper. On far too many occasions he would yell at her, curse and carry on about the silliest things.

Elizabeth's personality was the complete opposite of Edward's. She was easy-going, even tempered, just a warm, kind-hearted person. She sometimes had been the little "peace-maker" with her sister and brothers. Her mother often praised her for her patience with the younger siblings, even though they sometimes made her so angry. Most people who knew her would say that Elizabeth was a generous, thoughtful and caring person, and a lot of fun to be around. Her younger sister and two brothers would probably say the same thing, even though she had called them pests more than once. But she'd been seen playing gin rummy with John or checkers with Tommy on more than a few occasions. She and her sister Amy were close in age and had argued a lot, although there was no doubt that she loved her sister, and her brothers, too.

Unlike Elizabeth, Edward was an only child and appeared to have grown up always thinking of himself, not willing to make concessions. At age twelve or thirteen, he had made the decision not to become a farmer like his daddy. And of course his parents were willing to support him in whatever profession or career he chose, even though they hoped he'd change his mind as he grew older. During the few times Elizabeth had seen them together, his parents acted as if he were perfect in every way, especially his mother. She fussed over him like a mother hen with a baby chick, and Edward seemed to love every minute of it.

He now worked as an electrician at the Paper Mill in the town of Gillette; that was a job he really liked. After Edward and Elizabeth were married and moved out in the country not far from Gillette, Edward drove into work every day in a brand new pick-up truck that his daddy had bought for him.

He left home at six o'clock in the morning and returned home about 4:30 in the evening. That is, if he didn't decide to stop off with his buddies for a beer or two. He expected supper to be on the table by 6:00 p.m., or no later than 6:30. He would come in, sometimes take a bath, and then have a beer. After that, he was ready to eat his supper. It was the same routine, day in and day out. Nothing for Elizabeth to do except clean house, cook, wash and iron clothes.

For the first few weeks of their marriage, Edward had wanted to have sex almost every night, and sometimes during the day when he was at home. Elizabeth didn't particularly enjoy it, but being the ever-obedient wife she submitted without protest. She just hoped that Edward would tire of it after a while. And after a couple of months it did become less frequent, but no less aggressive and sometimes sadistic. There were times when she would grit her teeth to keep from crying out in pain.

From that sexual activity –– she couldn't bring herself to call it "making love" –– Elizabeth's hope was that she would conceive a child, and of course had been thrilled when she became pregnant. Having children had never been discussed, but wasn't there a tacit understanding; didn't everybody want to have kids, Edward included? Elizabeth hoped for only two, a boy and a girl.

She didn't know if she would be able to manage that, but she would try. Her mother had told her a few things she could do that would help prevent pregnancy, but she knew that none of them were fool-proof. And anyway, if she did have more than two, that would be all right. That is, if the years ahead with Edward would just go smoothly. She wanted to be a good mother and a good wife, too, but had begun thinking that the mothering part just might be a lot easier than the being-a-wife part. She didn't want to be a quitter, though; to give up so easily would be childish, she thought.

Chapter Four

Being cooped up in the house soon became too boring for Elizabeth, and she felt as if she had to get out and do something. She wanted to be outdoors more, or find something to occupy her time. Maybe she could grow a little garden; that was something to think about. And she just might one day venture down to that creek Edward had told her about. After all, she did like to fish. First, though, she'd have to ask him to get her a pole, lines and hooks, lures and all that. He might even go fishing with her some Saturday when he was off work. She didn't know, though, if he liked to fish. In fact, she'd never asked Edward what he liked to do, or if he had any hobbies.

She did remember that one time he'd mentioned that he liked to go deer hunting; maybe that was something they could do together. She'd been deer hunting a few times with her daddy and his brother, her Uncle Curt. She remembered being eleven the first time she went, and then a couple more times when she was twelve or thirteen. She'd never killed a deer, though, and didn't want to either. The truth was that Elizabeth could shoot okay, but didn't care that much for guns. Still, she thought it was fun to go hunting, sort of like camping out in the wilderness — just thick woods, not a real wilderness.

She missed her friends from school, although she'd never had any one special friend. With a pleasing personality, though, she was well-liked by most of her classmates. There had been two girls,

Susan and Vicky, who were nice and played on Elizabeth's softball team; she thought of them as friends. And there was a boy named Ralph that she'd gone hiking with twice. She went riding with him a few times, too; he liked horses as much as Elizabeth did. He was funny and could talk about all kinds of interesting things. But she'd had no contact with him or any of the others since she quit school.

Now she hoped to become friends with some of her neighbors. Houses were few and far between, so she would have to walk some distance if she wanted to meet them. While out in the yard looking around, though, she could see that one house looked no more than a quarter mile or so from hers, and that certainly wasn't too far to walk.

One bright, sunny afternoon, Elizabeth decided to wander around for a while; the dishes were done, the floors swept, the ironing finished. There wasn't much to do until it was time to start supper. So she decided to take a stroll down to that nearest neighbor.

As she reached the house, she could see that it was a white wood frame, and looked big from the outside. She'd glanced at it a couple of times when she and Edward had driven by, but it was some distance from the road. She had to walk up a long driveway before reaching the house. The yard was really kept up nicely, with a lot of flowers just starting to bloom. Everything looked so clean and fresh. A few hundred feet from the house was a barn-like structure which apparently was used as a garage; Elizabeth could see a big, dark blue pick-up truck inside.

She knocked and waited a few seconds before the door was opened. Standing there was a woman with the warmest smile Elizabeth had seen in quite a while. She appeared to be middle-aged, maybe close to fifty years old. She was tall, with salt-and-pepper hair, dressed in a loose-fitting white blouse, a long flared gray skirt, and her hair was tied up in a red bandanna.

"Well, come on in," the woman said, as she held open the door for Elizabeth to enter. "You're Elizabeth Johnson from down the road a ways, aren't you?"

"Yes ma'am," said Elizabeth. "I hope that I'm not intruding or inconveniencing you. I just wanted to stop by, introduce myself and say hello."

"Well, I'm so glad you did, and of course you're not intruding," the woman said. "I've been plannin' to come by there and see how y'all were doin'. But things have been out of whack; I had a bad cold, not feeling very well for about a week. My name's Mary Ann Butler; my husband, Frank, died about two and a half years ago and I'm here all by myself. Don't have any kids. So I'm just happy you decided to come by for a visit. Come on in and sit down. I'm just gonna run in the other room and put the rest of the clothes in the washin' machine.

"Sit down over there," she said, pointing to what appeared to be the living room, "and I'll be right back." From the other room she called out to Elizabeth, "Now you just sit tight, I'll be right there. I was loadin' the washin' machine when I came to the door. I'm tryin' to get bedspreads and things like that washed. I've already got my blankets on the clothes line airin' out."

She continued talking as she came back in and sat down on the sofa beside Elizabeth. "Frank and me were just sittin' on the back porch one Saturday afternoon, drinkin' iced tea, and watchin' the birds fly in and out of that little bird house he built for 'em, when all of a sudden Frank said, 'Mary Ann, something's wrong with me,' and he just keeled over, fell right onto the floor, out cold. 'Course we had no telephone – still don't, but I checked his pulse and it was real weak. So I ran out the door as fast as I could, down to old Mr. Clancy's house to use his telephone; couldn't drive there 'cause our truck had a flat tire. Mr. Clancy lives about a half-mile from here, maybe a little more.

"And the worst part of it all was that it probably took thirty-five minutes or more before a doctor from Gillette could get here, and by that time Frank was already gone. The doctor said it was a heart attack. Frank was only fifty-three years old; as a matter of fact, he'd just turned fifty-three a week before. He'd never been sick a day in his life.

"Well, listen to me, just carryin' on like a magpie. I'm gonna hush and give you a chance to say somethin'. I want to hear about your husband, where y'all are from, and all that."

"Well, Mrs. Butler, there's not a whole lot to tell," Elizabeth said. "I've been married almost two months. In fact, it'll be exactly eight weeks this coming Sunday. My husband's name is Edward Johnson and he works as an electrician at the Paper Mill in Gillette. He was living with his parents before we got married. They have a big farm; it's west of Gillette, a long way from here. Edward was already working at the Paper Mill, and it was quite a distance for him to drive. It's a lot easier for him now, being this close.

"But it gets pretty lonely for me with him working every day, and no friends or family close by. My parents live on a farm, too, just a few miles from Garden City. You probably know where that is, close to forty miles from here. I don't get to see them very often. I have a younger sister, Amy, who's thirteen. And I have two brothers; John is eleven and Tommy's eight. I miss them a lot, and if I think about it too much it makes me cry. It would be so nice if they lived closer."

Suddenly, Mary Ann Butler jumped up from her chair and said, "Goodness gracious, what kind of hostess am I! You must be thirsty. Can I get you a glass of iced tea or water maybe? Or you might like to have a coca cola; I've got some in the ice box. They'll be nice and cold. Now just tell me, what would you like? Then I want to hear more about you and your family."

Elizabeth had relaxed a little, but thought it might be too forward if she took something to drink. She said, "No ma'am, I wouldn't care for anything right now; thank you anyway. I need to be going pretty soon, and besides, I'm probably keeping you from your work."

"Aww, you are not. I want you to stay and visit for a while; I'm enjoyin' talkin' to you. Just tell me now if you change your mind about somethin' to drink. I know it's hard for you livin' out here in the country without your family and friends. Do you have any hobbies, things you really enjoy doin'? Do you like sewin', crochetin', things like that?"

"No ma'am," Elizabeth replied. "I can't sew or crochet. I've always been a tomboy; I like sports and outdoor things, horseback riding and playing softball. I like to listen to music too: Glenn Miller, Duke Ellington, Tommy Dorsey. My most favorite singers are Ella Fitzgerald, Patti Page, Doris Day and Nat King Cole; I love listening to them on the radio.

"As for my liking it here, I guess I really don't know yet. The reason Edward wanted to move out here was, first of all because the house and the few acres of land it's on belong to his daddy. I think he bought it in some kind of deal with a man who owed him money. But he told Edward that if he'd keep the place up and do some refurbishing of the house that we could live in it rent-free. The other reason that Edward chose this place was so he wouldn't be too far from the Paper Mill in Gillette – that's where he works. 'Course I told you that already, didn't I?"

Then Elizabeth got up from her chair and said, "Mrs. Butler, I guess I better be getting on home now. It won't be too long before I'll have to start supper, and Edward likes to have it ready on time. He usually gets home around 4:30 in the evening and wants to eat about an hour and a half or so after that. It was nice meeting you, and I hope you can come and visit me real soon. I would welcome your company anytime."

As she walked Elizabeth to the door, Mary Ann said, "I'm just so glad I got to meet you too, and I want you to call me Mary Ann, not Mrs. Butler; I would like that a whole lot better. And somethin' else I wanted to tell you is that I do a little painting, occasionally a portrait, and if you would let me, I'd like to do a portrait of you some day. I'm not all that good, and mostly I paint outdoor scenes, trees and flowers, that kind of thing. I even manage to sell a painting now and then." She gave Elizabeth a big grin, hugged her and said, "I'm also a certified midwife, so if you ever need me to deliver your babies, just let me know." That caused Elizabeth to blush. Then Mary Ann added, "Babies or not, you come on back soon."

As she walked home, Elizabeth wondered if Mary Ann guessed that she was expecting. Probably not; it was too soon for her to be showing even a little bit. She began to think that being several miles from town with a midwife close by would be real handy. She began skipping along, smiling to herself, anxious to tell Edward about her afternoon. She thought it would be so much fun to have a baby. They would read, play games, sing songs, dance and do all kinds of things. She could hardly wait!

She started supper when she got home, and was in a real good mood when Edward came in. She began telling him about visiting their neighbor, Mary Ann Butler, about her husband dying, how she was a midwife and a painter, but he didn't seem interested. Elizabeth thought at first he wasn't going to acknowledge the fact that she'd said anything, but finally he mumbled, "Well, don't you be spending all your time down there. Plenty here to keep you busy."

Edward probably intended for that to be a warning, but it wasn't going to work. She liked Mary Ann and hoped that they would become friends. If, and when, that happened she would spend as much time as she wanted visiting, just wouldn't say anything about it to Edward. All she had to do was see that the house was clean, the clothes were washed and ironed, and be at home in plenty of time to cook his supper. How would he know what she did the rest of the day?

And it would be so nice to have someone she could visit and talk to during the long months of her pregnancy. She hoped that the time would go by quickly, and that she would get through it without any problems. She was so anxious for that baby boy or baby girl to come into the world.

Fortunately for Elizabeth, there were no problems or complications, but she did gain a lot of weight and as the due date got closer, it was hard for her to get around.

Edward seemed to be a little more thoughtful and considerate of her during those last few months. He had even teased her about eating so much, saying he didn't know how she could consume so much food. She had smiled and said, "Remember, I'm eating for two."

Elizabeth had visited Mary Ann often until it became too hard for her to walk that far. Then Mary Ann had started coming down to check on her. Sometimes she would come in the morning and spend almost the entire day. Now and then she brought things that she'd cooked; it might be an entire meal that just had to be warmed up when Edward got home. She had been there several times when Edward came in and he would say hello, but not much more. Once in a while she tried to engage him in conversation, and didn't have much luck. But he wasn't rude to her or anything like that.

Mary Ann was so good to Elizabeth, and they spent a lot of time talking about babies. It was all pretty new to Elizabeth. At home when her brothers were little, she hadn't been too interested in what was going on with them. Now she was happy to be getting expert advice and suggestions from Mary Ann. She was overjoyed at the thought of having a baby and hoped so much that Edward would become more enthusiastic; right now, he just seemed indifferent.

Chapter Five

The birth of baby Jimmy was a glorious event for Elizabeth. He was delivered by Mary Ann, who had really become a good friend just the way Elizabeth had hoped.

Edward wasn't at home the night the baby was born; he was in town, drinking beer and playing pool. At least that's what he'd told Elizabeth when he came home, and there didn't seem to be any doubt since he reeked of beer and cigarette smoke. His only comment after seeing Jimmy was, "He's certainly a puny-lookin' little fellow; is he okay? Nothing's wrong with him, is there?" Mary Ann assured him that Jimmy was fine. After that, Edward went into the bathroom, took his bath and went to bed.

Elizabeth had been a little more than four months along when Edward had first taken her to the department store in Gillette to buy maternity clothes. Until then she wasn't showing much and was wearing long loose-fitting dresses. It was shortly after getting the maternity things that she had walked down to Mary Ann's and told her that she was expecting.

Mary Ann had been so excited at the news. It was as if the baby Elizabeth was expecting might be her very own grandchild. And Elizabeth would forever be grateful for having her around during that time. It would've been nice, of course, if her mother could have been there. But Elizabeth had understood why that just wasn't possible. It would have been too difficult for her mother to leave Amy and her brothers who were all in school.

Annette did make a few visits during Elizabeth's pregnancy, and again to see the baby a week after he was born. Her daddy and the kids also came that day to see Jimmy, and it was wonderful. They had such a good visit and Elizabeth was so happy to see all of them. It appeared to her that Amy, John and Tommy had grown a few inches since she had last seen them.

But it had been Mary Ann who was there when Jimmy was born, taking care of him and Elizabeth. She had even spent the first two nights right there with them, and ran back and forth from her house for a few weeks afterward.

The joy that Elizabeth experienced with her baby surpassed anything she was prepared for. She spent every minute she could with her precious Jimmy. He was a happy baby, wasn't fussy, seldom ever cried. Though very tiny, he appeared to be in perfect health. A few weeks after his birth, Elizabeth took Jimmy to be examined by a doctor who confirmed that he was as healthy as could be.

All mothers probably think that their baby is the prettiest, the brightest, the most lovable baby ever, but many would agree with Elizabeth that Jimmy certainly did seem to be special. He learned how to talk early, and how to walk months before the average baby walks. When he began talking, it wasn't gibberish; he usually spoke in complete sentences. And he was always smiling; he was just the jolliest, happiest baby you would ever want to see.

But Edward appeared to have little or no interest in Jimmy. He never picked him up, played with him or talked to him. He pretty much ignored the baby, seemed to resent him, and acted as if he were a burden that he didn't want to deal with. His actions were becoming more bizarre every day. And he was often verbally abusive, cursing a lot. He seemed to get mad so quickly, mostly about trivial things. If Elizabeth dropped a dish and it broke, he would carry on as if it had been fine china. He also began to criticize her housekeeping; it seemed that in his eyes she could do nothing right.

He didn't demand sex as often, but sometimes when he came home drunk he would just get on top of her and do what he wanted to do. Other times, if she wasn't already in bed when he came home, he would push her down on the sofa and rape her, except no one would dare call a husband forcing himself on his wife rape. But as far as she was concerned it was rape, because she would resist with all her might. He did use enough common sense and good judgment, though, to make sure that the baby was asleep in another room, for which Elizabeth was grateful. But soon she realized that resisting and saying no to Edward just didn't work; she was neither big enough nor strong enough to keep him off her. Eventually she just stopped trying; she knew it was smarter to lie there passively and try to think of other things, positive things. Thankfully, he usually finished quickly.

If it hadn't been for Mary Ann, Elizabeth didn't think she could've made it. Even though she was deliriously happy with Jimmy, she still sometimes became down and depressed because of the way Edward treated her and the baby.

At one point she even considered trying to take Jimmy and leave, although she didn't know where she would go. She had mentioned it to Mary Ann, but didn't tell her the whole story; not about how hateful Edward was acting, about his verbal abuse and his fits of anger. She did tell her that he showed no love for Jimmy, that it was only when yelling at him or spanking him that he even acknowledged Jimmy's presence. But no one had to be told that; it was obvious. She also told Mary Ann about him drinking too much.

But Mary Ann had talked her out of trying to leave, telling her that Edward might eventually show affection and love for Jimmy. And that maybe he was drinking more because things weren't going well at work. So Elizabeth stopped talking about it.

Actually, Mary Ann seemed to like Edward. He was always polite to her and sometimes would talk a little, but more often than not he would just go into the bedroom when she was around. Other times he would say that he was going for a walk, but Elizabeth knew that he kept whiskey in the little shed in back of the house, and that he would go in there and drink. She could sometimes smell it when he came in from his "walk." Of course he always had a supply of beer in the ice box, but hardly ever did he keep any other kind of liquor in the house.

It was easy to see that he was drinking more and more and behaving even more strangely. And one time when her parents were visiting, and Edward was at work, Elizabeth decided to talk to her mother about how unhappy she was and that she wanted to leave Edward.

Again, she just couldn't bring herself to go into all the details. She did tell her mother that he had a terrible temper, got mad and cursed a lot. And she told her that he didn't seem to care a thing about Jimmy, that he never held him, never played with him, never even talked to him unless he was yelling.

Annette had hugged Elizabeth and said, "Now sweetie, you need to think about this long and hard. You just can't expect marriage to be 'a bed of roses'. I can tell you first hand that it's not always what it's cracked up to be. You have to expect some problems; don't ever think that it's just fun and games."

Elizabeth started crying, and Annette said, "Oh, honey, it's gonna be all right. Things will get better. Edward's just not used to having a baby around the house. I think you should give him a little longer before you make some hasty decision. And besides, you've made a commitment, a promise before God that you'll 'love, honor and obey' and that's supposed to be 'until death do you part'." Then she smiled at Elizabeth and said, "Of course I don't like the idea of *obeying* anybody, and as you know, I pretty much don't do it."

Elizabeth wiped her eyes and couldn't help but smile a bit at what her mother had said. The mood had lightened somewhat and she was feeling better. "Okay, Mama, I just hope you're right, and that he will change. But the way things are going right now is not acceptable to me, and if they don't improve I'm gonna leave him. And I'm like you, that part about 'obeying' just doesn't sit well with me."

As an afterthought, Elizabeth added, "I want to try and save a little money if I can. Of course, any money I do save will have to come from what Edward gives me for groceries and other things that we need. But I hope to have some saved up if, and when, the rainy day does come."

They walked back into the living room where Elizabeth's daddy and her brother Tommy were playing with Jimmy. Clearly, they had fallen in love with that little fellow.

♪ Chapter Six

In spite of the problems with Edward, Elizabeth was happy when she discovered that she was pregnant again. She hoped for a girl this time — that would be perfect! She estimated that the baby would be born about three and a half months after Jimmy's second birthday. It probably wouldn't be so easy having two babies to take care of at the same time, but Jimmy was such a little grown-up in many ways; he was no trouble at all. And she was sure he would be potty-trained before the new baby arrived. Everything was going to work out perfectly.

Even though she was in an unhappy marriage with a man who showed no love for his child, Elizabeth continued to hope that Edward would eventually warm to his son. In the meantime, she thought Jimmy needed a sister or a brother and believed that she could give two children enough love, affection, and all the necessary ingredients for them to thrive and enjoy a happy, healthy life. It would be a joy, a pleasure to welcome into their lives another little boy or girl, even if she encountered difficulties along the way. She would make every effort to love her children unconditionally, teach, guide and discipline them.

Her joy and happiness now came from being in the presence of Jimmy, and that joy and happiness would surely double when there was a baby sister or brother. Jimmy was her pride and joy, but she would do her best never to show partiality or favoritism to either when the new baby arrived. She would try to give them equal attention, love and affection. Her Jimmy was still so small that he appeared to be younger than he actually was. It was possible that he might never grow to be a big person, although that couldn't be determined yet. He was thriving, was healthy, mentally and emotionally advanced beyond his age, so she wasn't going to worry about his small stature.

It was clear early on that Jimmy was an exceptional child, and not only in Elizabeth's judgment. Her mother, Annette, constantly reminded her that Jimmy was special, that his intelligence, his abilities far exceeded that of other babies his age.

He began walking at about seven months. It seemed as if he just suddenly went from crawling to walking without a long trial-and-error stage. Something else that surprised Elizabeth, and her mother as well, was that Jimmy began talking early. He knew quite a few words by the time he was a year old, but he was actually speaking in complete sentences by eighteen months; granted, they weren't very long sentences, but they were complete. Elizabeth's mother told her that she and her siblings had appeared to know only a few words before age two, and that it was difficult sometimes to even understand them.

Jimmy was also the little instructor, a miniature teacher when he was around other kids, and they didn't appear to resent that or consider him to be a little smart-aleck. Of course, he wasn't around kids very often. But on those few occasions, he wasn't overly aggressive or showing-off. It was clear, though, that there was a big difference between Jimmy and most other children his age. He just seemed to know things that others didn't, but was always patient and would repeat things over and over for them without frustration or anger. It was unfortunate that there were so few occasions when other children were around; there just weren't any little ones living near them.

Early on, Elizabeth had thought her baby boy was smarter because she read to him almost from the time he was born. And of course he was around adults most of the time. But she soon realized those things were only a part of it.

Sometimes Elizabeth was even a bit unnerved by her son's actions and the remarkable things he would say. At first it seemed unnatural for such a little fellow to know so much, and to see things others couldn't see. She refused, though, to think of his uniqueness as being in any way negative, and would not restrict or oppose his actions to the detriment of that uniqueness. She accepted the fact that he was just an unusual child, a special gift from God, and who was she to question that?

A few months into her second pregnancy, Elizabeth was astonished one day by what Jimmy said; it was evidence of his extraordinary ability to see things in the future, even at that early age. She'd heard stories about people who were called psychics or mediums, people who could see things before they happened, and those who could communicate with the dead, but she wasn't sure if she believed those things. Surely Jimmy wasn't a psychic, was he? But after what happened, she had little doubt that he possessed some kind of power outside the normal senses.

One day as he sat on Elizabeth's lap, both of them singing *Mary Had A Little Lamb* at the top of their lungs, Jimmy suddenly stopped and said, "Mommy, tell me about *Curly Locks.*" That was a poem Elizabeth's mother had recited to her, years ago when she was a child; she had loved that little poem, still did. It was written by James Whitcomb Riley, and Elizabeth had recently bought a book of his children's poems to read to Jimmy.

She had laughed at his mention of Curly Locks and asked him if he liked that more than *Mary Had a Little Lamb*. Jimmy's face lit up with that adorable smile, and he said, "*Curly Locks* will be special for my baby sister."

Elizabeth was so stunned that for a few seconds she just sat there, speechless. Jimmy was still a baby himself, barely two years old! And not a single word had been said to him about getting a baby sister or any baby for that matter. So how in the world could he possibly know that? And then Jimmy said, "When will she be here, Mommy?"

Elizabeth sat there, stupefied, at first not even knowing what to say. Surely Jimmy saw the surprise, the disbelief on her face; her eyes were probably so big that they appeared ready to pop out of her head. Finally she was able to question him, though she soon realized that it was a mystery she'd never understand, never solve. He was simply too young to give her a logical explanation. But from that point forward Elizabeth was convinced that the new baby would be a girl. Although shocked by such a revelation, she smiled with happiness as Jimmy clapped his hands, and said, "A baby sister."

She hugged him tightly and said, "But we'll have to wait a while for her to get here, Jimmy. It won't be too hard, though, waiting for someone so special." Jimmy just nodded and smiled.

♪ *Chapter Seven*

On Wednesday, May 28, 1947, Rebecca Lynn Johnson was born. It was another happy occasion for Elizabeth. Mary Ann was there for the delivery. Edward was there, too; that is, he was at home but sat outside on the porch during the couple hours of labor and the actual delivery. He even showed some interest in the new baby.

It was late in the evening when Rebecca was born and Jimmy had been in bed, fast asleep. But the following morning when he saw his baby sister it was clear that he absolutely adored her. He began calling her Becca, and eventually everyone called her that, never Rebecca.

Becca was a sweet baby, truly adorable, but cried a lot for her first few months, much more so than Jimmy ever did. She usually woke up a couple of times during the night crying, but would quiet down and go back to sleep if you walked her and sang her a song. Just feeding her was not always enough.

Elizabeth knew that it was not a good idea to compare Becca with Jimmy. And she would make a sincere effort not to do that. They were two individual babies; each was special in his or her own way and shouldn't be expected to behave exactly the same. But when Becca's sleep patterns began to change at about six or seven months, Elizabeth couldn't have been more pleased. Occasionally Becca would sleep through the night, and overall became a calmer, more contented baby.

Jimmy was in no way jealous or resentful of Becca. He played with her, talked to her, and even began reading to her when he was about three, and she wasn't quite a year. Actually, it wasn't clear if he was reading to Becca or if he was reciting the words from memory. However he did it wasn't that important as he sat there, book in hand, turning the pages always at the appropriate time.

Elizabeth believed that Jimmy really was reading the books to Becca. She believed that because by the time he was fifteen months old, he was able to say his ABC's and could make simple words from his alphabet blocks. She knew, of course, the fact that she'd been reading to him almost since the day he was born had helped. Nevertheless, she was so proud of him when she pointed to words in a book and he could tell her what they were.

And Jimmy was always curious about the content of the books. For example, he would ask his mother, "Where do the elephants live, Mommy?" and "Do the animals talk to each other?" She would answer all his questions to the best of her ability.

He would read aloud *The Three Little Pigs, Little Red Riding Hood, Henny Penny, Tales of Mother Goose,* or any number of other books as Becca sat still as a mouse, listening intently. At least that's how it appeared; it was as if she were completely mesmerized by her big brother.

Elizabeth was happy that both of her children liked books so much. And clearly, Becca loved it when Jimmy read to her; of course she loved anything that Jimmy did. When she had begun crawling, she would crawl or scoot around after him. And there was no doubt that he loved his little sister just as much, and thoroughly enjoyed playing with her or reading to her.

One day it became clear to Elizabeth that some of the books she'd read to Jimmy, and ones she now read to Becca were absolutely too violent. She realized that, even though written for children, *Henny Penny* was about one animal eating the heads off other animals. And in the book, *Little Red Riding Hood,* the wolf swallows a little girl and her grandmother, though eventually they're recovered from the wolf's belly, alive and well.

Of course the books were probably meant to convey some kind of message, a lesson for children to listen and obey their parents, and perhaps introduce them to the predators in the world. But Elizabeth felt that her children were too young for that. She began to search for other, more appropriate books. And there were plenty of those, too. Until the birth of her children, she hadn't known that so many children's books existed.

She had been a pretty avid reader as a child, was taken to the public library once in a while, but had never had the voracious appetite for books that Jimmy had.

On Saturdays when Edward was at home, he'd sometimes take Elizabeth and the children to the library in town before going to the store to buy groceries for the following week. The public library was where Jimmy really began to explore all kinds of new worlds through books.

When Elizabeth had a little extra money, she would buy the books he enjoyed most, the ones that were special to him. Most of the *Little Golden Books* could be purchased at the grocery store for .25 cents each. Eventually, Jimmy had accumulated a pretty big collection of those: *Little Red Hen, Poky Little Puppy, Saggy, Baggy Elephant* and more. Another book that both Jimmy and Becca came to love was one that was published the year Becca was born, called *Goodnight Moon,* and it was soon added to the children's collection. Both of them wanted to hear that story every night for at least a couple of years.

As Edward began to show a little interest in Becca, he paid a bit more attention to Jimmy, as well. Unfortunately, it was not always in a way that Elizabeth had hoped. It often led to spankings and verbal attacks that, in Elizabeth's mind, were totally uncalled for. Even the smallest infraction often resulted in Edward grabbing Jimmy up by one of his arms and spanking his bottom hard. Sometimes Jimmy cried, other times he didn't make a sound. Never once did he try to run from his daddy, nor did he try to free himself from the vise-like hold on his arm.

Elizabeth cringed when Edward spanked Jimmy, and had to bite her tongue to keep from yelling at him to stop it. She knew, of course, that children had to be disciplined and that an occasional spanking was probably necessary. But Jimmy was a well-behaved child, usually did what he was told without much resistance. That didn't mean, though, that his behavior was always exemplary. He was, in many ways, the typical little boy. He was rough-and-tumble, liked to play in the dirt, was curious about insects, frogs and snakes. He liked riding his tricycle, and playing with toy cars and trucks.

In other ways, Jimmy was far from typical. From the time he was just crawling around, Elizabeth could have a basket of eggs on the floor, or a jug of sun tea, tell him not to touch them and he wouldn't. His curiosity never extended to areas where he was told not to go. And unlike most babies, Jimmy had quite a long attention span. He would look directly into Elizabeth's eyes when she talked to him and seemed to be carefully listening to every word.

But Edward frequently spanked Jimmy for no good reason; in Elizabeth's eyes, seldom was there justification. Once, when Jimmy accidentally bumped into the coffee table and Edward's beer fell over, spilling onto the floor, he became furious. He began hitting Jimmy hard on his little bottom, over and over again, finally sending him to his bedroom. He told him to stay there until he decided to come and get him. After Jimmy was in his room, Elizabeth confronted Edward, telling him that he had been too harsh, that the spanking was much too severe.

That really set him off; Elizabeth was afraid that he was going to hit her, too. Instead, he shouted, "Mind your own damn business; you're letting that boy get away with any and everything, making him into a little sissy, sassy 'mama's boy' and I'm not going to stand for it." He stormed out of the house and didn't return until late that night.

Shortly after Edward left, Elizabeth told Jimmy that he could come out of his room. He said, "Mommy, I don't love daddy anymore." Elizabeth didn't know what to say, and just hugged him closely to her for a minute or two. It was breaking her heart to see him mistreated by his own daddy. She wished so much that Edward would show love and affection for his son. Why couldn't he just talk to him sometimes, play with him and take him places? Hearing Jimmy say, "I don't love daddy anymore" just about summed up how much Edward's lack of attention and love had affected him.

🎵 Chapter Eight

On February 2, 1950, Jimmy celebrated his fifth birthday and Becca pretended it was her birthday, too. Elizabeth had bought a couple of small gifts for her so that she wouldn't feel left out. But she liked the dump truck Jimmy received much more. It was clear that Jimmy loved that truck, but was willing to share, as he always did with his little sister.

There was no doubt, though, that the greatest joy for Jimmy on his birthday was when Elizabeth's Aunt Naomi came driving up in a truck with a piano in the back, and it was for him. There were two men with her aunt who unloaded the piano and set it up in the living room. The piano was old, had some scratches, and the veneer was peeling off in a couple of places. But it had been cleaned and polished, and still looked pretty good.

Jimmy was so excited that he could hardly contain himself. He ran to his great-aunt, hugging her and kissing her on the cheek over and over. Elizabeth was just as pleased; she told her aunt that was the nicest thing in the world she could have done.

After a moment's hesitation, Jimmy walked over to the piano and began touching the keys, and soon was playing a few notes. He wasn't eager to leave it when his mother insisted that he stop and eat some birthday cake with the rest of the family.

Before long, Elizabeth began to think that having the piano right there in the living room might not work out well; she realized that Jimmy would be spending a lot of time on that piano stool. The noise wouldn't bother her so much as it would Edward. That meant she would just have to rein Jimmy in when Edward was at home.

It was amazing how quickly Jimmy learned to play that piano. At first he would experiment with one or two fingers at a time, as if he wanted to be sure what sounds were possible from each and every key.

But soon he was playing a few simple little songs, and then one day, several weeks after getting the piano, Elizabeth heard him playing a song that had recently become popular on the radio, called *Mona Lisa*, by Nat King Cole. Of course on the radio it sounded as if there were a lot of different instruments playing, maybe an entire orchestra, but the sound that came from that old piano was just as beautiful, thought Elizabeth. Jimmy was sort of humming along, and now and then singing a few of the words. It made Elizabeth cry, but they were tears of joy.

Jimmy continued to practice on the piano, and was soon playing many songs he heard on the radio. His musical repertoire was growing every day; he could play a variety of songs, and he began to sing, more and more. He learned classical, country, popular, blues, and children's songs; a child prodigy, for sure.

When he played and sang *Tennessee Waltz*, those who heard it said it was as beautiful as Patti Page's version. He even knew when to substitute the word "him," for "her" as the friend "who stole my sweetheart from me." Elizabeth hadn't even noticed that the first time she heard him sing it. He also did a great job on *Sentimental Journey;* that had been a popular hit by Doris Day.

Becca would sit alongside Jimmy on the piano stool as he played *Mary Had A Little Lamb, The Farmer In The Dell, Twinkle, Twinkle, Little Star,* and other songs and nursery rhymes. He didn't know a tune for the poem called *Curly Locks,* which he said was especially for Becca. Instead of singing it, he would recite the poem and do his own little background music. Becca loved it!

One day Jimmy asked his mother if she might be able to buy some recordings with music from either of the two composers,

Wolfgang Amadeus Mozart or Johann Sebastian Bach. That surprised Elizabeth, and especially since he had pronounced their full names. She knew nothing about classical music, and asked where he'd heard about the two composers. She didn't think he had heard their music on the radio. Jimmy said that he read about them one day at the public library in Gillette.

She assured him that she would find records as soon as possible, having no idea how in the world she would do that. But she told him that they would first have to buy a record player, and promised that she would talk to his daddy about it at the right time, hoping that could be real soon.

One afternoon when Mary Ann stopped by for a visit, Elizabeth asked if she had any idea where she might buy records with the music of Mozart or Bach. And she could hardly believe her ears when Mary Ann said that she had recordings of music from both of those classical composers. She went on to say that she would loan them to Jimmy, along with her record player. Well, Elizabeth thought that was too much, and told her that she couldn't allow her to do that. But Mary Ann insisted that it would only be a loan until Jimmy had his own records and record player. Elizabeth gratefully gave in.

A couple days later, on a Saturday when Edward was at home, Mary Ann came by and asked him if he would help her put the record player and records in either her truck or his, so they could bring them to Jimmy. She was hoping Edward would show a little enthusiasm since Jimmy was so excited about having records to play on a real record player. Edward agreed to go with her, but seemed indifferent and had little to say as he walked with her to his truck and drove down to her house. His mood was a little different when he saw the record player.

"This is really nice," he said to Mary Ann. "And with those speakers and all I bet it sounds good, a heck of a lot better than our radio. I'm hoping that I can buy one of these pretty soon, and that way we won't have to keep yours very long."

"Well, I want y'all to keep it just as long as you want. I know Jimmy will love it, Becca too," Mary Ann told him. "Why, Edward, you just might enjoy listenin' to some of those records yourself. You do like country music, don't you?"

"Oh, yes ma'am, I like country music, I like it a lot. Hank Williams is my favorite singer; there're several Grand Old Opry singers that I enjoy listening to."

He suddenly seemed in a hurry to get back to his house, and said, "Well, let's get going here. It's gonna be hard to keep Jimmy away from this, but I'll see that he takes good care of it."

"Oh, my goodness, Edward, don't you worry for one minute about that. I know he'll take care of it – that's just the way that little fellow is – takes care of his and Becca's toys and everything. He's just an unusual child, a special one, don't you agree, Edward?"

"Well, yeah, I guess he is. Sometimes, though, I think his mama spoils him," he said as he and Mary Ann got in the truck and drove back to his house.

When Jimmy saw what they brought back, he was so excited he began hopping up and down as if he were on a pogo stick. He was almost as happy as when he was given the piano. Edward set up the player on a small table he had made to hold some of his tools and things; it had a little compartment like a magazine rack on the lower part. He had seemed proud of himself when he told Mary Ann that he had the perfect place for the record player and the records. And Elizabeth was pleased when he began to help Jimmy with the records. He was in a rare mood, almost a playful one, and that was very unusual.

Mary Ann had brought records other than Bach and Mozart, and she stayed a while to see what Jimmy would do after hearing some of the music. There were some country music singers: Hank Williams, Ernest Tubb, Eddy Arnold and there was a record of Muddy Waters, who was well known for blues. The classical ones got Jimmy's attention. After listening to one of Mozart's piano concertos several times, he thought he was ready to try it on the piano. Edward didn't complain at having to listen to a kind of music that he'd probably never heard before. Finally, though, he went outside, no doubt to have a drink of whiskey. Elizabeth knew that he had already had a couple of beers.

When Jimmy gave his mother a big smile and said, "I want to try and play that one," Mary Ann stopped the record player. Once Jimmy began to play, he did what Elizabeth thought was a pretty good job. He made a few obvious mistakes; they had to be pretty obvious for her to even notice. Of course he had no accompaniment, and naturally it didn't sound like the record. She and Becca sat beside him on the piano stool as he played it a second time, and she thought he did an even better job. Elizabeth started to think that one day her son might be a famous pianist.

Mary Ann could hardly believe her ears as she sat there listening to Jimmy play. After he finished, she went and gave him a big hug and told him how beautiful it sounded. She later told Elizabeth that she had never before seen anything like that; it was incredible that he could listen to something a few times, then sit down and play it. A true musical prodigy, if ever there was one!

It was probably an hour and a half before Edward came back in the house. Clearly, he had been drinking. He walked over to Jimmy, reached down and took his little hands in his own and said, not unkindly, "It's time now to stop playing, that's enough for today." Jimmy looked as if he might cry, but he didn't. He took Becca by the hand, went out the back door and out into the yard to play.

Mary Ann said that it was time for her to be getting on home and she left a few minutes later. But first she went to the back yard and said bye to the children. Jimmy thanked her again for the records and record player she had loaned him, and he gave her a big hug and a kiss. Clearly, he was still excited about everything.

Edward went to the ice box and got himself a beer, then put one of the Hank Williams' songs on the record player, and sat in the living room just humming along with the music. He was so unpredictable; he might sit there for the rest of the evening, drinking beer and never saying a word. Or he just might begin to curse and carry on about some imagined slight from a fellow worker at the Paper Mill. He might even explode over something the kids had or hadn't done a week ago. There was just no telling what he might do, and that was cause for concern. Elizabeth came close to uttering aloud the question, *am I afraid of my own husband?*

♫ Chapter Nine

Elizabeth desperately wanted to get out of her present situation. She knew it was not good for the children, and thought that they would be better off living without a father than with one who mistreated them. Of course she knew that it was preferable for children to have both parents, but she felt that it might be more damaging when one was abusive toward his children. She didn't like the idea of a divorce, and knew that many people would disapprove, her mother and daddy among them. But clearly that seemed like the only solution. Jimmy and Becca were entitled to a happy childhood in a wholesome, loving home, and that was not the kind they were living in. Elizabeth felt compelled to find something better, make a safer environment for them.

Occasionally, Edward would demonstrate that he could still behave like a human being should, especially, Elizabeth thought, when he began to spend a little time with Becca. He would actually pick her up once in a while and play with her. However, she was not exempt from his outbursts, his terrible temper. He would swat her bottom good and hard if she didn't stop crying when he told her, or for other things like accidentally spilling her milk in her high chair. And he would spank her if she pulled open a drawer or cabinet door.

Lately he was drinking more and more, which made his already combative personality even worse. It was becoming rare for him to come home directly from work; when he did come in, more often than not he was drunk.

Jimmy would be starting school in September, and Elizabeth was determined to take the kids and leave Edward before then. She wanted to move far away to a place where they couldn't be found. But where in the world would that be, and how was it going to become a reality?

She made the decision once again to talk to her friend and neighbor, Mary Ann Butler, about her predicament; this time she would tell her the whole story. After she and the children walked down to Mary Ann's one afternoon, she settled Jimmy and Becca out in the backyard where they could play. Then she pored her heart out to Mary Ann.

The words came easily as she began telling her how Edward had ignored Jimmy from the day he was born, acting as if he cared nothing for their child. She said that any attention their son received from his daddy was by way of a spanking or an angry verbal attack over something inconsequential. She told her that Edward was angry most of the time, and that he often ranted and raved over some minor incident; he cursed and called her names. She said his drinking was excessive and that he rarely came home directly from work, that when he did come in he was often staggering drunk. And she wondered how he could get up every morning and go to work after nights like that, but he did.

Mary Ann listened to every word, and obviously was concerned for Elizabeth. She told her that they would just have to come up with some solution. But at the moment there didn't seem to be one because neither Elizabeth nor Mary Ann could think of a place for her to go. It had to be a place where Edward couldn't find her. Mary Ann assured her that together they would figure out a way, and suggested that, in the meantime, if Edward became ugly and abusive that she should just walk out with the kids and come down to her house.

Elizabeth racked her brain trying to think of a solution to her problem, and suddenly she thought about her Aunt Naomi, her aunt who had given Jimmy the piano. She lived in Morriston, more than sixty-five miles away. She was sure that Naomi would let her and the kids stay there for a while until she could figure out something else. It was not likely that Edward would think of Elizabeth hiding out there. Thinking that she would get a letter out to her aunt in the next day's mail, she began feeling somewhat relieved. Maybe her prayers were going to be answered, she thought, as she began writing the letter to her aunt. It was as if a heavy weight was being lifted from her shoulders. First thing the following day, she would put the letter in the mail box out by the side of the road so that the postman could pick it up. Her aunt would probably receive it in three or four days. She would try to wait patiently for an answer.

Elizabeth wondered how things could have reached this point. She'd been married a little more than six years, only twenty-two years old with two wonderful children, but had a husband who was either crazy or just plain mean. She wasn't sure which.

Chapter Ten

After Edward left for work the following day and Elizabeth had given the kids their breakfast and got them dressed for the day, she walked with them out to the mailbox. She carefully placed the letter she had written into the box and raised the flag so that the postman would stop, even if there was no mail for them.

She and the children spent the day doing the things they normally did, reading, having lunch, then playing in the yard. Elizabeth put Jimmy and Becca into the little red wagon and pulled them around for a while. Becca loved riding in the wagon, but Jimmy always wanted to get out and pull it himself. He could do a pretty good job of pulling Becca around. Finally, it was nap time for everybody, and after that, time to start cooking supper.

The routine was much the same every day, but that was probably good for the children to have a routine, a schedule. While Elizabeth cooked supper, Jimmy played the piano for a while and Becca played on her little rocking horse. But 4:30 came and went, and there was no sign of Edward. Of course that was no surprise because these days, more often than not, he was coming home late. After she and the children ate their supper, she cleaned up the kitchen, putting the food in the oven to keep it warm. Edward might want to eat when he came in; she just never knew any more what he would do.

After Becca and Jimmy had their baths, heard *Goodnight Moon* and part of *Peter Rabbit,* both of them were sound asleep. Elizabeth looked at a couple of magazines for a while and then went to bed.

It was like a part of her dream when she heard Jimmy say, "Wake up, Mommy, wake up, Daddy's hurt and we need to help him." When she opened her eyes, there stood Jimmy at the side of her bed, looking terribly distraught. As she began to fully realize what he was telling her, she jumped out of bed and ran into the living room, thinking she'd find Edward, drunk, having fallen or something. But he was no where to be seen, and his truck was not outside.

In her efforts to get more information from Jimmy, she finally realized that he had actually had some kind of vision, not just a dream. What should she do? No phone and no transportation! Finally, though, she was able to think rationally; she knew that she had to go to Mary Ann's and ask her to drive her into Gillette and on to the hospital. That's probably where Edward would be if he had had a wreck in his truck. But then she decided it would be more practical, and possibly avoid delays, if she made some inquiries by simply telephoning the hospital. First, though, she should probably call Edward's parents; they had a telephone and if there had been an accident the hospital or the police would most likely have called them. She knew she had to hurry and get to a telephone some way.

She remembered Mary Ann talking about Mr. Clancy, who lived about a half mile from her, having a telephone. But Elizabeth had only met the man one time, and that was just briefly. She decided it would be best to go by and ask Mary Ann if she would go with her to Mr. Clancy's. She hurriedly dressed Becca, Jimmy and herself, and then headed for Mary Ann's house.

At first, Elizabeth tried to carry both children in her arms and run, but that was too much weight. She put Jimmy down and told him to run as fast as he could. Becca was laughing, thinking it was a lot of fun, even though it was the middle of the night and dark outside. But a flashlight and the full moon made it possible to see the road clearly.

Elizabeth wondered if she was being foolish, that possibly nothing had happened to Edward. Maybe Jimmy was just having a bad dream and unable to distinguish it from reality. No, she couldn't think like that! She was absolutely certain that something bad had happened to Edward, and knew she must hurry and find out what it was.

She was out of breath when they reached Mary Ann's house. There were no lights on inside, but she began knocking frantically until Mary Ann finally came to the door. She was in her nightgown, looking all disheveled, and clearly was frightened when she saw Elizabeth and the kids. She opened the door to let them in, and her words were a frantic shriek, "What's wrong, Elizabeth? What's happened?"

"Oh, Mary Ann, I don't know; Edward might have been in an accident, but there's no time to explain," Elizabeth said. "Can you take me to Mr. Clancy's so I can call the hospital or Edward's parents? Jimmy had some kind of vision and says that his daddy's hurt, and I have to believe it's true. Please, can we go to Mr. Clancy's?"

"Of course we can; just let me get dressed. It'll only take a minute," and Mary Ann left for the bedroom. She was back and ready to go in no time.

Jimmy was calm, but Becca was beginning to suspect that something bad was happening, and she started to cry as they rushed out to Mary Ann's truck. The motor wouldn't turn over when she tried to start it, and Elizabeth was about to panic. She silently prayed that the truck would start, and after a couple more attempts by Mary Ann, it finally did. *Thank you, Jesus,* Elizabeth said out loud.

"Amen to that," said Mary Ann, and off they went.

It only took a couple of minutes to reach Mr. Clancy's house. Elizabeth was starting to feel terrible, knowing that they were going to wake him from a sound sleep. But she was reassured by Mary Ann's presence.

Mary Ann made a beeline to the front door, Elizabeth and the kids following. She began furiously pounding, and the door opened right away. Mr. Clancy stood there, looking somewhat alarmed. He was a handsome older man, maybe sixty-five or seventy, a head full of gray hair. It didn't appear that he'd been sleeping; he looked hale and hearty standing there in his pajamas and robe.

"My goodness, Mary Ann, what's wrong? Y'all come on in. Hello there baby girl," Mr. Clancy said, as he chucked Becca under her chin, and patted the top of Jimmy's head.

"Mr. Clancy, you remember Elizabeth Johnson who lives down the road from me. And that's Becca and Jimmy," she said, pointing to the children. "We have reason to believe that something bad has happened to Elizabeth's husband and we need to use your telephone, if that's all right?"

"Why of course, it's all right. You know where it is, over there on that table. Just go right ahead. And yes, I do remember Elizabeth; such a charming young lady." He looked at her and said, "I do hope there's nothing seriously wrong. Should I make some hot chocolate for Becca and Jimmy while you two make the calls?" Elizabeth was discombobulated, but still able to think: *what a nice man, and so proper, enunciating his words with no hint of a southern accent, though he did use the term y'all.*

"No, no, Mr. Clancy, don't do that right now," Mary Ann said. "We may have to leave right away if we find out Edward's in the hospital. Elizabeth is going to call his parents first, and see if they've heard anything. They would likely be the first ones to be notified if he's been injured and is in the hospital, since they have a telephone. 'Course if they haven't heard anything, this is really gonna upset 'em. But that just can't be helped."

Elizabeth got the operator, gave her the Johnson's telephone number, and waited. It didn't take long for the call to go through. She identified herself when Rose Johnson, Edward's mother, answered the phone. It was immediately clear after a brief greeting from Rose, that she had received bad news about Edward.

49

Her tone of voice was not particularly friendly; that's what Elizabeth thought on all the other occasions when she'd seen her or talked to her. It was pretty clear that Rose Johnson didn't care much for Elizabeth. Right now, though, that didn't matter. Rose began by saying they had received a telephone call from a Gillette policeman about a half hour ago telling them Edward had been seriously injured in an automobile accident.

Suddenly, she paused and said, "Elizabeth, are you calling because you heard about the accident; if so, how in the world did you find out so quickly? The policeman said Edward was unconscious and they had found our telephone number on the back of his driver's license. He wouldn't even have known Edward had a wife or where you lived. That's strange. Where are you calling from; you don't have a telephone now, do you?"

"Mrs. Johnson, I'm calling from a neighbor's house; Jimmy had some kind of dream, a premonition or something. I'll try to explain that to you later. But please, just tell me what happened to Edward; what are his injuries? Is he going to be all right? Is he in Gillette General? I'll have my neighbor drive me there."

"Yes, Elizabeth, he's in Gillette General Hospital, and we don't know what his injuries are, but the policeman said it was clear that they were serious. He suggested that we go to the hospital as soon as possible, and we were just getting ready to leave. And if your neighbor can take you, it probably would be a good idea for you to get there as soon as you can. Just pray, Elizabeth; that's all any of us can do right now."

Elizabeth began to cry, but managed to say, "Of course I'll pray, and I'll leave for the hospital right away. I'll see you there, Mrs. Johnson. Bye, now."

She hung up the telephone, turned to Mr. Clancy and thanked him for the use of his phone. She and Mary Ann grabbed the kids and rushed to the truck. She was so glad when Becca fell asleep in her lap. Jimmy just sat quietly beside his mother, at one time looking up at her and saying, "He'll be okay, Mommy, Daddy is going to be okay."

Elizabeth knew that she would have to speak to Jimmy about all this at some point, find out how he knew that his daddy had been hurt. She hoped that he could tell her; did he sense what was happening, or did he see it in his mind's eye? It was not something she wanted to deal with, but knew she would have to, sooner or later.

♫ Chapter Eleven

Neither Mary Ann nor Elizabeth knew exactly how far it was to Gillette, but probably no more than twelve or fourteen miles. However, it was a narrow, gravel road, and their progress was slowed several times when they got behind some slow-poke driver. It was simply too risky to try and pass on the narrow road with the deep ditches on either side. It was just barely wide enough when two cars met; one of them would have to pull to the road's edge and stop, allowing the oncoming car to squeak by safely.

At last they reached the hospital. Since no children were allowed in patients' rooms, Mary Ann said she'd keep Becca and Jimmy in the Waiting Room or they might go to the cafeteria and get something; maybe some hot chocolate, if the cafeteria was still open. She told Elizabeth to look for them in one place or the other when she was ready to go. Mary Ann was so good with the children, and they loved her. Becca was awake now, but both children would probably fall asleep in a little while. After all, it was close to midnight. It had been about ten o'clock when Jimmy woke Elizabeth. It seemed like a long time ago, not just a couple of hours.

Elizabeth decided the best way to find out where Edward was would be to ask first at the Information Desk. When she gave her name and the name of her husband who was the patient, she was asked to wait there a moment. The Information lady made a quick telephone call and then asked Elizabeth to sit down and wait for a few minutes; she said that someone wanted to talk to her.

Her first thought was, Oh *Dear Lord, Edward has died, and they're sending someone in here to tell me.* But that wasn't what the policeman who approached her had to say. He looked ill-at-ease as he sat down in a chair alongside Elizabeth. He kept folding and unfolding his arms, then took out a pen and a little notebook from his pocket. He was tall, muscular, no older than Elizabeth but already had a receding hairline.

The policeman began by saying, "Ma'am, I'm Officer Thomas Martin. I was expecting Mr. and Mrs. Clarence Johnson, the parents of the injured man. I just spoke to Rose Johnson on the telephone; she said she was his mother, and that she and her husband would be here as soon as possible. Are you a relative, ma'am?"

"Yes, I'm Edward Johnson's wife; my name is Elizabeth. I've spoken with Edward's parents and they will be here shortly. In the meantime, please tell me what happened, is my husband all right? He's not dead, is he?"

"No ma'am, your husband is not dead, and from the information I've been given, he'll pull through. It's my understanding that he has two broken legs, a broken arm and possibly some internal injuries. Of course you'll be able to get more information from the medical staff. They have him in Surgery right now, and there's just no telling how long he'll be there. Unfortunately, that means you can't see him for some time, and I would like to talk to you about the accident, if you think you're feeling up to it. If not, we can wait until tomorrow when maybe you're a bit more settled. Do you think you feel like talking to me now? I've asked permission to use a conference room where it's quiet if you think you're okay.

"Mrs. Johnson, this is not a job I like, and I want to say, first of all, that I'm terribly sorry about what has happened; I sincerely hope your husband will be fine. But I have to tell you some things that I know won't be easy for you to hear."

Elizabeth couldn't imagine what would be worse than what he'd said already: that Edward had two broken legs, a broken arm and maybe some internal injuries. She couldn't hold back the tears as she said to the policeman. "Yes sir, I'm okay. I can't imagine what you have to tell me that is so bad, but I want to hear it now."

"Okay, ma'am, let's go down the hall here where it's nice and quiet, much more private. Would you like to have a cup of coffee or something to drink? I can get something for you if you want."

Elizabeth just wanted him to stop beating around the bush and tell her what was going on. She said to him, "No sir, I'm fine. I would like to get this over with as soon as possible."

The policeman led Elizabeth a few feet down a hallway and into a big room with a long table and a number of chairs. He told her to just sit wherever she would be most comfortable. She chose a seat where she could look out a window. Of course there was nothing to see except the lights of other buildings. But it gave her a feeling that the world was still turning round and round and maybe soon she could be a part of it once again.

Right now Elizabeth felt all alone, lost, helpless. Of course she knew that her friend, Mary Ann, was nearby with Jimmy and Becca, and that was somewhat reassuring. She was concerned, though, about what the policeman had said: *that it wasn't going to be easy for her to hear some of the things he had to say.* She wondered what in the world that could mean, and thought, *do I really want to hear this? Maybe I should have waited 'til tomorrow.*

What the policeman said next brought her out of her reverie. "I won't mince words, Mrs. Johnson. We have reason to believe that your husband was drunk when he had the accident. He was out on County Road 51, which you probably know is a dangerous road to drive on, just two lanes, one north and one south, and a lot of curves, not too easy to maneuver even when you're sober. Along most of that road, there's not even a shoulder.

"It appears that your husband lost control of his truck, went across a ditch and slammed right into a tree. There was a passenger in the truck with your husband, a young woman. We've been able to identify her as Sharon Hamilton, a waitress who works in the lounge at the Red Roof Inn; that's a big hotel here in Gillette. The sad part, Mrs. Johnson, is that Sharon Hamilton died as a result of the accident; she was pronounced dead shortly after she was brought into the hospital."

Elizabeth gasped, seemed to have difficulty breathing. Then she began sobbing, fumbling in her purse until she found some tissue. Her next words were almost inaudible, "No, surely that can't be true. Oh, my God, that can't be true, can it? That poor, poor woman; I'm so sorry. How could something like this happen? I must be in a bad dream, a nightmare. Oh, dear Lord! Are you telling me, officer, that a woman is dead because Edward was driving drunk?

"What an unbearable shock that must be for her family and friends," Elizabeth said, tears rolling down her cheeks. "But, Officer Martin, what was she doing with my husband? I don't understand."

Suddenly it hit Elizabeth like a ton of bricks, and she realized how ridiculous, how naïve she must sound to the policeman! Clearly, the reason the woman had been with Edward was because they were having some kind of illicit affair. She was embarrassed beyond words, and said to the officer, "Sir, I'm sorry for asking such a stupid question. Generally I'm not so simple-minded, so slow to catch on to things. I can assure you, though, that I'm now seeing the picture quite clearly; there's no need for you to tell me what he was doing with the woman."

"Well, ma'am, if you'll permit me to say so, I didn't think for one minute that you were simple-minded. And don't be embarrassed; naturally, you wouldn't have expected something like this. I'm sure you must be stunned by it all." Just then he reached over and patted Elizabeth's shoulder, saying, "I'm so sorry."

She was more than stunned, could hardly take it all in, and began to wonder how long it had been going on. She knew he'd been staying out late, drinking a lot, but thought he was with his buddies. She'd never for a minute entertained the idea that he was running around with other women. That seemed so out of character for Edward. But you never really know a person, she decided, even if you're married to him.

Elizabeth just sat quietly for a couple of minutes, wondering why Edward would do a thing like that. She guessed that he probably didn't care anything about her. But she believed that she'd done her best to be a good wife: learned how to cook his favorite foods, dressed as nice as she could, wore make-up and fixed her hair the way he liked it. She knew she wasn't real pretty, but thought that as she had gotten older she could be considered attractive. She was almost as tall as Edward, had long brown hair that had some natural curl, but wasn't real curly. Her eyes were greenish brown, and her daddy had once told her that she had a cute little nose. And never was there a visible ounce of fat on her body except when she was pregnant. She sometimes thought that she might even be too skinny. Maybe it was the sex thing that caused Edward to stray; she felt pretty sure that she'd failed, big time, in the bedroom.

Elizabeth looked at the officer and asked, "How did you find out that the two of them were romantically involved? And please don't call me ma'am; just call me Elizabeth."

The officer gave her a timid smile, saying, "Well, Elizabeth, as soon as we were able to identify the woman – she had a driver's license with an address in Gillette – we went to her home. It was a boarding house. The manager, a lady who runs the place, said that Sharon Hamilton had lived there about eight months, but didn't know much about her. However, she was able to tell me that Sharon worked at the Red Roof Inn. Then I went there to try and get more information from her employer.

"Her boss said that Sharon had worked there for six months, that she was a real good employee and well-liked by everyone. He said that Edward had been coming there for some time, and that it was probably a month ago when he began taking Sharon home after her shift ended. It soon became clear to everyone working with Sharon that she and Edward were boy-friend, girl-friend.

"Sharon wasn't married, and apparently no one knew that Edward was, so they all thought it was just a normal relationship, no reason for them to think otherwise. Her boss told me that Sharon was twenty-one years old. We were able to obtain her parents' address and telephone number from her personnel records at the Red Roof Inn, but so far we haven't been able to reach them. It was the bartender there at the lounge who told me that Edward had been drinking quite a bit last night before he and Sharon left, although he couldn't say with any certainty exactly how much he drank.

"Now, I guess that about wraps things up. 'Course we still have more to do, but I don't think we'll have to bother you any more. Again, I want to tell you how sorry I am about all this, and certainly hope that things will work out for the best. Undoubtedly, this is very, very difficult for you. One more thing I'd like to tell you, Elizabeth," he said her first name shyly, as if it might not be acceptable, "if you need assistance in any way, there are some social services that may be available to you at little or no cost: things like transportation to and from the hospital, child-care services, that kind of thing. If you'll stop by the Information Desk before you leave, they can provide you with more details.

"And as far as your husband is concerned, I seriously doubt that any charges will be filed against him. However, to be perfectly honest with you, we were at first sure that there was some kind of criminal negligence involved here. I'm now more convinced that negligence or drunk driving would be hard to prove in a court of law. I expect that your husband is being punished enough, and will be for some time, more so than the law would be capable of doing."

The police officer got up from his chair, looked at Elizabeth and said, "You take care of yourself, Elizabeth. If you just go back to the Information Desk, they'll be able to tell you if your husband is out of Surgery, and when you can see him. But please feel free to sit in here as long as you like." He reached out and shook her hand, saying, "I want you to take my card and if I can help you in any way, please let me know. Would you do that, Elizabeth?"

She told him that she would. He gave her a small business card, leaving her to sit there alone and think about everything that had happened in the last few hours.

It was almost more than she could grasp. She did know, however, that the plan she'd been attempting to devise that would enable her to take the children and leave Edward would now have to be put on hold, maybe indefinitely. At this moment she was more concerned about his well-being; how bad were his injuries, would he recover or ever be able to resume a normal life again? Or would she, herself, ever be able to resume a normal life?

♪♫ Chapter Twelve

Elizabeth didn't know how long she sat in that conference room, thinking, praying, wondering what to do next. She realized that, even though deeply concerned about Edward's present condition, she was extremely angry at him. He had, almost since the time she'd married him, been verbally abusive, inconsiderate, obstinate and controlling, but she had truly wanted the marriage to work. Then when Jimmy came along, Edward practically ignored his existence, spanked him for no good reason, never played with him or talked to him, showed no love for his son. He had been a little more attentive to Becca, but still was far from being an ideal father.

Now, adding fuel to the fire, he had been running around with another woman, and she just might not be the first one. In Elizabeth's mind that was proof enough that he really didn't care about her or their children. He probably was the type of man who should never have married; a family was not what Edward wanted or needed.

Slowly, Elizabeth made her way back to the Information Desk to get the latest word on Edward and whether or not she could see him now. As she passed the Waiting Room, she saw Edward's parents sitting there and went over to greet them.

Rose Johnson immediately began asking questions: "Have you seen Edward yet? What have they told you about his condition? We've been here more than a half hour and haven't been able to find out anything except that he's still in Surgery. What have they told you, Elizabeth?"

Elizabeth was at first hesitant, then said, "Mrs. Johnson, a policeman has been talking to me, explaining what happened and giving me details of the accident. It's very upsetting and right now I'm just not in the mood to discuss everything the officer told me. As far as Edward's injuries, he has a broken arm, two broken legs and possibly some internal injuries. However, a doctor did tell the officer that Edward would make it, that even though his injuries were very serious none of them appeared to be life-threatening. We can all be thankful for that. Now, I'm going to ask if it's likely that we can see him anytime soon. If not, I'll take the children home. They need to get some rest, and so do I.

"I'll ask my friend, Mary Ann, to drive me back to the hospital sometime tomorrow, or I should say later today; it seems I've lost all track of time. She and the kids are probably still upstairs in the cafeteria. I plan to call my mother and ask if she can come and stay at our house for a few days and take care of Jimmy and Becca. Then I'll be able to go to and from the hospital; I'm sure Mary Ann will drive me. I don't mean to appear rude, but if you'll excuse me now, I just can't talk about this anymore." She kept her emotions in check as she walked away, headed for the Information Desk.

The person at the Information Desk made a quick telephone call, then told Elizabeth that Edward was still in Surgery, but probably would be out soon. After that he would go to the Recovery room until he was awake. It might be some time yet before Elizabeth could see him.

She thanked the woman and went back to tell Edward's parents. She also told them she was leaving, repeating what she'd told them a few minutes before, that she would return later in the day. The Johnsons said they would stay at the hospital. They didn't mention wanting to see their grandkids, Becca and Jimmy. Of course that didn't surprise Elizabeth. They were not doting grandparents. Jimmy was five years old, Becca three, and they had seen them maybe once or twice a year since their birth.

60

But regardless of her past feelings toward Rose and Clarence Johnson, Elizabeth now felt deep sorrow for them.

She soon found Mary Ann, Jimmy and Becca in the cafeteria. Becca was sound asleep in Mary Ann's lap and Jimmy was sitting in a chair, looking very sleepy himself. Briefly, she explained the situation as they went downstairs. There was no sign of Mr. and Mrs. Johnson anywhere. Elizabeth saw no reason to search all over the place in order that they might see their grandchildren. They could have stayed in the Waiting Room for a few more minutes. *Did they even want to see Jimmy and Becca?* That was a thought Elizabeth would keep to herself. She, Mary Ann and the kids walked out of the hospital.

When they reached her house, Elizabeth asked Mary Ann to come in for a little while. Then after she got the kids in bed, she began to tell Mary Ann how grateful she was for all her help.

Mary Ann said, "Well, I'm just happy I could help you out a little. And I'll be back down here this afternoon to drive you to the hospital. I'll entertain Becca and Jimmy while you see Edward. Everything's gonna work out for the best, Elizabeth, even though it probably doesn't seem like it right now. You have to try and keep your chin up, girl. Edward's gonna be okay and eventually things will get back to normal, just you wait and see. Easy for me to say, I know, but worryin' won't help things a bit."

As Mary Ann walked to the door, she said, "I'll be back to get you this afternoon; try to get some rest if you can."

Elizabeth began crying and said, "Oh, Mary Ann, I feel like screaming, running away, maybe jumping off a bridge. I just don't know what I'm going to do. I don't think I can go through all this. I'm so angry at Edward, but I'm also sad for him."

Mary Ann put her arms around Elizabeth and held her for a few minutes as she wept, making sounds of such emotional pain. It was hard for Mary Ann to keep her own emotions in check. Finally, Elizabeth pulled away and said, "I'm all right now. Thank you so much for everything."

She stood in the doorway and watched Mary Ann drive away, thinking what a wonderful friend she'd turned out to be. What would she do without her? Of course she was a lot older than Elizabeth and dispensed advice and counsel freely, sometimes assuming the role of a second mother. But she was smart, caring and generous; also zany, amusing and witty. Mary Ann had a simple, uncomplicated attitude about life, believing that each person was in charge of his or her own destiny.

Elizabeth had been so thankful for her presence last night when all the trouble started. Of course, she wished very much that her mother could have been with her. And she hoped that she would be soon. Elizabeth's plan was to telephone her later when she got back into Gillette, and ask her to come and stay for a while during Edward's recovery. But in the meantime she would lean on Mary Ann as she had done so many times in the past few years.

Chapter Thirteen

It was about one o'clock in the afternoon when Elizabeth and Mary Ann, along with Becca and Jimmy, drove back into Gillette. When they reached the hospital, Mary Ann said she was going to drive around for a while with the children and probably take them to a nearby park she was familiar with. She said they would return in a couple of hours and would wait for Elizabeth in the Waiting Room.

Elizabeth was extremely nervous and anxious as she approached the Information Desk once again. There was a different lady there. After asking about Edward and if she could see him, she was given the floor and room number.

Now was the moment; how would she handle this? Of course Edward might not even be conscious, but whatever shape he was in she would have to consider the pain he was going through, how he must be suffering. She would need to put her own pain aside for the time being.

Elizabeth walked into his room and the first thing she saw was Mr. and Mrs. Johnson, sitting in chairs across from Edward's bed. They both appeared to be asleep. Then she looked at Edward, and was shocked. Elizabeth had thought she was prepared for the worst, but nothing could have prepared her for what she saw. There was Edward – at least she assumed that it was Edward – lying there with a face swollen beyond recognition, bruises everywhere that bandages weren't visible. He had tubes and wires attached to seemingly every orifice of his body, both legs in casts, outside the bed covers; also his left arm was in a cast. Elizabeth couldn't even tell if he was breathing.

She ran from the room, sobbing uncontrollably. On her way down the hall she was stopped by a nurse, who asked Elizabeth if she could help her. When she got no answer, the nurse simply led the unresponsive Elizabeth into an empty room and told her to sit down and try to relax, that she would get a doctor to help her. Elizabeth began to protest, trying to explain to the nurse what was wrong, in the best way she could between sobs. She felt so bad for poor Edward, and she was helpless to change anything.

The nurse was extremely kind and understanding, and after Elizabeth had calmed down a little, she told her to stay there for a few minutes, that she would be right back. In no more than a couple of minutes the nurse was back with a pill and a little paper cup of water. She told Elizabeth the name of the medication, and that it would calm her nerves after twenty or thirty minutes. The nurse said that she should stay in the room until she was feeling better, then she could return to her husband's room. She gave Elizabeth a little hug and said, "Now hon, you're going to be all right. Just sit here and try to relax. I'm going to be back in a few minutes and check on you." She gave Elizabeth a big smile as she walked out of the room.

It was only a short time before the nurse returned. Elizabeth had dozed for a few minutes, but heard the nurse come into the room. She heard her talking to someone, looked up and saw that a doctor was with her. The doctor told Elizabeth that he would just like to check and see if she was feeling okay before she went to see her husband. She assured him that she was fine, but he asked her a few questions, took her pulse, and then checked her blood pressure and listened to her heart. He said he was just making sure that everything was in working order. When he finished, the doctor smiled at Elizabeth and told her that now he was convinced she really was fine. He walked out of the room, but the nurse stayed and chatted for a while. A few minutes later they walked together down to Edward's room. At the door, the nurse patted Elizabeth's arm and said she'd be okay.

Bravely, she walked in and stood at the foot of the bed for a few minutes. Then Rose Johnson woke up, acknowledged Elizabeth's presence and quietly began filling her in on what had developed since she'd left the hospital earlier in the morning.

She began by saying, "We talked to Edward's doctor and he said his spleen was ruptured and had to be removed. I'm not sure I understand what the removal of the spleen will mean to his overall well-being, but other than that they found no internal bleeding or injury to other organs. There was also a very deep gash in the upper left thigh, and his doctor said that would have to be carefully monitored; they'll want to make sure it doesn't become infected. But the doctor feels certain that Edward will be fine eventually, even though it will be a long healing process, especially with so many broken bones. He wasn't sure about the length of time he'll have to spend in the hospital, but said it might even be a couple of months."

Elizabeth said nothing for a few seconds as she tried to take it all in. Then, "Has Edward been awake at all? Have you been able to speak to him?"

With tears now streaming down her cheeks, it was more difficult for Rose Johnson to speak, but she managed to say, "No, he apparently was awake for a minute or two at some point, according to one of the nurses. But he's been asleep since we've been in the room. We were told that with the anesthesia and other medication he had received that he might be asleep for some time, that we probably shouldn't count on him being awake and alert for a day or two."

There were no additional chairs in the room, so Elizabeth just stood for some time before saying to the Johnsons, "I'll be back in a little while," and walked out of the room, straight downstairs and out of the hospital. She had seen a café nearby and walked there to see about a pay telephone. There might have been one in the hospital, but first she would need to get some change in order to make a call.

As she neared the café she spotted a public telephone booth just a few feet from the entrance. She went into the café, sat down at the counter and asked for a cup of coffee when the waitress greeted her. She saw slices of pie in a glass case, and asked the waitress what kind they were. She decided on chocolate. The coffee and pie seemed to perk her up a little, give her some badly needed energy.

When she was finished, Elizabeth paid the cashier, then asked if she could have some quarters and dimes for a couple of one-dollar bills. She told her she needed change to make a telephone call. The cashier gave Elizabeth six quarters and five dimes.

She went into the telephone booth, closed the door and was about to sit down on the little bench, but noticed that it was covered in crumbs. She took a couple of tissues from her purse and wiped the seat, then from a little zipped pocket she took out a piece of paper where she had written down her mother's telephone number. She placed a dime into the coin slot, dialed the operator and gave her the number. The operator told her to deposit ninety more cents for three minutes; she put the money into the appropriate slots.

When her mother answered, Elizabeth began crying, but her mother recognized her voice immediately when she said, "Mama, it's me."

"Lizzie, what's wrong, honey?" her mother asked. She was the only one who had ever called her by that nickname. But when she was about ten or eleven years old, Elizabeth had heard the story of the infamous Lizzie Borden who had been accused of murdering her father and stepmother with a hatchet. It was then that she asked her mother not to call her Lizzie anymore. But occasionally it just slipped out, as it had done now. It didn't matter, though; she was just so glad to hear her mother's voice.

"Mama, can you come and stay with me for a week or two?" Elizabeth asked her mother after explaining about Edward's accident, and telling her that she needed her to take care of Becca and Jimmy for a while. Before she could finish, the operator broke in to the conversation to tell her that she had to deposit thirty cents for another minute. Elizabeth's mother asked the operator to reverse the charges and put them on her telephone bill. The operator agreed, and they continued talking, but Elizabeth didn't say a word to her mother about Edward being with a woman who had died in the accident. She would get around to telling her that at some point.

Her mother told Elizabeth that of course she would come, but that she would have to bring Tommy. Elizabeth's sister, Amy, was now eighteen and her brother, John, was sixteen, so it would be okay for them to stay at home with their daddy, but she thought Tommy, at age thirteen, should come along with her. Of course there was no school now, so that would work out fine. And Elizabeth thought that it would be a good opportunity for Becca and Jimmy to get to know their Uncle Tommy a little better. Her mother said that she would have Elizabeth's daddy drive her and Tommy there the following day.

They said goodbye and Elizabeth hung up, left the telephone booth and walked back to the hospital. She went directly to Edward's room where he was still asleep or unconscious, she didn't know which. His parents were still sitting there. She told them that she had telephoned her mother and that she'd be coming the next day to take care of the children. That would allow her to travel to and from the hospital, and Jimmy and Becca would be in good hands.

The Johnsons said they were going to drive to their home, get a few clothes and other things they would need, and return the next day. Their plan was to stay in a hotel there in Gillette, at least for a week or two, so they would be close to Edward while he was hospitalized.

Elizabeth told them that she was going to go ahead and leave, wait downstairs for her friend to return with Becca and Jimmy. She explained that they would probably be there soon since Mary Ann had said they would return in a couple of hours. It had now been a little more than two hours since she left with the children.

It was important that Elizabeth find out the name of the doctor treating Edward. She really wanted to talk to him, and wandered over to the Nurses Station after leaving Edward's room. After getting the name of his doctor, she asked a nurse when would be the best time to talk to him. The nurse explained that he usually made his rounds about eight o'clock in the morning, and that would be her best opportunity to speak with him. But Elizabeth didn't know if she would be able to get back to the hospital so early; at least, not for the next couple of days. After her mother arrived, she could ask Mary Ann to take her to the hospital early one morning. Even though Edward's parents had told her what the doctor said to them, Elizabeth still was anxious to get more detailed information, how long Edward might be in the hospital, would he be okay without a spleen, and if he would ever be able to walk normally again, things like that.

♪ *Chapter Fourteen*

Elizabeth was so happy when her mother arrived. Her daddy and all the kids were with her, but only Tommy would be staying. The entire family had arrived in late afternoon and her daddy, Amy and John stayed for only a couple of hours, then headed back home.

Becca and Jimmy had raced out to the truck to see their Big Mama and Papa the minute they drove up. Their grandmother didn't seem to mind the name of "Big Mama." When the children were old enough to understand, Elizabeth had explained to them that Annette was her very own mama, and told them that if they wanted they could call her mama, too. It was Jimmy's idea to call her Big Mama, and it had absolutely nothing to do with her physical size. As a matter of fact, Elizabeth's mother was a small woman, probably wouldn't weigh more than 110 pounds soaking wet. The name had stuck, and it was just Papa for their grandfather. They called Edward's parents Ma-Maw and Pa-Paw.

Elizabeth wished so much that both sets of grandparents lived close by so the children could see them often. She thought it was important for children to know their grandparents. There was no question that her mother and daddy loved Becca and Jimmy very much, and would have liked to spend more time with them. However, she just couldn't be sure how Edward's parents felt about the kids. Thus far, they hadn't openly demonstrated much affection toward them. Of course it might be that they just weren't demonstrative with their love and affection. And, too, they had only been around them a very few times; it might be different if they saw them more often.

Right now, she was just pleased that at least one grandmother would be spending some time with them, and with her; she loved her mother dearly. And it was great that Tommy came along; he would be a big help with Jimmy and Becca. Elizabeth would be away at the hospital or taking care of other things much of the time, but would feel comfortable leaving the children with her mother and brother. It was clear that Tommy liked playing with them, and the kids were absolutely thrilled to have him there.

The day after Annette Bolin arrived at Elizabeth's house she began to take over cooking and a lot of other chores so that Elizabeth would be free to go to and from the hospital. Annette could tell that her daughter was worried and upset, besides being run down and exhausted. She told Elizabeth how glad she was that she had a good neighbor like Mary Ann. Annette had met Mary Ann a few times before on visits to Elizabeth's house, and really liked her; they seemed to have some common interests, a lot to talk about. Also, they were close to the same age. She didn't know Mary Ann's exact age, but her best guess was forty-five, maybe fifty. It wasn't easy to tell by her physical appearance, but forty-five or fifty was based on things she talked about, references she made, and years that certain events occurred. Annette would be forty-six years old in just a couple of months.

During the first few days of their visit, Elizabeth learned a lot of things about her young brother that she hadn't even known. Of course he had only been seven years old when she left home. He was real easy going and funny too, always telling some kind of silly little joke, and he loved to tease. She discovered, too, that he liked to whittle. A day or two after his arrival, he found some wood and began making wooden toys for the kids, did a good job too. He whittled out a little choo-choo train, a perfect little horse and a wooden car. Elizabeth told him she didn't know that he was so talented, and really bragged about what all he could do with his pocket knife and a piece of wood. He obviously was pleased at hearing that.

Elizabeth had begun to check the mailbox every day after she'd get home from visiting Edward at the hospital, thinking she might hear from her Aunt Naomi. Of course it might be too soon to get a reply to her own letter, but she wanted to try and keep her mother from seeing it when it did come. She didn't want to have to explain it all, not just yet. She knew it would now be impossible to leave while Edward was recovering. She still wanted a divorce, but to take the kids and leave now would be impossible. Her plan to start Jimmy in a school in some other town would have to be postponed.

It was about a month before school would begin in Gillette, and she and Jimmy had talked about him being away all day when it started. So far, the idea of school was intriguing for him; he was anxious to go. But Becca wasn't at all excited about Jimmy going off to school in a few more weeks. She wanted him to stay right where he always was, at home with her, playing, reading and doing fun things. Elizabeth had done her best to explain to Becca that kids had to go to school, and there they would learn all kinds of new and interesting things, besides meeting other kids and having lots of fun.

She had told Becca that it wouldn't be too long before she, too, would be going to school. That bit of information did nothing to pacify her, and sometimes she would cry when she talked about Jimmy "going away." Jimmy also did his best to reassure her, telling her that he would be home early enough every day for them to continue playing and doing lots of things together. He told her that mommy had promised that when they got a little older, she'd take both of them fishing down at the old creek. Now that was something for Becca to look forward to. She talked about that creek a lot, and the thought of going there to fish cheered her up a little.

Elizabeth knew that not only was it going to be hard for Becca when Jimmy started school, but for her as well. She would miss him terribly, and knew that it would take some time before she would get used to it, and probably longer for Becca. She wasn't sure now about many things, but knew that she would get Jimmy to school every day, regardless of what other problems she was faced with. And from the looks of things, there were plenty of problems ahead. She liked for things to go smoothly, just wasn't very good when there was a major disruption in her daily life.

What really troubled Elizabeth more than anything at the moment was how, when school did start, she could take care of Becca and also go to the hospital every day. She hadn't asked her mother how long she would be able to stay, but she and Tommy definitely would have to return home before school started.

She knew, of course, that Mary Ann would help her out in every way possible, but she hated to ask her to drive her into Gillette every day and then take care of Becca, too. But there didn't seem to be any alternative at this time. She knew nothing about their finances, but assumed that they didn't have money to pay someone to come to the house every day to care for Becca.

Their financial situation was a big worry for Elizabeth; Edward had taken care of all that. She did know that he had health insurance for himself, as well as her and the children, through the Paper Mill. So hopefully, the biggest part of the medical bills would be paid by the insurance company. But she didn't know if they had any savings, or if Edward would continue to draw a salary while he was disabled. Oh, it was all just too much for Elizabeth! She knew now that she should have taken more of an interest in their finances, although Edward might not have been agreeable to that. She was beginning to feel that she needed some independence, didn't like the idea that all her life she had been totally dependent on someone else. First it was her parents, and since she'd left home, it had been her husband. Now it looked as if her husband would be dependent on her; maybe not financially, but in a lot of other ways.

When she thought about money, Elizabeth knew that she would have to start asking Edward questions about those kinds of things as soon as he began to feel better. He might not want to talk about them, but he really didn't have a choice. He needed to tell her, whether he wanted to or not.

She had saved a little money along as Edward would give her grocery money, money for clothes and things for the children. And that had been mostly in anticipation of one day leaving Edward. She didn't know exactly how much she'd saved; she kept it in a gallon jug that she had hidden in the attic. As she accumulated a bit of change or a couple of dollars, she would go into the attic and put it in that jug.

Maybe she would have to get a job now. She could probably work as a sales lady in a store, the way she had once dreamed about working at McLaughlin's in Garden City. Or she might be able to do waitress work. If she did get a job, then she definitely would have to hire someone to baby-sit. Maybe she could get an older woman, a widow, to live with them for her room and board. Then she told herself just to hold on, and not get ahead of herself; those plans would have to wait.

That evening, after finishing supper and cleaning up the kitchen, Elizabeth just wanted to be alone and think, not that she would likely be able to solve any of the problems. She bathed the children and got them ready for bed. The excitement of having company and so many things going on had tired them out, and they fell asleep before she finished reading them a story.

Her mother and Tommy were playing Chinese checkers and she went out on the back porch, sat down and watched the hundreds of lightning bugs flying all around. She remembered, as a child, the many evenings she would go out into her parents' yard and catch the lightning bugs in a jar; such a sight that was. She loved watching the jar light up, but of course her mother always made her set the bugs free. She had told Elizabeth that eventually they would die in that jar, and of course she didn't want that to happen.

The memories of her childhood kept going through her mind, the fun times the family had, and how much she had enjoyed playing softball. She regretted not finishing school, and wished her parents hadn't allowed her to drop out. Of course she had been a bit rebellious in those days, frequently complaining and expressing her dissatisfaction about so many things. She had resented not having a room of her own, having to share it with her younger sister, and she complained that she couldn't have her friends over because the house was so small.

And a real source of embarrassment was the thread-bare sofa in the living room and the other ratty old furniture. She had thought not having a telephone was some kind of conspiracy, a deliberate scheme by her parents. Having to draw water from a well until they finally got a pump was absolutely mortifying, the ultimate in humiliation. Oh, there were so many things she complained about, but she would give anything to go back to those days.

No, no, she said to herself, *I must stop that kind of thinking*. She was sure that happier times would be coming soon. She had two beautiful children whom she adored; they were her life. And she knew that it just wasn't right for her to be complaining, or wishing she could go back to her childhood. She had been blessed in so many ways, had so much to be thankful for.

Elizabeth sat there on the porch for a long time, acknowledging that it was really a beautiful world in spite of all the problems staring her in the face. She loved the sound of the crickets and katydids, and could even hear the frogs down by the creek. There were millions of bright stars in the sky; occasionally she would see one fall. She was able to pick out the Big Dipper and there was an almost-full moon. She loved watching those lightning bugs, hearing the chirping of the birds, and the sound of so many other little creatures. But when the mosquitoes started bothering her too much, she decided it was time to go inside.

As she was swatting at mosquitoes and thinking about all kinds of things, Elizabeth heard the night call of a whippoorwill, and that was supposed to be a bad sign. It meant that someone you knew had just died, or would die soon. She didn't want to believe those superstitions, but it was hard not to, having heard them all her life.

She remembered stories from her grandmother that supposedly strengthened the validity of those things: something to do with an owl hooting and what do you know, poor ol' Mrs.Whoever down the road fell and broke her arm. And what about the time her neighbor, Mr. Downey, saw two blackbirds sitting together in a tree? Who would have guessed that the next day he'd get a check from the Internal Revenue?

Most of the superstitions were about death or just bad luck of some sort. But there were a few, other than two blackbirds together in a tree, that would bring good luck as well: if you made a wish when you saw a red bird, your wish would come true. If your nose itched you would have company that day. And if the palm of your left hand itched, you would be getting money. Seeing a ladybug in your house meant something good was about to happen.

Elizabeth didn't know the origin of the superstitions, but some were ridiculous. Why would it be bad luck to walk under a ladder? Because it might fall on you? Or why be leery of a black cat walking in front of you? And there's one that topped the *most absurd list:* It's bad luck to see a car with only one headlight. No joke! But fear not; you can nullify that by spitting. That's right, just spit and the bad luck goes away.

If you break a mirror you can expect a whopping seven years of bad luck. And there's reason for concern if a mirror in your house should fall and break by itself. In some cases, though, throwing salt over your left shoulder can change your luck. No clue as to how that might work.

Elizabeth got up from the porch, ready to go back into the house and forget all about those silly superstitions. She especially wanted to forget about hearing that whippoorwill. Suddenly, she heard Tommy say, "Hey Jimbo, something woke you up?"

And Jimmy answered, "Yeah, where's Mommy? Isn't she here?"

Elizabeth heard her mother say, "She's out on the back porch, Jimmy. Did you have a bad dream? Come here, baby, sit with me for a while."

Jimmy saw Elizabeth as she was entering the living room, and ran to her. She could tell by the look on his face that something was wrong. She reached down, hugged him close and said, "It's okay, sweetheart, I'm here now; I'll read you a story so you can go back to sleep," and she walked with him back to his bedroom.

Jimmy began to talk very fast, and was so worked up that it was hard to understand him. He climbed up on his bed, and Elizabeth tried to calm him down, saying, "Okay, sweetheart, tell me again now. I'll close your door and it'll just be the two of us. Just talk slowly to your poor ol' mommy; it takes her a while to catch on to things." She gave him a big smile, hoping a little joking around would help to relax him. But he obviously was agitated and hurriedly started explaining.

"Ma-Maw fell and someone came in and they took her out on a bed, and put her in a big car or some kind of truck."

"Took her out of where, sweetheart? Where was your Ma-Maw; do you know?"

"In a room with Pa-Paw."

"Do you know where they took her?"

"No, Mommy, I don't know."

"Was she hurt when she fell, Jimmy? Do you know if she was awake, was she talking to the men who took her out?"

"Her eyes were closed, and she didn't say anything."

"Did Pa-Paw go in the big car too?"

"I don't know."

"Okay, sweetheart, now maybe Ma-Maw isn't hurt at all, so let's not get too worried until we know more about what happened. But is it okay if we talk a little about how you know all this? Can you tell me why you think your Ma-Maw fell, and also how did you know that your daddy had been hurt?"

"I see it happening, Mommy. It's like dreaming, but it's real. Remember when you told me that dreams weren't things that really happen, and for me to keep them separate? I'm doing that. It's kinda like a dream, but I can tell when it's not a dream."

"Oh, Jimmy, my love, I just wish that I could understand it better. Can you tell me if there's a voice speaking to you when you see these things happening, or do you just see a picture?"

"I just see a picture."

"Does it make you scared when you see it, Jimmy?"

"No, but it's usually something bad happening to somebody and that makes me sad. And then I think it would be better if I didn't see it."

Elizabeth was so confused, and she needed to ask more questions. But she didn't want to upset Jimmy and decided that she could ask the questions at another time. Then, trying to sound cheerful, she said, "Well, sweetheart, we'll have to wait until tomorrow to find out more about Ma-Maw's fall. Are you ready to go back to sleep now? I'll read you a story if you want me to."

"No story, Mommy, but can you stay here 'til I go to sleep?"

Elizabeth lay down on the bed beside Jimmy, and said, "Yes sir, my little superman, I can, I can." He was smiling his endearing smile as Elizabeth kissed him on his cheek, and minutes later he was sound asleep.

Chapter Fifteen

It was about ten o'clock the next morning when Elizabeth and Mary Ann arrived at Gillette General Hospital. Mary Ann went in and sat down in the Waiting Room, as Elizabeth prepared for the difficult trek upstairs to see Edward. Of course this morning was a little different. The primary reason for Elizabeth being at the hospital today was to find out from the staff if something had actually happened to Edward's mother, Rose Johnson. Earlier, on Mary Ann's arrival to pick her up, Elizabeth had explained all about Jimmy's revelation the night before. And now she was so nervous. She felt tightness in her chest and a little shortness of breath as she slowly made her way upstairs, wishing she could avoid what lay ahead.

She walked into the room and saw no one but Edward, still appearing to be asleep or unconscious. There was no sign of Mr. or Mrs. Johnson, so she headed for the Nurses Station; she had to find out what had happened. A nurse informed her that Mrs. Johnson had been brought into the hospital after suffering a stroke. Elizabeth couldn't believe what she was hearing, and had to ask for a place to sit down. Now she felt lightheaded, with the sensation that she was about to fall. *How could this be happening*, she wondered.

After a couple of minutes of trying to regain her composure, Elizabeth asked the nurse what was Mrs. Johnson's present condition, and if she could see her. She also asked about Mr. Johnson, whether or not he was with his wife.

Befuddled, almost in a daze, Elizabeth tried to concentrate on what the nurse began to tell her. The nurse knew, of course, that she was Mrs. Johnson's daughter-in-law and she was kind and sympathetic as she told Elizabeth that Mrs. Johnson's condition was dire, that she was in a coma. She added that the doctors were hopeful there might be some change within the next twenty-four to forty-eight hours. Naturally, not even the doctors could know if she would recover; it was just a waiting game. "And, yes," the nurse said, "Mr. Johnson is right there at her bedside." Then she gave Elizabeth the room number, which was just a short distance down the hall.

Elizabeth had known since her marriage to Edward that Mrs. Johnson didn't really like her, and the feelings were pretty much mutual. She definitely didn't want to appear hypocritical, but felt that she had a duty, an obligation to go see Mrs. Johnson and extend her empathy and concern to Mr. Johnson. In this kind of situation, she could only feel compassion for the woman. She didn't want to see anyone sick or in distress, and would certainly pray for Mrs. Johnson's recovery.

She realized as she neared the room that she was holding her breath. She stopped just outside the door, tried her best to breathe normally, said a little prayer and entered the room. There was Mrs. Johnson in the hospital bed, hooked up to all kinds of apparatus: tubes, bottles, cords, and she showed no signs of life. And not far from the bed was Mr. Johnson, seated in a chair, sort of slumped to one side and snoring.

Elizabeth didn't want to disturb him and since there was really nothing she could do there, she quietly left the room. She was reminded once again of Jimmy's extra sense, what he himself had called extrasensory perception. He had read about that at the library. She began thinking that maybe it was something everybody has to some degree; some people may never allow it to surface! *But, no,* Elizabeth thought, *I don't believe that for one minute. It surely must be a unique, incomparable kind of specialness that God has allowed only a few to possess.*

And Elizabeth knew that if she spent a lot of time thinking about those things, about what her little boy could perceive through some supernatural means, she would be overcome with a feeling of despair or dread; and she did not want that to happen. She loved her son so much, and had recognized early in his life that he was blessed in a special way, with extraordinary gifts, and she wanted to embrace that, not fear it. She knew, though, that she would always have that feeling of awe and a kind of reverence.

After a few minutes of what she considered to be mental numbness, Elizabeth began to think more clearly and headed downstairs to the Waiting Room, where she found Mary Ann. She told her she was ready to go home, that Jimmy had been right about his grandmother, that she'd suffered a stroke the night before and was in a coma. She told Mary Ann that there appeared to be no change in Edward, that he was asleep or unconscious, and there was no reason for her to stay at the hospital. She figured that a lot of people would think it was her duty to remain with Edward regardless of whether or not he was awake. But she believed that it was more important to be with her children.

She was disappointed, hurt and angry, felt like telling Edward what a devil, a fiend, a wicked man she thought he was, and that maybe his suffering would teach him a lesson. But she knew it was wrong to think that way; it was uncharitable thinking and what some people might call "unchristian."

Of course, she realized that most of her thoughts about Edward could be considered unchristian. She was thinking more and more that she cared less and less about him. Oh, yes, without a doubt, she would continue to be the dutiful wife, go to see him at the hospital and take care of him when he was released. And naturally, she felt sorry for him, pity for him. She knew that she would do certain things simply because her husband was a human being. It simply was not in her nature to be heartless and without compassion toward anyone, and especially the father of her two children.

When Elizabeth arrived home, her mother, Tommy, Becca and Jimmy were out in the yard playing. She got out of the truck, said goodbye to Mary Ann and joined them. On one side of the house were Tommy and Becca. On the other side were Annette and Jimmy. They were playing a game of *"ante-over,"* the ball being thrown back and forth over the house and a lot of running going on. The one who threw the ball would yell ante-over and someone on the other side tried to catch it. It was more fun and a bigger challenge when there were several people on each team, but you had to do the best you could with whatever number of players you had.

Elizabeth joined Tommy and Becca's team, giving them an unfair advantage. But Jimmy was as swift as a deer, and his Big Mama was pretty good at running, too. The object of the game was to run around the house after catching the ball, touch or hit a player on that side, and then he or she would become part of your team. The winning team was the one that ended up with the most players.

When the fun was over and they all went inside the house, Annette asked Elizabeth if she would call the telephone company the next day, and make an appointment to have a telephone installed. She said she knew that Elizabeth's daddy would be willing to pay for the installation. They would have to worry later about how the monthly charges would be paid if Edward didn't want to pay them. And there was no way of knowing how he would react to having a telephone installed in his house without his permission. But they would cross that bridge when they came to it.

Annette told Elizabeth that she had no choice, that no longer could she afford to live so far from town without a telephone or any kind of transportation. There was nothing right now that could be done to provide transportation, but something could be done about having a telephone. Annette thought it was strange that Mary Ann Butler didn't have one. Apparently the poles and installation of equipment needed for service out in their area had been completed some time ago.

Of course Elizabeth knew that Mr. Clancy, who lived a short distance from Mary Ann, had a telephone and that he was on a party line. But she didn't know if there were other people in the area who had one.

Over the past few years Elizabeth had met two other families living in her area, but didn't know if they had telephones. Mr. and Mrs. Harper lived a couple of miles from Elizabeth and Edward. They had a small farm, grew their own vegetables and some really delicious watermelons. More than a few times, they'd brought watermelons to Elizabeth and Edward. They were an older couple with no children living at home, but had a grown son who was a lawyer and lived in another state.

There was one other family Elizabeth had met, Clint and Virginia Olson and their two sons. The boys were twelve and fourteen years old. The Olsons also had a small farm, but Clint was a carpenter as well and had a little shop on his property. Elizabeth didn't know, though, what exactly he built. The family seemed real nice the few times Elizabeth had been around them. The boys, Jeff and Roger, were extremely polite and well-mannered. They were the only children living in the vicinity as far as Elizabeth knew.

She had tried to meet everyone living within a reasonable distance, hoping to find families with small children, playmates for Jimmy and Becca, and there were none. That was certainly a disappointment, but Elizabeth was thankful that her children had each other and loved playing together, though she did wish for more close neighbors and friends.

♫ *Chapter Sixteen*

Supper that evening was a rather quiet and subdued time, and after the dishes were done, the kitchen sparkling clean, Jimmy asked about his Ma-Maw. Elizabeth had made up her mind not to talk about that subject until Jimmy brought it up. Although she had expected him to ask questions when she got home from the hospital, he had not.

Now he began to question her. "Mommy, did you see Ma-Maw? I don't know what else happened 'cause I didn't see her anymore."

With an effort to lessen the severity of her mother-in-law's condition and wanting to be honest, but not too blunt, she said, "Well, sweetheart, I saw your Ma-Maw, but she wasn't awake. She had what is called a stroke. That means a blood clot stopped the flow of blood to her brain for a while, or a blood vessel ruptured. Either way, there can be severe damage to the brain. A person needs blood to circulate through the brain and all the rest of the body in order for it to function properly. A blood clot blocking the flow of blood, or bleeding from the brain when a vessel ruptures are both very serious.

"Right now your Ma-Maw is being taken care of in the hospital by the doctors and nurses, but they don't know yet if she will recover. We'll have to pray that she'll get well again. So when you go to bed tonight, I want you, and Becca, to say a prayer for her. I will see her again tomorrow, and if she's awake I'll tell her hello for you. How's that?"

"Okay, Mommy. What's a blood clot?"

This was too hard for Elizabeth. She didn't know much about medical things, but didn't want to just dismiss it, nor did she want to give him the wrong information, so she said, "Jimmy, you know how when you cut your finger and after a little while the blood stops coming out? Well, that means the blood has clotted. And that is the way the body works. Because when it's just a little cut, if the body is doing what is natural, there will be a clot, or a solid lump of the blood that forms and makes the bleeding stop.

"I'm not too sure about all of this myself, but in your Ma-Maw's case the body did something that was not normal. If it was a blood clot, also called an embolism I think, it must have been big enough to plug up or block the blood vessel that was supposed to be taking the blood to her brain. And I'm not sure of this either, but it seems logical that if the clot breaks away or medicine or something can get rid of it, then the blood could once again flow through the vessel like it's supposed to do. The problem might be, though, that in the meantime with no blood traveling to the brain it could be severely damaged, causing other physical problems, sometimes very serious. Does that make sense to you, Jimmy?" Elizabeth gave him a big smile and then looked over at Becca, who seemed just as absorbed in what was being said as Jimmy.

He didn't say anything for a few seconds, then, "Of course that makes sense. I once saw a book in the library that showed pictures of blood vessels, veins and arteries, but I didn't read about clots. That was when I was looking at pictures showing the anatomy of a human body. I sure hope Ma-Maw gets well and that her brain isn't hurt."

"I hope so too, sweetheart. We'll remember to pray for her before going to bed. And of course Big Mama and Tommy will probably say a prayer for her too."

Becca, at three years old, was not as talkative as Jimmy, but suddenly she wanted to participate in the conversation, and said, "'Member, Mommy, when I was barefooted out in the yard and cut my toe on a piece of glass? It bled a long, long time."

"Yes, Becca, I do remember that. You were such a big girl, too. And you're right; it did bleed for a long time. We were so glad when it stopped, weren't we?"

Becca was concentrating so hard as if she were trying to think of other occasions where she cut herself. She suddenly blurted out, "And when I skinned my knee on the cement step, it didn't bleed so much, right Mommy?"

"That's right, honey. You've had a whole bunch of skinned knees and elbows, haven't you? And you may have some more, but I want to remind you and Jimmy, as well as Tommy, to be very careful when Tommy is whittling with his knife. I don't want any of you getting cut; that might cause a lot of bleeding, too. Just be real careful! Tommy, are you listening to me?"

"Yeah, yeah, I'm listening," Tommy said. "I'll be careful and I won't let them touch the knife, so don't worry about it. As a matter of fact, I've put the knife away for now; I'll take it out again when I'm ready to whittle."

So with assurance that Becca and Jimmy were in good hands while they were with Tommy, Elizabeth got up and began getting the kids ready for bed. After their baths, she read them a story and they said their prayers, with special prayers for their Ma-Maw. Elizabeth told them good night, but Jimmy wasn't ready to go to sleep. He said, "Daddy will get well and come home, won't he?"

"Yes, Jimmy, your daddy will get well, but it's going to take a long, long time. You remember how long it takes for your birthday to come around, and how long it takes for Christmas to get here? Well, it may seem that long before your daddy is completely well again. He may be able to come home in a couple of months, but he won't be able to walk around, go to work, cut wood for the fireplace, or do any of those things for a very long time.

"Remember, I explained to you and Becca that your daddy's legs were broken in the accident, and one of his arms was broken too? The doctor could see on an x-ray machine that takes pictures where the bones were broken. Then somehow he managed to push the broken bones together – I think it's called 'setting' the bones – so that after a lot of time passes the broken parts will fuse, actually grow together again. But in order to keep the bones tightly in place so they can't move around, the doctor put a plaster cast over both legs and the arm. It's probably very uncomfortable for your daddy, but that's the way to get the bones to heal as they should. We can talk about this some more at another time; you should go to sleep now. I'll see you tomorrow. Good night, Jimmy."

"Good night, Mommy" was barely audible as Elizabeth kissed him on the cheek, and said a silent prayer that God would always watch over him and her precious Becca.

♪ Chapter Seventeen

Everything that took place in Elizabeth's household soon became routine and predictable, with her mother handling the cooking, the washing and practically all the things that had to be done in order to give the appearance of normalcy. Her brother, Tommy, was the one who watched after Becca and Jimmy much of the time, but their Big Mama always knew where they were and what they were doing. And Elizabeth went back and forth to the hospital, knowing that she would soon have to take care of the business matters: finding out about their finances, the health insurance for Edward, what bills they owed, when they were due, whether or not he would be receiving a salary while he was laid up.

On her fourth day of visiting Edward at the hospital, Elizabeth found him awake when she entered his room. He was alone, and she was so nervous that she hardly knew what to say to him. He still looked terrible, but some of the swelling in his face had gone down, and he was more recognizable.

Her first words were, "How are you feeling, Edward?" And that elicited a response Elizabeth wasn't prepared for.

Instead of talking about how he felt, he said in such a soft voice that she could hardly understand him, "Elizabeth, I'm sure you know by now that I was with a woman when I had the accident. I just want to tell you that the woman meant nothing to me. She had been coming on to me for sometime, and I took her to a motel once, and I was just taking her home the night of the accident."

Elizabeth was shaking, but tried to keep an even tone as she spoke. She was doing her best to conceal the anger that threatened to surface, and said, "Yes, Edward, I'm aware that you were with a woman. I'm also aware that the woman died in the accident.

"The police suspect that you were drunk when it happened. The bartender at the Red Roof Lounge told them that you'd been there for several hours, and drinking most of the time. But he couldn't say with absolute certainty how much beer or whiskey you drank.

"I'm sure that you're in a lot of pain, Edward, and since being awake, have spent some time thinking about what happened, what you have to look forward to, and how long it might take you to recover. And I'm truly sorry that you have to go through this kind of thing. However, you brought it on yourself; you've made your bed, now you have to lie in it. Literally! That probably sounds cruel, Edward, but you know as well as I do that your wounds are self-inflicted!

"I will stand by you during your stay here in the hospital and your recovery at home. But I want you to know, here and now, that there is no way in the world that I can ever trust you again. And as far as what you've just told me about your relationship with that poor woman who died, well, Edward, I don't for one minute believe a word you've said. Now, I simply do not want to talk about that anymore, at least for the moment." Then she asked him, "Have you been told about what happened to your mother?"

Edward frowned, panic in his eyes, and said, "No, what happened? Nobody told me anything. What's happened to Mama, Elizabeth?"

Oh, how she wished that someone else would have told Edward about his mother's stroke. She didn't want to do this, was even afraid that it might have a negative effect on his well-being, his recovery. After all, he was still in a very bad shape. But she knew that she had to tell him about his mother and proceeded. She said, "I'm so sorry to have to tell you this, Edward, but your mother has had a stroke. She's here in the hospital, and according to the doctors, her condition is not good; she hasn't regained consciousness."

With his one good arm, Edward covered his face and began sobbing. After what seemed like several minutes, and making wordless, sort of wailing sounds of grief and pain, he wiped away the tears but was barely able to speak, finally mumbling, "What do the doctors say, Elizabeth; will she recover? I know Daddy must really be upset. Please try to find out what you can about her condition. I guess they didn't want to tell me, afraid it would be too upsetting. Damn right it's upsetting, but I should have been told.

"According to the nurses, I've been asleep most of the time since coming out of surgery, but I'm fully awake and alert today. Damnit, they should have told me that my mama had a stroke. Where's Daddy, Elizabeth? Is he with her?" Suddenly, it was like all the air went out of him, a balloon being pricked with a pin, and he began crying again.

She knew that she should try to console him, say something that might comfort him a little, but she just didn't know how to do that. Instead, she said to him, "Now Edward, it's not good for you to get all upset like this. And just think about it, what could you have done if you'd been told? Not a single thing, and you know it. Please just try to relax and get some rest. Can I get you anything?" Elizabeth hesitated, and after getting no response, went on, "I will do my best to find out more about your mother's condition. As a matter of fact, I'll go to the Nurses Station right now, and see if there's been any change." She gently touched his good arm, and said, "Edward, I'll be back in a little while," and then she walked out of the room.

The nurse Elizabeth spoke to said that Mrs. Johnson still hadn't regained consciousness, and that was all she could report at this time. She gave her the name of the attending physician, a Dr. Joel Harrison, and said he was expected to return to the hospital later in the afternoon, but she didn't know exactly what time. The nurse was one that Elizabeth hadn't seen before, and she had to go through the whole story of being the daughter-in-law of Mrs. Johnson, married to her son Edward, who was a patient down the hall. She explained that she had, only a few minutes ago, told her husband about his mother's stroke, and that he was terribly upset. She told the nurse that she would be in her husband's room for a while, and asked if someone could let her know when Dr. Harrison arrived. The nurse assured her that she personally would come and get her.

Elizabeth slowly, deliberately forced her legs to move, and began walking back to Edward's room. He was still awake, and looked even worse than he had a few minutes before when she left the room. He started to say something, but seemed to gasp and struggle for breath, so Elizabeth ran out of the room, almost colliding with a nurse walking down the hall. She tried to remain calm as she told the nurse that something was wrong with her husband, and that she should check on him right away.

The nurse followed Elizabeth into Edward's room, and it was immediately clear to both of them that he was in distress. The nurse went to the side of his bed, touched his wrist, taking his pulse Elizabeth guessed, and began talking to Edward in a soothing, gentle voice. Then she put her hand on his shoulder and kept talking to him, telling him that he was going to be fine, that he should try to relax and breathe normally.

Elizabeth just stood watching, nothing else she could do; gradually Edward began to breathe more easily. When she thought he was okay, the nurse gave him a big smile, patted him on the arm, and told him that she'd be back in a while to check on him. Elizabeth followed the nurse from the room, then quietly asked her what had happened, and if Edward really was going to be all right. The nurse said he'd be fine, that he probably had become agitated and so emotional when he heard about his mother's stroke that it had caused him to hyperventilate, just temporarily interrupting his natural, normal manner of breathing.

Elizabeth went back into Edward's room and told him that she hadn't seen his mother's doctor, that he was not in the hospital. And that the nurses were unable to give her any information. She told him that she would wait for a while, that perhaps the doctor would be returning. Edward made no comment, and closed his eyes. She sat there for a while in the chair beside his bed. She was hoping that Dr. Harrison would return to the hospital so that she could talk to him.

After waiting around for almost another hour, she decided to leave, not knowing if, or when, he might return; she would have to try again tomorrow. Edward's eyes were still closed, but she didn't think he was asleep. As she got up to leave, she said goodbye and told him that she would probably be back tomorrow. She began walking toward the door slowly, thinking he might say something. But there was no response from him; maybe he really was asleep.

Mary Ann was in the Waiting Room, looking at a magazine when Elizabeth got downstairs. She looked up, smiled, and said, "Hey there girl; how was Edward doing, and did you find out anything about your mother-in-law? But wait a minute – maybe you shouldn't talk about all that right now. Why don't you tell me everything later? It might be best to try and think about other things for a while."

Elizabeth laughed and said, "You're reading my mind again. Actually, you're getting pretty good at that, Mary Ann. What I really would like to talk about is food. I'm starving! How about you? I thought maybe we could stop by that little drive-in place that we pass on the way into town, if that's okay with you."

Mary Ann feigned a sassy little glare and asked, "Now, who's readin' whose mind? Food is all I've been thinkin' about. That magazine I was lookin' at was filled with pictures of desserts; I was just about ready to eat a page. 'Course I could've gone to the cafeteria, but wanted to wait 'til you got here. I was hopin' your stomach would be tellin' you it was time to eat."

They left the hospital, got in Mary Ann's truck and drove the couple of miles to the drive-in restaurant. Elizabeth knew they wouldn't have to get out of the truck to order their food, and that was just as well as far as she was concerned. She didn't even know how to explain what she was feeling; she just knew that it was bad.

Gradually, though, she began to feel a little better as Mary Ann chattered away about everything except Elizabeth's immediate problems. She was almost always cheerful and upbeat, and had a positive attitude about things. And that's exactly what Elizabeth needed, especially at this time, because worry had started to gnaw away at her.

While they drove away from the hospital in Mary Ann's truck, Elizabeth felt as if she never wanted to move again, didn't want to do anything. All she really wished for, besides getting some food in her stomach, was to hold Becca and Jimmy close to her, read to them, play games, sing along as Jimmy played the piano, listen to him recite poems to Becca, and just close out the rest of the world forever. That was ridiculous, of course. But one thing was for sure: she must try to forget the problems for a little while, and enjoy the here and now with her family. She didn't want to get sick herself or suffer a nervous breakdown. That certainly wouldn't help matters. Naturally, she planned to do everything she could to help Edward, as well as his mother, but what could she actually do that might help them, other than pray? Praying for them and visiting were the only things she could think of.

Maybe she needed to be concerned more about how all these changes, the disruption of their lives, were going to affect her children. She thought it was important that they not know how upset and troubled she really was. That wouldn't be good for them, so she would just have to *pretend* for a while. As she reflected on all that, a kind of peacefulness seemed to take over her body and mind.

She and Mary Ann indulged in gigantic hamburgers, onion rings and coca colas at the drive-in, and she was feeling pretty good when she reached home. She asked Mary Ann to come in and stay for a while. Annette was in the kitchen, cooking, and Tommy and Becca were outside. Jimmy was sitting at the piano playing some of his favorite songs. A few minutes after she and Mary Ann greeted Annette and Jimmy, they sat down on the sofa, and Elizabeth exhaled deeply and closed her eyes.

When Jimmy began playing and singing *In The Good Old Summer Time*, Elizabeth and Mary Ann joined in. In a few minutes, Annette came out of the kitchen and began singing too. After going through all the verses they knew, Jimmy said, "Let's sing it one more time." Everybody laughed, and began singing again. By that time, Tommy and Becca had come into the house. Becca was the only one who didn't know the words, but she tried her best to sing along. It was such a change of pace, so much fun for all of them.

During the singing and all the fun, Elizabeth remembered that she was supposed to have called the telephone company while she was in town. That had completely slipped her mind. Oh well, tomorrow was another day and she would take care of it then. Her mother was right; they definitely needed a telephone out here.

With everyone asking her to stay and eat supper with them, Mary Ann didn't hesitate to say that she would love to. After the dishes were washed and dried and the kitchen floor swept, it was time for games, checkers and gin rummy in particular. Becca fell asleep on the sofa, and Elizabeth had to wake her up to get her ready for bed. Jimmy and Tommy played several games of checkers, with Jimmy only winning one. Tommy was really good at those games. Jimmy kept saying, "Let's play again," and finally Elizabeth just had to put her foot down, and insist that it was time for a bath and bed.

After the kids were in bed, Elizabeth, Annette and Mary Ann talked and talked, about everything under the sun, including Edward. It was late when Mary Ann went home. Before going to bed, Annette told Elizabeth that she and Tommy would stay until the week before school started. But she would need to get back home by that time, go shopping and get clothes and things that Tommy would need for school. She told Elizabeth that they would figure out what to do about getting someone to stay with her while Edward was in the hospital; she definitely needed someone there to help with the kids. And she reminded Elizabeth to be sure and contact the telephone company about getting a phone installed as soon as possible.

Elizabeth fell asleep almost as soon as her head hit the pillow, and it was a dreamless sleep. She assumed it was dreamless since she had no recollection of any dreams when she awoke the following morning. All she remembered was that she had fallen asleep immediately after going to bed, and apparently had slept like a log.

Chapter Eighteen

It was a little later than usual when Elizabeth got up the following morning. Her hope was that she and Mary Ann would still be able to get to the hospital early enough to see Dr. Harrison and ask him about Mrs. Johnson. They had agreed last night that they would try to leave around eight o'clock, or shortly after. And she was pretty sure she could be ready by that time. Becca and Jimmy had eaten breakfast and were dressed and ready for the day. Apparently they had gotten up early, so now all she had to do was eat her breakfast and get ready to go. She was grateful for the good night's sleep, and knew she had her mother to thank for the kids being so quiet. She had certainly needed the rest; that probably had helped lift her spirits a bit.

A new day was here and Elizabeth believed that she was ready for it. She didn't want to feel overwhelmed or anticipate problems that might not even arise. There would be a solution for everything, and she felt confident that things would somehow work out for the best. When it happened it might not be exactly what she wanted, what she had prayed for, but surely it would be the right thing. Even though she didn't think of herself as being religious, Elizabeth did have a lot of faith in a power greater than herself. She knew that there was a God and that He would guide her through all her struggles.

She knew, too, that she just might not be able to hang onto that kind of optimism indefinitely, but she would certainly try.

Her confidence, her feelings, her attitude would probably go back and forth, up and down, fluctuating from day to day. She decided, though, that it wouldn't be so much what did or did not happen, but how she handled things.

As she sat down at the table and ate her breakfast, she vowed to herself that she would make this day a productive one, devising a plan for what she would do when the time came for her mother and Tommy to return home.

She was Edward's wife, and his money and business dealings shouldn't be a secret from her. She would just have to talk to someone, a lawyer, an accountant, anyone who could advise her, counsel her about what to do in her present situation. Of course it would cost money to retain a lawyer, but she would just have to borrow the money from her parents or from Mary Ann. It was important now that she get some things settled.

Elizabeth felt good as she left for the hospital a few minutes past eight o'clock. Immediately after getting into Mary Ann's truck, she told her that she'd made up her mind to talk to a lawyer about some things. Mary Ann said that she knew a lawyer right there in Gillette, and if Elizabeth wanted her to, she would call him and make an appointment. Elizabeth was so pleased, and said that she would love for her to make the call. She asked her to try and make the appointment for that day.

After reaching the hospital shortly past 8:30 a.m., Mary Ann said she was going to the nearby café for a cup of coffee. She assured Elizabeth that she wouldn't forget to call the lawyer's office as soon as it opened. She told her that she would return to the hospital around ten or ten-thirty, and go directly to the Waiting Room and wait for her there.

Elizabeth went straight to the Nurses Station when she got upstairs, and asked if Dr. Harrison was there yet. A nurse told her that he was presently in the hospital making his rounds, and suggested that she wait in her husband's room and she would let Dr. Harrison know that she wanted to see him. Just as she turned away, the nurse said, "Oh, here's Dr. Harrison now." She walked over to the doctor and told him who Elizabeth was and that she would like to speak to him about Mrs. Johnson's condition.

Dr. Harrison was an older man with gray hair and a mustache. He gave Elizabeth a faint little smile and nodded at her, speaking softly as he told her that the chances of Mrs. Johnson even surviving were slim. He explained that there was nothing more they could do for her, and as far as he could tell there had been no change since she was first brought to the hospital. He did, however, try to end on a more positive note, saying, "Of course we can't be sure what will happen, and we'll watch her carefully and hope for some improvement. I'm sorry, though, that I can't be more optimistic; it's just a waiting game at this point."

Elizabeth thanked the doctor and continued on to Edward's room. She didn't look forward to telling him what the doctor had just said, but knew she had to do it.

There was a man talking to Edward as she entered his room, and she assumed that he was the doctor who was caring for him. She introduced herself and he told her that he was Dr. Milton Jones, Edward's attending physician. He had a face covered in freckles, was probably in his fifties, average height, with thick gray and auburn sideburns, but very little hair on the top of his head. He had a nice smile and beautiful, white, straight teeth.

Elizabeth asked Dr. Jones if she could talk to him for a few minutes, that she had several questions she'd like to have answered. He told her that he'd be glad to try and answer her questions, but that first he wanted to finish with Edward. He suggested that she wait for him in the hallway.

A few minutes later Dr. Jones came out of Edward's room, and Elizabeth first asked him what kind of problems Edward faced without a spleen, if its removal was a serious threat to his recovery. She also wanted to know if Edward would be able to walk again, and if there was any way of knowing how long he would be confined to the hospital.

Dr. Jones explained that people can live without a spleen, but that it was an important part of one's immune system, that it filters out foreign substances from the blood, removes worn-out blood cells and that kind of thing. He said that the risk of infection was much greater without the spleen, particularly early on after its removal, but that eventually other organs such as the liver could take over some of the functions.

As for Edward's ability to walk again, the doctor said that it would probably be quite a long time, maybe six months or more, and that he would probably end up walking with a limp. He would need a lot of physical therapy, and it was just too early to say what the outcome would be. Also, it would depend a lot on the body's ability to heal, as well as his emotional state, which, understandably, was not so good at the present time.

"Without the spleen," Dr. Jones said, "even more careful monitoring is needed in order to prevent an infection." Then the doctor seemed a little hesitant for a second or two, before he continued speaking. "A bad gash in his left thigh will have to be watched carefully. His broken arm will probably heal quickly since it's a clean break. But his broken legs are a different story. His left leg was broken in two places, and although there's only one break in the right one, the kneecap was also damaged."

He then looked at one of the nurses who was passing by and said, "Catherine, I need to talk to you for a minute, so don't disappear. I'll be through here shortly."

The nurse nodded and said, "Okay."

Dr. Jones turned back to Elizabeth and said, "Sorry about that, now back to Edward. I don't think there's much more I can tell you, except that he will be in the hospital for at least a couple of months, maybe even longer. Then he will need physical therapy for quite a while, maybe three days a week at first. No guess at this point just how long that will be necessary; it might take several months. A lot will depend on Edward himself and his attitude. I regret to say that right now he seems angry and bitter, and unable, or perhaps just unwilling, to do much in the way of helping himself. Of course I realize that it must be extremely difficult for him to accept that kind of devastation to his body, and him still a young man.

He reached out to shake Elizabeth's hand, said he had to finish his rounds, and told her to try and remain optimistic about Edward's recovery. He wished her well and said he was sure that he'd be seeing her again.

Elizabeth thanked Dr. Jones, and he gave her a big smile as he walked away. She went back inside Edward's room and asked him how he was feeling. He mumbled something that Elizabeth couldn't hear. She wasn't yet ready to tell him what Rose Johnson's doctor had told her a little earlier; she would eventually get around to that. Right now, she wanted to try and talk to him a bit. She asked him what the hospital food was like, if they had him on a special diet.

She was surprised when he looked at her and said, "They don't have me on any kind of diet as far as I know. I guess I can eat anything I want, but I don't like what they've been givin' me so far; it's hardly fit to eat. So I was wonderin' if you would bring me some fried fish and hush puppies. I don't have much of an appetite, but I know it would be a lot better if I could have some good ol' fried fish. I would prefer catfish, but any kind would be all right. I think a little cole slaw would be good too, and some onion. Will you be able to do that, you think?"

Elizabeth thought it strange that he had suddenly become so talkative. About the only time he'd had anything to say during the past couple of days was when she'd told him about his mother having the stroke. She could see now, though, that the talking had tired him out; he had sighed and closed his eyes when he finished.

Of course she didn't know if bringing him that food would be allowed, but told him if the doctor said it was okay then she would try to bring him some in a day or two. She said that first she would have to make certain he wasn't on a special diet.

He suddenly regained a bit of energy and responded with, "I don't give a damn what the doctor says. Just bring me some fish and hush puppies. I'll get well a lot sooner if I don't have to eat this hospital crap." His next words were, "Did you ask the doctor how long I'm going to be in here? And what about Mama, did you find out anything?"

"The doctor said you'll be here for at least two months, possibly longer," Elizabeth told him. "I know it's not easy being in here, Edward, but do try to make the best of it. And try to be nice to the nurses and the rest of the hospital staff. If you treat them decently and with respect, they'll treat you decently, too. Don't yell at them, or go acting mean and crazy. As far as the fish and hush puppies, I'll do whatever I can to see that you get them."

He just turned his head and didn't say anything, but Elizabeth knew that he expected an answer to his other question, the one about his mother. She felt obliged to tell him what Dr. Harrison had told her, so she said, "I talked to your mother's doctor a little while ago, and I'm afraid the news is not good, Edward."

That statement certainly got his attention and he turned his head back toward Elizabeth. In a voice much louder than before, he asked, "What d'ya mean, what did that doctor say to you?"

"Well, Dr. Harrison said that your mother is still in a coma and that the chances of her recovering are very slim. He told me there was absolutely nothing more they could do for her, but that they would watch her closely for any signs of improvement. He said it's just a 'waiting game'."

Clearly, that upset Edward; tears began rolling down his cheeks and his breathing became somewhat labored. But that was only a temporary setback. The tears soon stopped and his voice was harsh and his look menacing as he said, "I wish I could get up out of this bed and I would tell her doctor a thing or two. I bet those damn doctors aren't interested in tryin' to help her, and they're probably not interested in tryin' to help me either. They're just a bunch of money-grubbing vultures."

He was quiet for a minute or two, then started crying again, almost sobbing as he said, "Oh, dear God, I don't want Mama to die. Please, God, don't let her die."

Elizabeth couldn't help but feel sorry for Edward, but she just didn't think she could hug him and try to console him that way. Frankly, she had absolutely no desire whatsoever to hug Edward, then felt terrible for thinking like that. So she just stood by the side of his bed and almost whispered, "I know this must be so hard for you, Edward, and I'm truly sorry. I sincerely hope that your mother won't die, and I'll pray that she doesn't. I just wish there was something that could be done to make you feel better, to make the pain and anguish go away. But one day, Edward, you will feel better, so try to think positive thoughts. And remember, doctors are sometimes wrong. Until more is known, we need to have hope."

She walked away from his bed, turned and said, "Edward, I need to go home now and see about the kids, and there are other matters, too, that I have to take care of. So I'll see you either tomorrow or the next day. I'll do my best to get that fried catfish for you."

Elizabeth began walking away, but turned back and said to him, "You know, Edward, that I can't continue coming here every day after my mother goes back home. Now that I think of it, I guess I hadn't even told you yet that my mother and my little brother, Tommy, are staying at the house helping us out. Mama does the cooking and practically everything else that has to be done, and she takes care of Becca and Jimmy when Mary Ann brings me here to the hospital.

"I'm going to try to find someone who can stay with the kids on a permanent basis. I want someone who is trustworthy and will be good with Becca and Jimmy, a person who can live in the house with us. Mama and Mary Ann are both trying to help me find somebody. I'll definitely let you know what happens just as soon as I know something myself."

Suddenly Elizabeth felt completely exhausted and even a bit dizzy, but she knew the cause was nothing more than fatigue, anxiety and uncertainty. She decided that it was time to go, to get out of the hospital as soon as possible. She said to Edward, "I have to leave now, but I'll see you soon. And I do hope that you'll start to feel better. I'll say 'bye for now."

There was no response from Edward, and she walked out and headed straight for the downstairs Waiting Room. But she began to have more troubling thoughts, like how in the world was she going to live in the same house with Edward again, and would she ever be able to share his bed. *No, no, absolutely not, I won't do that,* she thought.

Elizabeth tried her best to get all those unpleasant thoughts out of her head as she walked into the Waiting Room. She was disappointed when she saw no sign of Mary Ann, but had only been sitting there for a few minutes when she walked in.

Mary Ann told Elizabeth that she had called the lawyer whose name was Harold Franklin, and that he could squeeze her in for a few minutes around one o'clock. She said that she and her husband Frank had hired him for some legal work a couple of years before Frank died. They had liked him a lot and had both agreed that he was honest, reliable and very capable.

Elizabeth and Mary Ann walked over to the café that was close by, ate lunch and then walked directly to Mr. Franklin's office. It was only a few blocks from the hospital. They didn't have to wait long before being ushered into his office.

Mr. Franklin remembered Mary Ann and they chatted for a couple of minutes before he asked Elizabeth how he could help her. She explained her situation in detail, stressing her need to get information about Edward's finances and about his health insurance. She wanted to know if his job was being held for him and if he was entitled to, or was receiving, any compensation from the Paper Mill while hospitalized. If so, how long would that continue? Had sick leave and vacation time accumulated?

The attorney took a lot of notes and after finishing their talk, said that he would get back to Elizabeth in two or three days. They agreed that he would send her the information through the mail since she had no phone. Or, he suggested that she might want to call him or stop by in a couple of days if she got the chance.

After leaving the lawyer's office, they went to a pay telephone and Elizabeth called the telephone company about getting a phone installed. She was told that she would have to come into the office, sign some papers and pay a deposit. After getting the address, they went back to Mary Ann's truck and drove to the telephone company office. That was completed in about an hour, with installation of the phone scheduled for the following week.

Relieved at seeing the lawyer and also scheduling a date for installation of a telephone had helped to cheer Elizabeth. She felt as if she had done something constructive, accomplished some things that she'd been putting off.

They were both tired and anxious to get home, but first Mary Ann had to stop at a paint store for a gallon of paint. She planned to paint her back porch within the next few days. Elizabeth was still finding out things about Mary Ann. She already knew that she was an intelligent woman, great at arts and crafts, a good cook, but until now Elizabeth hadn't known that she could also do carpentry work and paint. And she had recently told Elizabeth that she always changed the oil in her pick-up, that she had done that even before Frank died. And of course she was an artist and a midwife, a truly amazing woman.

The thought of her being an artist made Elizabeth think of the first time she had met Mary Ann and she'd told Elizabeth that someday she wanted to try to paint her portrait. Well, thankfully, it had been mentioned only once since that time. And Elizabeth had explained to her that she would rather not have her portrait done, but thanked Mary Ann and told her how nice it was of her to offer.

After arriving at Elizabeth's house, they discovered that Annette had supper just about ready, and she asked Mary Ann to stay and eat with them. Mary Ann loved Annette's cooking and just couldn't refuse. As usual, everything was delicious: a meat loaf, creamed potatoes, fresh butter beans, corn-on-the-cob, rolls, iced tea and coconut pie for dessert.

Annette wouldn't let Mary Ann or Elizabeth help with the dishes, so Mary Ann went home soon after eating.

The kids seemed tired and worn out, got their baths early and went to bed. They did stay awake long enough for Elizabeth to read them a story. And shortly after that she took her bath and collapsed into bed, falling asleep quickly.

♫ Chapter Nineteen

Elizabeth's night of sleep had been a deep, rejuvenating one, and she felt so good when she got up that she began to have little pangs of guilt. *How could she feel so good when her husband was so badly injured and confined to a hospital?*

However, those feelings of guilt vanished rather quickly, and after breakfast was finished she made a decision. While all of them sat at the table, laughing and talking, she suddenly got their attention by tapping a spoon against her coffee cup. "I won't be going to the hospital today," she said, looking as if she might not be feeling so well. But right away her expression changed, and with a mischievous grin, she declared, "Instead, all of us are going on a picnic down by the creek. We'll take lots of food and some cold drinks; we'll take that big ol' cooler. It's going to be a warm day but things will keep just fine with a lot of ice in that cooler. We'll even take fishing poles; I know that Mary Ann has at least a couple that she'll let us borrow. As a matter of fact, we should ask Mary Ann to come with us. Do I hear any objections to us having a picnic today?"

There was a resounding "no ma'am" from the kids, and they began giggling. Jimmy got up from the table and helped Becca out of her high-chair, grabbed both her hands and they began dancing around the table. As they danced, he sang a little ditty to the tune of *The Farmer In The Dell.* It went like this:

"On a picnic we will go,
On a picnic we will go,
Hi-Ho we have no dough,
So on a picnic we will go."

Everyone began laughing and that was all Jimmy needed. He tried making up a couple more verses but was having a hard time rhyming, so he soon gave up.

Annette got up from the table and said that she'd better get busy in the kitchen, frying some chicken and making a bowl of potato salad. She said they could take light-bread and that way she wouldn't have to make biscuits or cornbread.

Elizabeth could tell that Tommy was excited too. He began telling her that he liked living out there with them and wasn't looking forward to starting school in three more weeks. She told him that once school started he would probably feel differently, and reminded him that he would be able to see old friends and probably make some new ones. He made a frown and said, "I don't know, maybe."

Elizabeth said, "Oh, Tommy, you know you'll make new friends. You might even meet a girl that you'll like." She gave him a wink. "Don't you think that's a possibility?"

"Well, actually I have thought a little bit about that. But I don't want to be friends with any of those girls that were in my classes last year. I just hope there'll be some new ones."

Elizabeth ruffled his hair and said, "You'll find a girlfriend; count on it. Now, let's get ready to go."

Before getting herself and the kids ready, Elizabeth ran down to Mary Ann's house, asked her to go with them and to please bring along the fishing poles. Mary Ann said the picnic sounded like a great idea and that she could probably be ready to go within thirty minutes or so. And that was about all the time it took for her to get to Elizabeth's house. She was carrying two fishing poles and all the paraphernalia needed for a little fishing.

By ten-thirty, the food and drinks were all packed into the cooler. Paper plates, napkins, wash cloths and blankets were stacked in a box by the door, and everybody was dressed and ready to go. It wasn't a very long walk to the creek, but there was so much to carry that they loaded up Jimmy's little red wagon with some of the things, and took off for their fun day down by the creek.

That "old creek" they talked about so much, but seldom went there, was really a pretty big body of water. Elizabeth knew that she would have to watch the kids carefully. But it was really nice there, plenty of shade trees where they spread their blankets and placed the cooler.

Tommy had a sling-shot and decided to wander around a while and see if there was anything he could shoot. Annette told him that he shouldn't shoot at any little animals, like a rabbit or squirrel, because he would only injure them and they would suffer terribly before dying. He promised that he wouldn't use the sling-shot for anything like that. Annette was a bit puzzled as to what he would use it for, but she didn't ask him any more questions, just told him to be very careful and not to wander off too far. Jimmy wanted to go with him, but Elizabeth wouldn't allow that, telling him that he could use one of the fishing poles. She bet him a nickel that he would be the first one to catch a fish. It turned out that he was the first, and it really tickled him when that happened. Elizabeth had to take the fish from the hook, and they filled a bucket they'd brought with water and put the fish in that.

Mary Ann caught several fish and by the time they went home there were six or eight fish in the bucket, some of them pretty big. Elizabeth reminded Jimmy that he owed her a nickel, and he told her that he would pay her as soon as he got a nickel. She laughed and said, "That's okay, I can wait."

It was such a fun day; besides fishing, they hunted for special rocks and found some really pretty ones. They played *tag* and *hide-and-seek*. It was about noon when they took the food out of the cooler and ate their lunch. Everyone agreed that Annette's fried chicken and potato salad were delicious. After they'd eaten, Becca took a nap. Jimmy was still too energetic to take a rest, and Elizabeth took him for a walk through the woods. But Annette and Mary Ann rested for a while.

At about two o'clock they packed up their things and went home. Elizabeth thought she'd be able to make it through the rest of the week without much trouble after having such a wonderful day. The kids had a great time, too. Annette and Mary Ann said they hadn't had so much fun in ages. That was probably the truth.

It was another early-to-bed night. They snacked on left-overs at supper time, got their baths and were in bed by about eight-thirty. But even after the wonderful day, Elizabeth was unable to fall asleep right away. Her mind was in high gear and she couldn't shut it down; too much to think about. It seemed like hours that she lay awake; she didn't really know how long it was because she wouldn't look at the clock. Finally, she fell asleep and slept soundly until almost seven o'clock the next morning.

She had become resigned to the fact that things were going to be really tough for a while, but when had they been easy? Certainly not since she had married Edward. And that was no exaggeration; the past six years had been difficult. Her happiness, the easy times or fun times came from her two beautiful children, not from her husband.

Elizabeth knew that she would make it through the tough times. There was no choice, she simply had to. She would wait until Edward recovered and could take care of himself before making plans to leave him. But she had made up her mind to try and find some kind of job after Jimmy started to school. And she knew that eventually she would find someone to live with them and take care of Becca, cook the meals and do at least some of the housework. That might not be so easy, but she was determined. She was beginning to think that perhaps all these trials and tribulations had made her stronger, and above all, more independent. She knew that she had relinquished any independence she'd ever had at the time she married Edward. She had totally succumbed to his dominance, his control. But no more! *That was then*, she thought, *and this is now.*

♫ Chapter Twenty

The following two weeks went by quickly. The routine was the same; almost every day Mary Ann drove Elizabeth to the hospital to see Edward. She assumed that his condition was improving, but there was no way to tell by looking at him or hearing him talk. He seemed bitter and angry and never had much to say to Elizabeth; that is, unless he was griping or complaining about something.

Of course Elizabeth knew it was a terrible situation for him to be in, and she tried to picture herself in that predicament. She realized that it would be horrible, but believed that it could be made somewhat easier if he just would accept the fact that there were no other options available to him, not at this time. His attitude could make a world of difference.

One day when she arrived home from the hospital, she found a letter from her Aunt Naomi, who apologized for not having written sooner. She'd been away on a trip, then had neglected answering her mail promptly. Aunt Naomi assured Elizabeth that she and the children were welcome to stay with her as long as they would like. Her house was big enough and she lived alone, so it would be wonderful to have them there with her, indefinitely, if they wished to stay.

Elizabeth knew that she would have to write her aunt again soon and let her know what had happened to Edward. She would tell her that it wasn't possible for her to leave Edward now, nor in the foreseeable future. She would express her gratitude to her aunt for her generous offer, and tell her not to rule out the possibility of her and the kids showing up on her doorsteps one of these days.

The new telephone had been installed and Elizabeth was delighted, even though it was a four-party line. And she was so pleased when she received a lot of the information she'd requested from Harold Franklin, the lawyer she'd consulted. He supplied her with all of Edward's financial records. Before that, she hadn't even known what bank he used. Not only did Edward have money in a checking account, but also a sizeable amount of money in a savings account.

She had completed forms from the bank, making her a joint account holder and that gave her access to the money. She learned how to write checks and a few other things she'd had no knowledge of before.

Elizabeth was extremely pleased when she found out that the Paper Mill was continuing to pay Edward. He had accumulated a lot of sick leave, as well as several weeks of vacation. The problem was that the checks were being mailed to Edward's father. He was listed on Edward's job application as "next of kin" and the person to be notified in case of an emergency. That really made Elizabeth angry. She asked Mr. Franklin if there was any way to have that changed, and have the checks mailed to her. He told her it could be changed, but that it would probably take some time. Well, that was okay as long as it could be done. Mr. Franklin said that he would start working on it right away.

Elizabeth was so grateful for the help she'd received from the lawyer, and so happy that Mary Ann had recommended him. He was a pleasant man, seemingly very competent and made every effort to make sure his clients' needs were met. He didn't put things off, did exactly what he said he would do.

The week before school started, Annette and Tommy had to go back home, and that was a sad day for everyone. Elizabeth cried when they were ready to leave, and told both her mother and Tommy how much she had enjoyed them being there. She said there was no way to fully express her appreciation for all their help. Annette told her to try not to worry about things, saying that they would do their best to come often for a visit. She reminded Elizabeth that they could talk pretty often now that she had a telephone.

Elizabeth knew that there was very little time left for her to do all the things she needed to do to get Jimmy ready for school. She had to get to a department store and buy new clothes and shoes for him. And she had to buy him school supplies, such as a book satchel, pencils, tablets, colors, paste and scissors.

After her mother and Tommy left, Elizabeth had to take Becca and Jimmy with her each time Mary Ann drove her to the hospital. Mary Ann was a life-saver; she would take the kids to a park or find other ways to entertain them. Sometimes they sat in the Waiting Room and she would read to them. According to Mary Ann, they always behaved well; she said they never gave her one minute of trouble. Of course Elizabeth was pleased to hear that.

On Thursday of that week before school was to start, instead of going to the hospital, Mary Ann drove Elizabeth to a department store. She spent a couple of hours buying clothes for Jimmy. He went in with her and helped choose his things. Afterward, they walked a couple of blocks to a Woolworths Five and Dime, where she bought the school supplies. Jimmy was really excited about everything, but when he told Becca that it was only four more days until school started, she began to cry. He opened his box of colors and let her draw on a sheet of paper from his tablet. She finally quieted down, but Elizabeth could see that it was going to be a real problem when Tuesday rolled around. That's when school would start since that Monday was Labor Day. Of course it wouldn't only be Becca who would be upset. She would be as well, and tried not to think about it.

That night after the kids had their baths and while Elizabeth was reading them a story, suddenly Jimmy became restless and just stared into space for a minute, seemingly paying no attention to the story. Then he turned, looked directly into his mother's eyes and said, "Mommy, I think Ma-Maw Johnson died."

Elizabeth didn't think she would ever get used to this kind of thing. She tried to remain calm as she said, "Why do you think that Ma-Maw has died, sweetheart? Did you see something, or hear something? Please try to tell me what just happened, okay?"

At first it appeared as if Jimmy hadn't heard his mother speak, but then he reached out for her hand, and said, "I didn't see anything, but I had a funny feeling inside my body and then the words, 'Ma-Maw died' were in my head. The words were just there," and then his little voice trailed off as if he were very tired.

Becca had already fallen asleep and Elizabeth didn't want her to wake up, so she held onto Jimmy's hand and took him into the living room. She put him on the sofa and sat down close to him, then hugged him and held him in her arms for a while. She could never be exactly sure what she should say to her son when he had one of these premonitions or whatever they were. But she did ask him if he wanted to talk about it before she called the hospital. He told her that he didn't want to talk about it anymore.

She told Jimmy to lie there on the sofa and try to go to sleep, that she would call the hospital and see what had happened. Her hands were shaking as she reached for the telephone. Again, she felt so thankful that at last they had a phone. On the day it was installed she had put a list of emergency numbers right beside it, and of course one of the numbers was for Gillette General Hospital.

Elizabeth picked up the receiver, listened to make sure no one was using it; after all, it was a party line with three other users. Thankfully, no one was there, so she dialed the operator, gave her the number of the hospital and asked her to ring it. When a woman answered, "Gillette General," she asked if she could speak to someone who would know the condition of a patient there. After giving the woman the floor and room number and the patient's name, she was transferred to the Nurses Station. Elizabeth asked if they had any information about Mrs. Rose Johnson.

At first the nurse's tone wasn't particularly friendly. She began to question Elizabeth, who became frustrated at having to repeat her story over again. Finally convinced that Elizabeth was the patient's daughter-in-law, the nurse said, "I'm so sorry to have to tell you this, but your mother-in-law has died. We've contacted her husband, who had only left the hospital an hour or so before Mrs. Johnson died. He requested that we go ahead and contact the funeral home, which we've done. He also suggested that his son, your husband Edward, not be told about his mother's death at this time. And our Administrative personnel have agreed that might be best."

Elizabeth thanked the nurse and said that she would be at the hospital the following day. She said she'd like to speak to someone who might know what negative effects the information could have on Edward. The nurse informed her that she should go directly to the Administration Office and they would refer her to someone. She again told Elizabeth how sorry she was, and hung up the telephone.

Jimmy was now sound asleep on the sofa, and Elizabeth picked him up and took him to his bed. He seemed as light as a feather, and before laying him down, she just stood and held him for a few minutes, then gently laid him on the bed. Tears were streaming down her face as she walked out of his room.

She didn't know if there was anything she could do or needed to do after confirming the news that Mrs. Johnson had died. After thinking about it for a while, she decided that she would go to bed and try to get some sleep. Surprisingly, she fell asleep rather quickly, for which she was grateful.

After breakfast the next morning, she walked down to Mary Ann's house with Becca and Jimmy. She told Mary Ann that Edward's mother had died. After the children went out to play in the yard, Elizabeth told Mary Ann what had happened: how Jimmy knew that his grandmother had died, and that she had called the hospital to confirm it.

Mary Ann said, "Elizabeth, that child has a special gift; you've known that almost since the day he was born. Even though it is a gift, and there's a reason that he has it, sometimes it probably seems like a burden as well. I myself wouldn't know how to handle it, and I'm sure it's not easy for you. But I think you just have to accept it and try to get an understanding of what Jimmy thinks about it all. Does he talk about it much?"

"No, he doesn't want to talk about it, and so far I haven't pressured him to do so. It appears, at least when I've been with him and it happens, that he almost goes into a kind of trance, then he tells me what's happening and that's it, it's all over. I've asked him if he wants to talk about it, but he doesn't. He does try to explain what he feels, what he sees or hears, but that seems to be difficult for him. I don't think he really knows how to explain it."

"Do you want to go to the hospital sometime today? I guess it will be up to you to tell Edward about his mother, or maybe his daddy has stopped by and told him."

"No, no one plans to tell him about it right away. Last night the nurse I talked to said that it might not be a good idea to tell him. And yes, I would like to go to the hospital sometime this afternoon if you can take me. That nurse told me to go directly to the Administration Office when I get there and they'll refer me to someone I can talk to; he or she will know the best way and best time to tell Edward.

"In all honesty, I wish someone else could do that. I don't look forward to it at all. Maybe I'll just ask the person who talks to me if he or she will do it. Now that I think about it, that's what I'm going to do, because I just don't believe I can do it myself. It was bad enough having to tell him that she'd had a stroke. Edward loves his mother very much, probably more than anybody in the whole world, and his life will be so different without her. I know it will be very hard for him to accept. And there's just no telling how he'll react. He seems to be such an angry, bitter man right now, just so unhappy and miserable. Hearing that his mother has died might just send him over the edge. I guess I never really knew him, but I certainly don't know him now."

A little later they all drove to the hospital, but it turned out that Elizabeth didn't have to talk to Edward about his mother dying. In spite of what his father had said about not telling Edward, he had stopped by and told him. A nurse saw Elizabeth as she started to enter Edward's room and told her about it; she said that Edward had become hysterical, just went berserk. They had to restrain him, and then give him a shot of something to knock him out. Elizabeth felt some relief, but in spite of his past behavior her heart went out to him. She knew that the death of his mother would cause him a lot of grief, pain and suffering. And that it had to come when he was already suffering and in such a bad shape seemed to make it so much worse.

Elizabeth went in to see Edward even though she knew he would be out as a result of the medication he'd been given. She actually thought he looked more peaceful than he had on other days. She stayed for a few minutes and then went back to the Waiting Room for Mary Ann and the children.

Elizabeth asked Mary Ann to stop at the drive-in restaurant after they left the hospital. It would be a real treat for Becca and Jimmy, something they hadn't seen before. She knew they would love to have hamburgers and French fries. They had only been to a restaurant once; actually it was just a little café in Gillette. Edward had taken them there when Becca was barely a year old and Jimmy was about three. Frankly, she couldn't even remember why Edward had done that; maybe it was some special occasion that she couldn't recall.

Sure enough, the kids loved the drive-in and ordered hamburgers and chocolate milkshakes. Jimmy ate all of his, but Becca couldn't quite finish her hamburger. She did drink all of the milkshake, though.

After getting home, Elizabeth placed a call to Edward's father. She asked about Mrs. Johnson's funeral, when and where it would be. She told him that she would have her friend, Mary Ann, drive her and the children to the funeral. Mr. Johnson expressed his appreciation but told her that wasn't really necessary, that there would only be a short service at the gravesite with Rose's brother and a couple of her closest friends.

At first Elizabeth wasn't really sure how to take that, but decided it wasn't in any way meant as a personal affront. She had to believe that Mr. Johnson was sincere, that he wasn't deliberately trying to keep Elizabeth away. She would just take him at his word.

Later that night, Jimmy asked what would happen to Ma-Maw Johnson now that she had died. Elizabeth didn't want to be blunt or insensitive, but thought she should try to explain things in an honest and forthright way. She told Jimmy that Ma-Maw's body would be put in a casket and the casket would be put into the ground at a cemetery. She didn't like having to tell him that it would be completely covered with dirt, but she did.

She also told him that a headstone showing Ma-Maw's name, the date she was born and the date she died would be placed there. She talked about one's soul actually leaving the body when the person died. Of course it was difficult trying to explain what a soul might be like, and Elizabeth was sure that she hadn't done a very good job. She told Jimmy that the soul of Ma-Maw had probably gone to Heaven, or would get there at some point. She expressed her belief that Heaven would be very different from what we see and experience here on earth, that it would probably be a wonderful, perfect place.

Neither Elizabeth nor Edward had ever taken the children to church, but they'd gone with their grandparents a time or two. And on a few occasions, Elizabeth had talked to them about death, about God and Heaven. It was hard to know how much they understood. Jimmy was inquisitive and perceptive, and might actually grasp more than Elizabeth thought he could.

But she wanted to make the explanation about his grandmother's death as simple as possible. When she finished, Jimmy said, "Will we see Ma-Maw again after we die?" He closed his eyes for a minute and then repeated the question, "Will we, Mommy? And will she look the same when she gets to Heaven?"

The questions were difficult for Elizabeth to answer, but she responded with honesty and openness. "I think it's certainly possible, Jimmy, that we'll see her in Heaven. And I just don't know if she'll have a body. Sweetheart, those things are sort of like mysteries, a lot of guess work and assumptions. We just have to accept that some things are not easy to understand. But with faith we can look forward to a life after death, a different kind of life. So I can only say that your Ma-Maw is probably in Heaven, has a body and you just might see her again some day. I truly hope that you will."

She was pleased that her answers seemed to satisfy him, at least for the moment. She kissed him, told him that she loved him so much, and then said, "Now you should go to sleep, my sweet boy."

"Good night, Mommy; I love you." Jimmy closed his eyes and was soon sound asleep. Elizabeth stood there for a while and watched her beautiful child as he slept. He really was special, and she loved him and Becca so very, very much. They were her reason for living.

♪ Chapter Twenty-One

Tuesday, the day after Labor Day, was one that Elizabeth and Becca would probably always remember: Jimmy's first day of school. The school bus was scheduled to come by between 7:15 and 7:30 a.m. Elizabeth had almost panicked when she got up that morning, just thinking about her little boy having to be away from her all day long. He would be growing up now; the time would fly by and before long he would be a grown man. Then she had to laugh at herself, at how silly she was being. She managed to get through breakfast okay, get him dressed in new pants and shirt and his brand-new shoes. On their little shopping trip to town Jimmy had chosen those shoes and most of his new clothes, as well. He looked so cute as he, Elizabeth and Becca walked to the bus stop.

Elizabeth had sat down the day before and, once again, tried to explain to Becca that Jimmy had to go to school, but would be back home every afternoon. She told Becca it was only natural that she would miss him terribly, but that after a few days it probably wouldn't be so bad. She had bought Becca a little clock, told her what time Jimmy would get home from school, and then showed her where the hands on the clock would be at that time. Becca seemed to like that a lot; anything to distract her, even briefly, would be welcome.

They were at the bus stop for only a few minutes when they spotted the bus coming, and Jimmy became so excited. Clearly,

117

he was eager to start school. Even though she hated to see him go, Elizabeth was sure that she and Becca would soon get used to him leaving them every morning. She guessed that he would be an exceptional student. He was very smart, knew his ABC's, could read and could add and subtract a few numbers. A problem that might arise could be boredom; she hoped that he wouldn't lose interest because of being more advanced in some areas than other students might be.

Just before the bus stopped, Jimmy hugged Becca and told her not to cry, that he would be back before she could count to one-hundred. And of course Becca couldn't count to one-hundred so he laughed at his own little joke. But Becca wasn't laughing about anything. She held on to Jimmy and he finally had to gently push her away. In a faint little quivering voice, she said, "I love you, Jimmy." He told her that he loved her too, then hugged his mother and bravely stepped onto the bus. He took a seat by the window and gave his mother and Becca that big, sweet smile and continued waving until they could no longer see him.

Elizabeth was trying so hard to hold back the tears as she picked Becca up and headed back to their house, but the tears just couldn't be held back. Becca couldn't hold hers back either, and laid her head on Elizabeth's shoulder, her little heart breaking. It would get easier for her, though; Elizabeth was sure of that. She just wished there were kids nearby for her to play with. But she planned to spend as much time as possible with her. She would play games, read and just try to keep her occupied, one way or another.

That first day with Jimmy gone was even harder than Elizabeth had imagined. And there were times when Becca would just start sobbing. Elizabeth cried just about as much as Becca. Shortly after they had lunch, Elizabeth said to her, "Let's not cry anymore, sweetheart. Jimmy will be home in about two more hours, and I bet that two hours will go by really fast."

Sniffling, Becca said, "Okay, Mommy, I'll try not to cry anymore. But can we please go to the bus stop now and wait there for Jimmy?"

"Not yet, Becca. Let's read one more story, then we'll walk down to Mary Ann's house and stay for a little while. By then, it will be time for us to go to the bus stop. Is that okay?"

"Okay," Becca replied, but her heart wasn't in it. She did check her little clock a couple of times. Even though she couldn't tell time, the clock seemed to give her some connection to Jimmy and Elizabeth was glad she'd bought it.

After reading the story, they walked down to Mary Ann's. She gave Becca a couple of chocolate chip cookies she had just baked that morning, along with a nice cold glass of milk. She told Becca that she was being such a big girl and that Jimmy would be very proud of her.

That seemed to bolster Becca's spirits a bit, and she started playing with the kitten Mary Ann had found on the side of the road a few days before. After cleaning the little thing up and feeding it, Mary Ann had decided to keep the kitten. Someone had probably just thrown it there, and she thought that was so cruel. She had named him Zippy; she didn't even know why she'd named him that, said it had just come to her.

The bus was expected to arrive somewhere around three o'clock. At about fifteen minutes before, they walked to the bus stop. Mary Ann went with them.

The pure excitement and joy in Becca's eyes when she saw that bus coming was something to see. If every toy she ever wanted had suddenly been put in front of her, she wouldn't have been happier.

As soon as Jimmy stepped off the bus Becca ran to him, hugging him so hard that he almost fell down, and she just wouldn't let go. Finally, he got free and hugged his mother, then Mary Ann. He began telling them all about school. It was pretty clear that he liked it, at least that first day. He held Becca's hand as they walked home, and she was so happy, just chattering away, asking him all kinds of questions. No one would have guessed that she, as well as her mother, had been crying most of the day.

The next couple of days were no easier for Becca as Jimmy left each morning. She cried and cried and would beg him not to go. Jimmy would try to reason with her and tell her that they would do something special when he got home that day. He told her that it wouldn't be long before summer when there would be no school, and then they could play all the time. He also reminded her that time would pass real fast, and that in a couple more years she'd be going to school too, that they would be riding the bus together. But that didn't seem to appease her. Clearly, more time was needed for her to adjust.

As hard as it was for Elizabeth, those early days of Jimmy going to school were twice as hard for Becca. She worshipped her big brother, had practically been his shadow since she could crawl. And he was always so patient and seemed to thoroughly enjoy playing with her, reading to her or singing to her.

Some days Becca was irritable and whiny, and occasionally had a temper tantrum, which was so unlike her. Only a few things could cheer her up, and riding to the hospital with her mother and Mary Ann was one of them. She never tired of riding in the truck. Once in a while, she would talk about her daddy and ask when he was going to come home. But it seemed that she was reminded of him only when she went to the hospital. Neither she nor Jimmy seemed to miss him.

There appeared to be no change in Edward. He was still being restrained much of the time, but on some days he wasn't so drugged that he slept constantly. However, Elizabeth began to think that there was no point in even going to see him since he never talked, hardly even acknowledged her presence.

She had spoken to Dr. Jones a couple of times. He seemed disappointed that Edward was making so little progress; so little, that is, when it came to his attitude, his emotional state. The doctor thought that a psychiatrist might be able to help him. Apparently, the problem had been discussed at length with other doctors, and all were in agreement that a psychiatrist should be brought in if Edward didn't improve within a few weeks. His behavior was erratic and Dr. Jones thought he was capable of harming himself or the staff, although clearly he wasn't very strong. But the doctor wasn't sure that being weak and suffering from severe injuries was enough to stop him from becoming violent.

Chapter Twenty-Two

Although Elizabeth thought the day would never come when Becca would stop crying over Jimmy forsaking her for school, it finally did. It was obvious that she still missed him terribly, but seemingly had resigned herself to the fact that she couldn't stop him from going. She looked forward to the weekends, though, days when Jimmy could be at home with her. She seldom let him out of her sight.

The routine of seeing Jimmy to the bus stop every morning continued, and they met him every afternoon. Becca was always tickled pink to see him get off that bus. Even with everything else that demanded her time, Elizabeth hadn't missed a day of seeing Jimmy to and from the bus stop.

She was still going to the hospital to see Edward two or three times a week, but could see little improvement. On the days when he was heavily sedated, Elizabeth assumed that was because he was being aggressive and belligerent, difficult to handle. But she chose not to ask the nurses about that. She would just sit in a chair by his bedside for a while and then leave. She had brought a bouquet of flowers a few times, flowers that she'd picked from Mary Ann's yard. And since she'd been told that he could eat candy, she occasionally brought him a Baby Ruth or a Peanut Pattie; he had always liked those. It wasn't clear if he ate them or if it was the hospital staff, but they would be gone the next day. She also brought mints and gum to help relieve his dry mouth.

When she had brought the fried fish, cole slaw and hush puppies he'd asked for, he ate very little. It wasn't that he didn't like it; he just didn't have his appetite back yet.

In spite of the problems, Elizabeth seemed to be fine most of the time. And Mary Ann had told her one day how pretty she looked, that there was a kind of glow to her face. Elizabeth had chuckled about that, but obviously was pleased to hear it. She was even feeling some freedom for the first time since she'd been married.

One day, in her new-found freedom, she asked Mary Ann to teach her how to drive. Mary Ann thought that was a wonderful idea, said she'd be happy to teach her and Elizabeth was thrilled.

But the problem was that she didn't know what to do with Becca while Mary Ann would be giving her the driving lessons. Mary Ann asked why they couldn't have her in the truck with them, but Elizabeth didn't think that was such a good idea. And even if she found someone to stay with her for a couple of hours, Becca just might not like that since she already was discontented, sad and unpredictable with Jimmy away at school. And Elizabeth certainly wouldn't want someone to have a problem with her. She told Mary Ann that she should first talk to Becca about it, and if she agreed to stay with someone, she would try to find a neighbor who would be willing to keep her for a couple of hours a few days or however long it would take for her to learn to drive. She believed that it wouldn't take too long, feeling confident that she could learn to drive a pick-up truck easily.

Fortunately for Elizabeth, after a talk with her, Becca agreed to stay with someone while she learned to drive. As a matter of fact, Becca thought it was a great idea that her mommy was going to learn how to drive Mary Ann's truck.

Elizabeth decided to ask Virginia Olson, a neighbor who lived about a mile away, if Becca could stay with her while she took her driving lessons. She'd met Mrs. Olson and her family several times, had actually gone with her once to a meeting in Gillette; that was an attempt to get the road leading to their houses paved. They hadn't succeeded.

It turned out that Virginia was eager to have Becca spend some time with her. So the following day Mary Ann began the driving lessons. For four more days they continued the lessons, spending at least a couple of hours at it each day. And Becca's time with Virginia Olson turned out to be no problem at all. According to Virginia, she was "a perfect little angel." Of course the Olson's poodle, Buffy, probably helped a lot; she was a tiny little thing and was snow white. Becca loved that little dog, and began begging her mother for a dog of her own, which Elizabeth said she'd think about.

After five days, Mary Ann was sure that Elizabeth could drive a truck or any other vehicle. Now all she had to do was go get her driver's license. She was once again confident, knowing that getting her license would be just as easy as learning to drive and wasn't at all worried about that. She just wished now that she had a car, and maybe sometime in the near future that could become a reality. But with all of Edward's medical expenses, and possibly losing his job as well, it wasn't a consideration right now. And of course that kind of expenditure couldn't happen without his approval; that is, unless she had her own money.

The people who knew her could see a real change in Elizabeth. She had become more assertive, outspoken and independent. Mary Ann certainly could see the change, and knew it was a good thing.

Having recently talked to Mary Ann about cars, how to buy, where to buy, cost, etcetera, it seemed like a strange coincidence to Elizabeth when Jimmy came home from school one day with quite a story. He recounted a bizarre incident that had occurred that day, probably unbelievable to most people, but knowing Jimmy it had to be true.

Becca and Elizabeth had, as usual, met Jimmy at the bus stop, and after all-around hugs, he said, "Mommy, I have something to tell you, but I'll wait until we get home. It's real important, and we have to tell Mimi, too." Some time ago, he and Becca had started calling Mary Ann Mimi.

Elizabeth had no idea what he could be talking about, but after getting back to their house and giving him a snack, she sat down with Jimmy at the kitchen table and asked what he wanted to tell her.

What Jimmy revealed was another real shocker for Elizabeth. As he began the story, he had a slight frown on his face, unusual for Jimmy; a smile was much more natural for him. He said, "Mommy, I saw Frank at school today. You know who Frank is, don't you?" Elizabeth looked a bit puzzled, but said nothing. He continued, "That's Mimi's husband who died. But I saw him at school today. Actually it was after school while I waited for my bus when he came up to me and started talking. He was real, Mommy. You have to believe me!"

Elizabeth said, "I believe you, Jimmy. But first I would like to ask how you knew that it was Frank? Tell me about it, and I won't say a word until you're finished."

"He told me that he was Frank. I was just sitting on a bench waiting for the bus, and then there he was. He said, 'Hi Jimmy, I'm Frank. Your neighbor, Mary Ann, was my wife, and I would like for you to give her a message for me. Will you do that, Jimmy?' I said, 'Yeah,' and then he told me what I needed to do.

"He said that I should tell Mimi about some money he left in a safe place. He was saving up to buy a new car, and he had put the money in an old trunk out in their garage. He told me it was in a little leather pouch at the bottom of the trunk under some old blankets and other junk. That's what he said, 'junk'. Mommy, he said that it was $800.00. He had been worried that she would never find out about the money unless he told someone. I asked him why he didn't just tell her himself. He said that she wouldn't be able to see or hear him, explaining that only a few people had that special ability, and that I was one of those people. Frank said that if I hadn't come along, he might never have been able to send such a message to Mimi, except he called her Mary Ann."

"Okay, Jimmy, can you tell me if he looked like a regular man, was he dressed in a suit, work clothes, how was he dressed? Did he sit down on the bus bench with you? Please, sweetheart, I'm sorry for all the questions, but I would like to know more about what you saw and heard. What did Frank look like? Was he a pale shadowy figure like Casper the Friendly Ghost? Remember the storybook about Casper?

"What I want you to see Jimmy, is that I don't understand all of this, but I'm trying. You must realize that not everyone has those gifts. Of course they're wonderful gifts, and they make you very special.

"Did you tell anyone about seeing Frank? You know, we've talked about this before; it's best not to tell others because some people are superstitious and they become afraid. We'll certainly tell Mary Ann what Frank said, but I don't think we should tell anyone else. Is that okay with you? Now, just tell me what Frank looked like; describe him if you can. It wasn't scary for you, was it?"

"No, Mommy, I wasn't scared; you always ask me that. And I didn't tell anyone. He looked like a regular man, not like Casper. He was wearing a suit and a necktie, had hair and some of it was gray; he talked like everybody else talks. I listened to what he had to say and then told him that I would first tell you, and that afterward we would tell Mimi. He smiled and just stood there for a minute. Then he said 'Thanks, Jimmy' and that was all; he wasn't there anymore."

Becca had been sitting alongside Jimmy and was listening to the conversation. She began talking rapidly, excitedly, "Jimmy, maybe you can talk to Ma-Maw Johnson. See if you can do that."

Jimmy smiled and said very grown-up-like, "Oh, Becca, I don't think I can do that unless Ma-Maw decides that she wants to talk to me. If she does, then I'll tell you all about it; how's that?"

Becca just nodded her head, and then, as if nothing at all unusual had happened, Jimmy said to her, "Come on, let's go play in the back yard before it gets dark. Is that okay, Mommy?"

"Just for a little while. It won't be long before I'll have supper ready. And you're right, it's going to be dark before you know it."

As the two children went outside to play, Elizabeth sat for a few minutes just thinking about what Jimmy had told her. She decided that after supper the three of them would walk down to Mary Ann's. Even though she believed Jimmy, it just didn't seem possible that he could have had a conversation with a dead man. But she wasn't going to question it further, nor try and figure it out. Of course she was past trying to figure those things out.

On the one hand, Elizabeth wanted to shout from a mountaintop what a special child she had. She wanted to tell the world that her Jimmy could see into the future, that he could speak to dead people. But on the other hand, she wanted it all hidden, kept a deep secret because she knew that there were people who would say he belonged in a freak show, that he wasn't normal. There would be condemnation, even fear. A few ignorant people would say that Elizabeth had done something outrageous, committed some sin against God and that her strange son was punishment. There were just too many people eager to pronounce judgment on them if they knew about Jimmy's unusual abilities. Most people are ready to denounce things they don't understand.

She had reminded Jimmy that they must not tell others about his special abilities, but she needed to once again relay that to Becca, and maybe do a better job of explaining why. She wasn't sure, though, that such a secret could be kept forever. She believed she could withstand the criticism and condemnation, but she didn't want her children subjected to that, not at such a young age.

While she cooked supper, Elizabeth asked herself if she really thought that a leather pouch with $800.00 in it would be found in Mary Ann's garage, and the answer was, *yes, absolutely!*

Chapter Twenty-Three

Mary Ann had been a little concerned when she spotted Elizabeth and the kids walking toward her house just as it was getting dark. It was rare for them to come late in the evening. She hoped nothing was wrong. After a few minutes of chit-chat, Elizabeth began telling her what Jimmy had seen and heard after school that day. Elizabeth encouraged Jimmy to help her tell Mary Ann the story, but he only spoke a couple of times, adding a few details.

It was more than a little shocking for Mary Ann; she just sat there for a few minutes, completely flabbergasted. Then she smiled at Jimmy, and said, "Little man, I've always said that you were special, but each and every day you amaze me more. I love you a whole bunch," and she looked over at Becca and said, "you too, punkin. Now, Jimbo, if I show you some pictures, do you think you could tell me if any of them look like the Frank you saw today?"

"Yes ma'am," Jimmy said. "I think I can."

Mary Ann began walking out of the room, saying to Jimmy, "Okay, I'll be back in a few minutes to show you the pictures. Just sit tight. Oh, I should've asked if y'all wanted somethin' to drink. Elizabeth, get somethin' for Becca and Jimmy to drink, as well as for yourself." And then she disappeared into the other room.

It was at least five minutes or so before Mary Ann returned to the living room. She said, "I wasn't able to find the pictures I wanted right away." She sat down beside Jimmy, and began spreading out several pictures on the coffee table in front of them. They were all pictures of men, and she asked Jimmy if he saw Frank in any of those pictures. He began looking at them and it was only a few seconds before he pointed to one of them and said, "That's Frank."

"You're right, Jimmy, that's my Frank. It's a picture of him about a year before he died," Mary Ann said, trying not to appear too stunned by Jimmy's identification of her husband. Then she tousled his hair and said, "Okay, Jimbo, let's go out to the garage and see if we can find some money." Abruptly, she stopped and asked Jimmy, "Did Frank say anything else, any other kind of message for me, Jimmy?"

"No ma'am, he just said to tell you about the money," Jimmy said.

For a few seconds Mary Ann appeared to be a little sad, even disappointed, then started laughing as she said, "Well, I was hopin' he might have said that he loved me and missed me. I guess he does, though, or he wouldn't have come back to tell me about the money."

She and Jimmy started toward the back door, with Elizabeth and Becca following right behind them. When they got to the garage Mary Ann said, "I think we'll find that old trunk at the very back, right up against the wall. When I come to the garage, I seldom look over there at the storage area, but we'll soon find out if it's there, and what's in it."

The garage was really big and had originally been a barn, Mary Ann said. They walked to the back wall, and there it was: a big old brown trunk. Mary Ann grabbed an old rag from the top and brushed some of the dust off and then opened it. There were quilts, bedspreads and curtains, which Mary Ann took out and placed on the floor.

A few small boxes and what appeared to be dishes wrapped in newspapers were then lifted from the trunk. Then at the very bottom, there was a small leather pouch. Mary Ann picked it up, looked over at Jimmy and smiled, saying, "Here we go!"

Her hands were shaking as she pulled the little draw string and peeked inside the pouch. Then she closed her eyes for a few seconds and whispered something that no one else could hear. Opening her eyes, she began to shake money from the pouch as she shouted, "Look at all that money!" The bills were flying all over; they were one-hundred dollar bills, eight of them.

Jimmy, Becca and Elizabeth began laughing when Mary Ann reached down and picked up the money, saying, "Gotta be careful with this; sure don't want to lose it. Just look at these! I haven't seen a hundred dollar bill in a long time. Look here, Jimbo and Becca, see who's on these hundred dollar bills? Why, it's wise, ol' Benjamin Franklin; isn't he a cutie?"

Then Mary Ann did a funny little dance around the trunk, stopped, looked at Jimmy and asked, "By the way, Jimbo, did Frank say what kind of truck or car he had planned to buy?"

"No ma'am, he just said he was saving up to buy a new car. I don't think he mentioned a truck," Jimmy told Mary Ann.

As Mary Ann started back toward the house, she became quite serious, and said, "Y'all probably think I'm being silly and just plain disrespectful about all this. Maybe you think it's not showin' proper regard for my husband, Frank. But Lord knows, I don't mean it that way. I loved Frank so much, and miss him every day. He would've got a kick out of me carryin' on like this."

Elizabeth told her that it hadn't crossed her mind that she was being disrespectful. She had heard Mary Ann talk about Frank many times, the close relationship they had had and how much she loved him.

They went back into the house, sat at the kitchen table for a while, talking and eating devil's food cake. Mary Ann could really make good desserts. Her devil's food cake, banana pudding, chocolate pie and chocolate chip cookies were the best Elizabeth had ever tasted, and that was really saying something, because her very own mother could make some delicious desserts.

Suddenly Mary Ann said, "I know what! Let's celebrate this streak of luck by goin' to the carnival in Garden City next weekend. I read about it in the newspaper. Would y'all like to go next Saturday, not tomorrow, but the Saturday after that? It's not that far for us to drive and I'll pay for everything. How does that sound? Becca, Jimmy, have you ever been to a carnival?"

Becca asked, "What's a carnival?"

Mary Ann answered, "Oh, my sweet Becca, a carnival is a lot of fun with rides, games, cotton candy and corn dogs. And there are sideshows with all kinds of peculiar and strange people. Oh, it's lots and lots of fun, Becca. What do you say? Want to give it a try?"

Elizabeth interrupted the chatter by saying, "Now, Mary Ann, that sounds great, but you know you shouldn't be spending your money that way. We just can't let you do that. You're much too generous, all the things you constantly do for us. You're wonderful and I --- no, *we* are so grateful for everything. But we just can't keep taking and taking from you. I thank you, though, from the bottom of my heart."

"Oh, Elizabeth, my dear, sweet friend, I'll hear no more of that! You all are the only family that I have and how in the world can you deprive me of doin' somethin' for you that I really want to do and can now afford to do? Please, Elizabeth, just let me do this. It will be as much fun for me as it will be for Becca and Jimmy. So, how about it?"

Elizabeth shook her head and gave Mary Ann a look of exasperation, then smiled and said, "Oh, good gracious, Mary Ann, I guess I just can't say no."

Becca and Jimmy began to jump up and down, with Jimmy yelling, "Hip-hip-hooray, Mommy says it's okay; thank you, Mommy." And of course Becca soon chimed in, which made Elizabeth laugh. It really was funny how she tried her best to imitate Jimmy in everything that he did.

She responded to them both by saying, "It's not me you should be thanking. It's Mary Ann you have to thank."

Jimmy ran to Mary Ann and began to hug her and say, "Thank you, Mimi," and Becca did the same. It had only been in the past year or so that they had started calling Mary Ann Mimi. One day

Jimmy had asked his mother if it was all right to call her that. He told her that Mrs. Butler was too hard and didn't seem like the right name for her. Elizabeth had told him to ask Mary Ann if it was all right, and of course she thought it was just fine. There probably wasn't much Jimmy could do that would warrant disapproval from Mary Ann.

♫ Chapter Twenty-Four

It was a bit later than usual by the time Elizabeth got Becca and Jimmy ready for bed. They hadn't wanted to leave Mary Ann's house; everybody was having so much fun. After baths, Jimmy pleaded for a little time at the piano before going to bed. Becca sat beside him as he played *Under The Double Eagle*, which Elizabeth loved to hear him play. Then he played *The Old Piano Roll Blues*. After that, Elizabeth told them it was time to hit the sack and they giggled, with Jimmy saying, "Are you gonna put us in a sack, Mommy?"

"Well, I'm thinking about it," Elizabeth said, doing a little giggling herself. She began reading them a bedtime story and both were asleep before the end of it. Becca still slept in her crib, and every night after story time Elizabeth would pick her up and put her in the crib. She had recently told her mother that she wanted a big bed like Jimmy's.

Elizabeth didn't feel guilty when she woke up late the next morning after sleeping a full nine hours; it had been nice, sound, restful sleep. It was Saturday and there was no school for Jimmy. He had completed three full weeks of school, and didn't seem to have any complaints. Everything he told Becca and his mother about school was positive, and she hoped that attitude would continue. She was pleased, too, that he had made some friends. He said there were two boys and one girl who told him they were going to be his best friend. He seemed a little puzzled as to how all of them could be his "best" friend.

Of course Becca was no longer crying when Jimmy went to school, and she didn't spend the whole day talking about him, but it was clear that she still missed him terribly. One day she had asked Elizabeth what was she going to do when she, Becca, started to school. When Elizabeth told her that she'd probably cry every day, Becca said, "Please don't Mommy; if you cry I'll cry. I don't want to do that 'cause I'll be a big girl then."

Elizabeth replied, "Okay, sweetheart, I'll try my best not to cry, but you know I'll miss you a lot. I'll also be very proud of you. You're so smart and you'll get good grades in school, I bet. It's going to be a lot of fun, too. And after a day or two, you'll like school so much that you might not miss your mommy at all."

"Oh yes I will, Mommy," Becca said.

Elizabeth, in one way, would be glad when Becca started school because she did need to meet little friends her age, and school would be the perfect opportunity. On the other hand, she would hate to see that time come. She realized, though, that she couldn't keep her children safely tucked away with her for the rest of their lives.

But she wasn't going to think about those things now, nor about the problems she would face when Edward was released from the hospital. She was in a good mood and hoped to stay that way for a while. The potential challenges of the future wouldn't change that, at least not on this day.

She hadn't told the children yet, but after breakfast she was going to take them down to the creek for some fishing; they were still using Mary Ann's fishing poles. And she knew that Jimmy would take his binoculars, too, for a little bird-watching. It was a wonderful day, blue skies, warm and sunshiny, and all seemed right with the world at that moment.

They had just finished breakfast when Mary Ann appeared. She tapped on the screen door and then came on in. Elizabeth told her that they were going fishing and invited her to come along. She said she couldn't because she was going into town, and wanted to know if Elizabeth needed anything from the store, or if maybe she and the kids would like to ride into town with her. Elizabeth asked Becca and Jimmy which they would rather do, and they chose fishing. Before Mary Ann left, she told them not to forget about the carnival next Saturday. Becca and Jimmy, in unison, shouted, "We won't forget, Mimi."

After cleaning up the kitchen, Elizabeth told them to choose some snacks to take with them to the creek and then they would get going. They had learned to wear long sleeve shirts so it wouldn't be so easy for the bugs to bite. But the last time they'd gone to the creek, the insects hadn't been bad at all.

Elizabeth took one of the fishing poles and Jimmy the other one. After walking the short distance to the creek, Elizabeth chose a spot a few yards from Jimmy, telling him if they were far apart there was a better chance for both of them to catch fish. She kept an eye on him, though, and Becca too. She didn't want them getting too close to the edge of the creek.

Becca sat with Jimmy, and even though they both knew the chances of getting a bite from a fish were better when it was quiet, Jimmy just had to talk. He began telling Becca about the Knights of the Round Table and King Arthur. He explained that some people thought it was just a legend, but that he believed King Arthur was real. And Becca appeared to be enthralled. Elizabeth smiled to herself, thinking how great it was to be the mother of those two lovely children.

In spite of his incessant chatter, Jimmy was still the first to catch a fish. He asked his mother to take the fish off the hook for him. He seemed to have an aversion to doing that, something Elizabeth didn't quite understand.

Between her and Jimmy, they ended up with seven fish. Later, Elizabeth threw all of them back in the water; most were too small to cook. And besides, she didn't plan to do any cooking for supper that night; they would just eat sandwiches. She knew that she wouldn't have been able to get away with just making sandwiches for a meal if Edward had been there.

When Jimmy had tired of fishing he decided to search for birds with his binoculars, and had some luck, too. He knew a lot about birds, could identify many from having seen pictures in books. He became excited every time he spotted one and loudly called out what he was seeing.

Back at the house an hour or so later, Becca and Jimmy lay down on the sofa the minute they walked in, and both were asleep almost immediately. Evidently the fishing, bird-watching and just the warm, wonderful day at the creek had worn them out. After a few minutes of folding some clothes that she had washed the day before, Elizabeth, too, lay down for a nap. It had been a great day.

Chapter Twenty-Five

The following week was a challenging one. Elizabeth had seen Edward only two times the past week, and on both those days he was yelling and cursing about how awful he was being treated by the nurses. He was sure they were trying to poison him, and said that he wasn't going to eat any more food that they brought him. And according to what a nurse told Elizabeth, he had hardly eaten anything for a couple of days. She said that if he didn't eat soon they might have to feed him intravenously, and they didn't want to do that if it could be avoided. Elizabeth asked the nurse if she should try and bring food to him, and the nurse told her that would be a mistake. She believed when he got hungry enough that he would eat the hospital food. His actions were causing problems for Elizabeth, as well as the hospital staff.

Also, one of the nurses told Elizabeth that Edward might be losing his mind, and Elizabeth didn't think that it was the job of the nurses to speculate about his mental state. She believed comments like that were uncalled for. Besides, "losing his mind" surely was not a real medical term. She planned to call Edward's doctor sometime in the near future in an effort to get more information. She wanted to find out if he had followed through on his plan to have a psychiatrist see Edward.

His physical condition, if not his mental state, was improving. It had been a little more than two months since the accident and the casts had been removed. Of course he hadn't walked yet and probably couldn't for quite some time. If, and when, he got a little stronger, he might be able to walk a short distance with crutches. But according to the nursing staff his belligerent, combative behavior was getting worse and he had become almost impossible to deal with.

Thankfully, Elizabeth was successful in putting the situation with Edward out of her mind when Saturday rolled around. It was the day of the carnival in Garden City and she was ready for it; so were Becca and Jimmy. It was a much bigger event than even Mary Ann had anticipated. There were all kinds of rides: Ferris wheel, roller-coaster, merry-go-round, and a tilt-a-whirl. The tilt-a-whirl looked pretty dangerous to Elizabeth and Jimmy really wanted to ride on it, but she wouldn't allow that. She didn't even think that she'd like to get on it herself; it looked too scary. Finally Jimmy settled for the Ferris wheel. He sat with Mary Ann and Becca sat with Elizabeth. They rode it twice because Becca and Jimmy thought it was the greatest thing ever.

There were a bunch of booths and concessions at the carnival. Jimmy tried one where you shoot a play rifle loaded with a cork and try to knock down wooden ducks. You could win a big stuffed elephant or some other stuffed toy by knocking down three. He didn't win. Or you could throw softballs into a row of holes designed for a perfect fit, but the balls never seemed to go in.

The penny arcades were a lot of fun, and there was a glass-enclosed fixture that looked a bit like a telephone booth with all kinds of nice prizes inside. All you had to do was pick up the prize you wanted with a little crane you operated by turning a handle. It looked easy to do, but wasn't.

Men with megaphones were yelling, "Come one, come all" to see wondrous sights for only a quarter, or in some cases, "one thin dime." And according to the spiels from those "barkers," the side shows were something to behold. You could see the fattest man alive or the tattooed lady, supposedly covered all over with tattoos.

And there was a bearded lady, a wolf-man, a fire-eater, and even an alligator woman who was said to have scales all over her body.

By the end of the day, Becca, Jimmy, Elizabeth and Mary Ann were all very tired and sun-burned, as well. They'd had such a great time, and the entire outing was compliments of Mary Ann; she had made it all possible.

Mary Ann asked Elizabeth if she'd like to drive back home and Elizabeth jumped at the chance. She knew it would be good experience for her, but the idea of driving such a distance did make her a little nervous. She had driven into Gillette a couple of times, but that was only about twelve miles. And Mary Ann had been sitting right alongside her in the truck, just as she would be now, so this was a good opportunity to get more practice.

After the first few miles, Elizabeth began to relax and to thoroughly enjoy the drive. Mary Ann bragged on her when they got home, and told her that she drove as if she had been doing it for years, which pleased Elizabeth. She was reminded of how badly she wanted a car of her own, and hoped to get one pretty soon.

Becca and Jimmy had slept during the drive home. After getting out of the truck, Elizabeth picked up Becca and Mary Ann got out with Jimmy in her arms. The children woke up as they got inside the house, and put up a good argument against a bath because they both were so sleepy. Elizabeth said that they had to get a bath before getting into their beds, but accomplishing that task turned out to be rather difficult. Mary Ann did what she could to help, and then said it was time for her to go home. Elizabeth gave her a big hug and thanked her for the wonderful day.

Even though Elizabeth was tired, she sat down and wrote a long letter to her Aunt Naomi. She had been intending to do that for days, but just hadn't gotten around to it. It seemed as if every time she started to write, something else would come up. She told her aunt the story of what had happened to Edward, and about the woman who was with him dying in the accident. She explained that she still planned to leave him, but didn't think it would be possible until he had fully recovered and was able to return to work.

She told her about Edward's erratic behavior in the hospital, how he thought the nurses were trying to poison him, and how he cursed and called them terrible names. She mentioned the incident when the nurse had said that he might be "losing his mind." By the time she finished the letter, Elizabeth had written four pages.

Even though she seldom saw her aunt these days, Elizabeth really thought the world of her. When she was a child, she had seen her quite often, as well as Uncle Fred, Naomi's husband. They had no children, and Elizabeth and Amy would sometimes spend a week or two with them in the summertime. And since Uncle Fred had died, she was all alone. Elizabeth's mother, Annette, was Naomi's younger sister, and she'd tried hard to get her to move closer to Garden City. But she didn't want to do that, at least not yet, said she would rather live in the home she and Fred had shared for more than thirty years. She seemed content living alone, and kept busy with her flowers and vegetable garden. And of course she had a lot of friends there.

After finishing the letter, Elizabeth sat at the table for a while thinking about her childhood, and how it seemed such a long time ago. Finally, she got up, took her bath and went to bed. But she had a hard time falling asleep. Her mind seemed to be working overtime. When she decided to look at the clock, it was almost two in the morning. A few minutes later, she could feel herself dozing off.

The ringing of the telephone woke her up that Sunday morning. As she got up to answer it, she glanced at the clock and it was only 7:00 a.m. She couldn't imagine who was calling her at that time. Automatically, she thought that something terrible must have happened.

With her hand shaking and her heart racing, she answered the telephone. It was Dr. Jones, Edward's doctor, calling. As soon as he identified himself, Elizabeth said, "Oh, Dr. Jones, what's happened to Edward?"

He replied, "He's okay, Elizabeth, and I'm sorry for having to call you this early, but I wanted to make sure I got in touch with you before you got out to do other things. And I shouldn't have said that Edward's okay, because he really isn't. What I meant was that nothing any worse has happened. His behavior, however, is something that we are obliged to deal with as soon as possible.

"I've conferred with a psychiatrist; his name is Dr. Nathan Hudson and he has spent several hours with Edward. However, it appears that he accomplished little with those visits. He says that Edward is uncooperative, angry and aggressive. He told me that he is also delusional, that he's suspicious of everybody and thinks they're out to harm him. I agree with Dr. Hudson that he is mentally unstable, and that he may be suffering from a nervous breakdown. I believe the death of his mother has caused further deterioration of his mental state.

"Elizabeth, we need your permission – actually we need your signature – before we can transport Edward to another facility in the city of Farmingdale. It's a mental hospital where not only the mentally insane are treated, but the emotionally disturbed and those suffering from a nervous breakdown and other mental disorders. Would you be able to come to the hospital tomorrow morning and sign the necessary papers?"

"Dr. Jones, this is so unexpected and I don't know what to say. Of course, I guess I can come in and sign papers, but first I'd like to ask you some questions. Will I be able to talk to you if I come to the hospital? Just tell me the best time to come, and I'll do my best to be there. Right now, I want to think about this and consider what it all means. Farmingdale is a long way from Gillette, isn't it doctor? I wouldn't be able to visit him."

"Yes, it is far, about 150 miles I believe, in the northern part of the state. True, it would be difficult for you to visit him, but it is the closest hospital used to treat patients like Edward. If you can be at the hospital Monday around 9:30 or 10:00 o'clock, Elizabeth, I'll be there and we can talk more. Is that okay?"

"Yes, Dr. Jones, I'll be there. Thanks for calling me about this."

Elizabeth hung up the telephone and just stood there thinking about Edward and wondering what was wrong with him. Was he insane? She tried to think of all the questions that she should ask Dr. Jones, finally got a page from Jimmy's tablet and wrote down several things. One big question for Dr. Jones would be if he and the psychiatrist believed that Edward could be cured.

After Becca and Jimmy were up and had eaten their breakfast, the three of them walked down to Mary Ann's. When the kids went out to play in the yard and she was alone with Mary Ann, Elizabeth told her about the phone call from Dr. Jones, and asked for her advice, tears welling up in her eyes.

Mary Ann began by saying, "Now Elizabeth, you've been doing so well, don't let this be a setback. Of course, it's a terrible thing, but you've known for weeks that Edward's behavior was becoming stranger every day. I bet those nurses are even afraid to go in his room. And I bet, too, that it takes at least a couple of 'em to hold him down to give him his medicine. They're probably constantly complainin' about the situation, and I don't blame 'em a bit.

"We'll go to the hospital tomorrow morning and you can look in on Edward and see for yourself how he appears. But I do think you should sign those papers. Maybe they can help him at that mental hospital. I personally know nothin' about those places, and probably shouldn't even be tellin' you this, but unfortunately their past stinks to high heaven; horrible stories have been told. I don't know that any of them are true, and I don't think you should let those kind of tales trouble you. I'm sure things have improved over the years.

"At least there they probably have big, strong men who are orderlies and can handle patients like Edward who become hostile. Years ago, those kinds of places were called Insane Asylums, may still be called that by some people. And it may very well be true that at one time the asylum was just a place to house the crazy people they didn't know what to do with. But surely there are new medicines, better methods of treatment that are much different nowadays.

"Anyway, Elizabeth, what else can be done? Now, you have to try and stop worryin' about that. Let's you, the kids and me go ride around for a while. How does that sound? You have to keep your chin up, girl. And you know I'll be with you all the way, tryin' to help in any way I can."

"I know that, Mary Ann, and I'm so grateful for your help. I don't know what I would do without you. And yes, I think going for a ride would be a good thing. I know that Jimmy and Becca would much rather go for a ride in your truck than play in the back yard.

"You know what I would really like to do? I'd like for us to take them to that real nice park in Gillette; you know, the one you've taken them to before. They love those slides and the see-saw and swings. I hope that some day soon I can buy a swing and have it put up in the back yard. And there are some other things I want to get and put out there in the yard. One thing Jimmy has talked about that he would like is one of those small trampolines. He's seen pictures of the big ones that are used in gymnastics, but thinks there are smaller ones as well. Of course I don't know a thing about them, and have no idea how much they cost, but I'm going to get one for him if I can."

Mary Ann knew more about things like that, and said, "Well, you know they just may have some of those in the Sears and Roebuck catalog, and I'll take a look later. That really would be a fun thing for Jimmy and Becca, wouldn't it?" She smiled and added, "Why, I might even like one of those myself. We can also check sometime in that store in town that carries sports equipment. I can't remember the name of it, but I know where it is. Now, let's get the kids and go to that park. Sounds like a great way to spend a Sunday afternoon."

Then she and Elizabeth went out to the back yard to get Becca and Jimmy. They were thrilled to find out they were going to the park. And even Elizabeth was cheered up a bit by the idea. The rest of the day was going to be just fine.

♫ *Chapter Twenty-Six*

Elizabeth got Jimmy off to school on Monday morning, then got herself and Becca ready to go to the hospital. After a lot of thought, she'd decided that she would sign the papers committing Edward to the mental hospital in Farmingdale, but she still had questions for Dr. Jones.

As Mary Ann and Becca waited in the downstairs Waiting Room of the hospital, Elizabeth went upstairs to Edward's room. His wrists and legs were tied to the bed with restraints, and he was asleep. She left his room and went to find Dr. Jones.

After a series of questions were satisfactorily answered by the doctor, Elizabeth signed the papers that would commit Edward to a mental hospital 150 miles away from Gillette. Dr. Jones assured her that it was the only alternative, the only reasonable solution to Edward's problems. He sounded optimistic about Edward's recovery, saying there were medications that could help him, but he had no idea how long it might take for him to get better.

He also tried to reassure Elizabeth about the kind of facility it was, told her that as far as he knew it was a reputable place and that the patients were treated humanely. He said there was much more scrutiny now for those type of institutions than in years past.

After she joined Becca and Mary Ann in the Waiting Room, Elizabeth sat down and tried to explain to Becca about her daddy being sent to another hospital. It was hard for her to know what to say, but she did her best to make it understandable. How do you explain to a small child that her daddy has a sick mind, as well as a sick body?

At home that evening, Elizabeth received a telephone call from her mother, Annette. After explaining the latest developments with Edward, she told her mother how pleased she was that Harold Franklin, the lawyer she had hired, finally had gotten her listed as Edward's "next of kin" and his beneficiary instead of Edward's father. Mr. Franklin had contacted Clarence Johnson and asked him to send the checks directly to his office. In turn, he forwarded them on to Elizabeth. There would only be a couple more weeks of pay since Edward's sick leave and vacation time were running out. But the checks Mr. Johnson had amounted to quite a bit of money, and Elizabeth was so happy about that.

Annette and Elizabeth talked for a while about how Amy, John and Tommy were doing, and then Annette gave Elizabeth some real good news. She had found a woman who she believed would be perfect to live with them and take care of Becca and Jimmy. She was a colored woman by the name of Louise Powell. She was widowed with no children of her own, had worked a number of years for a family who lived in Garden City. There she had done housework as well as take care of three young children. The family was getting ready to move to another state and Louise would be without work.

Apparently she was a middle-aged woman whose husband had died a few years earlier. They had lived in a small house in the colored section of Garden City, a house which Louise still owned. Her husband had been a math teacher at the Garden City school for colored children. After his death, Louise needed a job and went to work doing about the only kind of job available to colored women, and that was housekeeping and caring for the children of white folks.

Annette had found out about Louise Powell from one of her neighbors who was the sister of Jonathan Campbell. And Jonathan Campbell and his wife were the couple Louise Powell had worked for during the past several years.

According to Mr. Campbell's sister, Louise was loved by the family. She was great with their three children, and they couldn't have been more pleased to have her working for them.

But Annette wanted to hear that directly from the Campbell's, so she had called and spoken with Mrs. Campbell, who gave a glowing account of Louise's time with them. She said that she was a sweet, soft-spoken woman, hardly ever raised her voice, even when there were times that she had every right to. She was peppy and spry, full of energy and had the patience of Job; the kids loved her. Mrs. Campbell said Louise was not only good with the children, but was a very good housekeeper as well. She could think of nothing negative to say about her, and recommended her highly.

Luckily, Louise Powell had a telephone and Annette had called and asked her if she would be interested in working for Elizabeth. After saying that she was interested, Annette told her that Elizabeth would contact her soon and work out all the details.

Elizabeth was thrilled with the news, and after getting the woman's telephone number from her mother, she said that she would call her right away. But after hanging up the telephone, she settled down and calmly began trying to figure out things before making that call. She decided it would be best to wait until the following day to contact Louise. That would give her more time to think about it.

She had already made up her mind that she was going to get a job, and maybe that could take place sooner than she had originally hoped. Now that she wouldn't be visiting Edward at the hospital, and if things worked out with this Louise Powell, perhaps she could begin looking for work right away. She still liked the idea of working in a department store as a sales person. Even though she had never done anything like that, she was sure she could. Elizabeth believed that she had the personality for that kind of job, working with people. She was outgoing, friendly and even-tempered, and people liked her. Those were all things in her favor, assets for anyone working in sales.

After supper, it was time to talk to Becca and Jimmy about the possibility of a woman coming to live at their house, and taking care of them while Elizabeth was away at work. She had talked to them a couple of times about possibly getting a job just to see how they felt about the idea, and they had seemed to be all right with it.

She also wanted to talk to them about their daddy being sent to another hospital and tell them what the doctor thought was wrong with him. Of course she had already told Becca a little about it, and Becca had told Jimmy as soon as he came home from school. But now Elizabeth went over the story again with both of them. When she finished, Jimmy asked a few questions: how long would his daddy be gone, would he be well when he came home, and would they ever get a chance to go to Farmingdale and see him? Elizabeth didn't have answers for all of his questions. She did say that a visit wouldn't be possible; it was much too far. She suggested to Jimmy that maybe he could write him a letter once in a while. He had nothing to say to that, but admitted that he was getting used to his daddy being gone, that he really didn't miss him much anymore.

Without commenting on Jimmy's last remark, Elizabeth began talking to them about the woman, Louise Powell, who might be coming to live with them. She told them that she was a colored woman, asked if they wanted to meet her, and they did.

Then Jimmy asked his mother what was the difference between a colored person and a white person, other than the color of their skin. Of course she should have expected a question like that from Jimmy, but still she wasn't prepared to explain it. She tried, though, and ended up telling him that as far as she was concerned there really was no difference. She explained that most white people thought of colored people as inferior, and didn't believe that they were entitled to the same rights and privileges as white people. She described how they were forced to live in separate neighborhoods, go to different schools, and couldn't even shop in the same stores with white people, couldn't eat in restaurants with them either.

Elizabeth tried to explain to Becca and Jimmy that that kind of attitude was called prejudiced or bigoted, and that she believed it was wrong. She said that in her eyes all people were equal and that they were in God's eyes too, adding that everybody should be treated with dignity and respect. She told them that they should never discriminate against a person based on how he or she looked, saying that included all kinds of physical deformities as well as the color of one's skin. She reminded them that they should never laugh at, or make fun of someone just because they looked different. Then she gave them a brief history lesson about slavery and the Civil War that took place long ago in the United States.

For a minute Jimmy looked as if he were going to ask more questions, but didn't. Elizabeth concluded her little monologue by telling the children that she would call Louise Powell the next morning and try to set up a time that they could get together. She thought it would be good if they could see her in the afternoon as soon as Jimmy got home from school.

In fact, Elizabeth decided that if the woman was willing, she would ask her to drive out to their home for the meeting. That would give her the opportunity to see where they lived and meet the children in their own environment. Also, it just might help Louise Powell make up her mind more quickly. Jimmy thought it was a great idea for Louise to come to their house, and of course Becca thought so too. Whatever Jimmy said was usually echoed by Becca.

♪ *Chapter Twenty-Seven*

On the following afternoon, not too long after Jimmy got in from school, Louise Powell arrived. Elizabeth had called her that morning, and Louise was more than willing to drive out there. But she wasn't familiar with the area and had to be given explicit directions.

Everything Elizabeth had been told about Louise Powell seemed to be true. She was soft-spoken, pleasant and personable, had a beautiful smile, and chatted with Becca and Jimmy as if she'd always known them. Both appeared to feel at ease and comfortable with her.

Louise stayed about an hour and a half, had a cup of coffee and a brownie, telling Elizabeth that the brownie was delicious. They discussed what her duties would be, how much she would be paid and what days off she would have. Of course her salary wouldn't be very much since she would be getting her room and board. And it was agreed that she would have Sundays off. She would also have at least a couple of days off at Thanksgiving, and a week at Christmas time.

Elizabeth thought that Becca and Jimmy should be included in the interview, and Louise had agreed. When she asked if they had any questions, Jimmy began by saying, "Ma'am, do you like sports, you know, things like playing catch, or shooting marbles? Becca and I like to play hide-and-seek too."

Louise smiled at Jimmy and said, "You know what, Jimmy, I love sports. However, I must admit that I've been mostly a spectator in the past. I did play some ping-pong a few times, but wasn't too good at it. I think, though, that I could learn how to play catch, and I already know how to play hide-and-seek. I can't think of any reason why there wouldn't be time to play together. Although I've never played marbles, I'm sure you can teach me how. You and Becca must remember, though, that I would have other things to do if your mama decides to hire me. But playing would certainly be on my list of things to do."

Jimmy gave her a big smile and said, "That would be great. Mommy always plays with us and if she's away at her work, then you would be the only person we'd have to play with. We're going to have lots of fun, don't you think?"

"I certainly do, Jimmy, and I'm looking forward to it. Since I'm a pretty fast learner, and with you teaching me, it might not take me too long to learn how to play catch and marbles. And you know what? I really like to play checkers, too. How about you, Jimmy, do you play checkers?"

"Yes ma'am, I like to play checkers. But my uncle Tommy beats me almost every time, so I don't know if that means I'm a bad checker player or if Tommy is especially good," Jimmy said, as he smiled at Louise.

"Well, hopefully we'll find out about that pretty soon. I bet, though, that you're a better checker player than I am. Even though I love to play, I'm not the best player in the world," Louise said, as she turned to Becca and asked what her favorite game was.

Becca had been sitting quietly just listening, and seemed to be happy now that she'd been included, and she said, "My favorite game is hide-and-seek, and playing with Jimmy's dump truck. He calls it a dump truck, but I call it a gravel truck. Mommy says it can be either one."

"Well, I'll be anxious to see that truck. Do you haul gravel in it?" Louise smiled and winked at Becca.

"No ma'am. We don't have any gravel, but I haul dirt in it, and sometimes rocks."

Elizabeth then took over the conversation, telling Louise that if she wanted she could go ahead and move her clothes and things in anytime. She explained that although she didn't have a job yet, she would be looking. Louise said that she couldn't move in and start work until the week after Thanksgiving. She told Elizabeth to call her, though, if she needed her for a day or two while she looked for a job.

Elizabeth assured her that Mary Ann, her friend and neighbor, could stay with Becca while she searched for work. And of course Jimmy would be in school.

After Louise left, the children were jumping up and down, happy that she would be living with them; they really liked her. Jimmy asked his mother what he and Becca should call Louise, and she suggested that they call her Miss Louise. Then told them that maybe they should wait and ask her when she moved in. Becca said she would like for her to move in right now, but Elizabeth explained that she probably had a lot of things to do before she could be ready. She was so happy that the kids liked her, and of course she liked her too. Things were beginning to look up.

After she and the kids ate their supper, Elizabeth called Mary Ann on the telephone. Mary Ann had finally had a telephone installed after deciding that she really needed one now. No one could understand why she had waited so long.

Elizabeth asked her if she could take her into town the following day so that she could put in job applications at a couple of places. Mary Ann said she'd be more than happy to take her to town and that she'd be there to pick her and Becca up around 9:30 in the morning.

But the next day was a disappointing one; Elizabeth didn't find a job. The department stores had no openings but suggested that she fill out applications, which Elizabeth did at two different stores. She was told that they would give her a call if an opening became available. She hoped for the best, but wasn't too optimistic.

When Jimmy came in from school that day, he was very excited. He told Elizabeth that the school was having an assembly at Christmas time, that it would be the week before school closed for the holidays. The talent portion was open to students from first through sixth grades, and could include singing, playing a musical instrument, reciting poetry, almost any kind of talent. Jimmy said he told his teacher that he could play a piano and sing, and that he would like to be in the program. He began laughing as he told Elizabeth about it, said he didn't think the teacher had believed him. She took him to the auditorium and had him sit down at the piano and show her. He played *White Christmas*, but didn't sing.

He said that the teacher seemed surprised when she heard him play, and told him it sounded wonderful. She said that he certainly could be in the program, and that he, along with his parents, should decide what song would be best. It didn't have to be a Christmas song, but the teacher would need to determine its appropriateness.

Jimmy was sure that he could do well and really wasn't worried, but wanted his mother's help in choosing the right piece to play. Obviously he was confident, but in no way could he be considered arrogant or conceited; quite the opposite, in fact. Jimmy simply knew without being told that he could play a piano very well, and that his singing wasn't bad either. It was nice for him to hear that from other people, but wasn't necessary for his self-esteem. He had a special talent, a talent that few children had, or even adults for that matter, and he didn't need a confidence booster. He was self-assured, positive, unflappable; nothing wrong with that! And it certainly couldn't be interpreted as conceit or arrogance.

Elizabeth and Becca were as excited as Jimmy about the up-coming event, and Elizabeth told him that the three of them would decide the best number for him to play. The program was scheduled to take place a week before the Christmas holidays began, but there would be a few practice sessions before that.

Jimmy talked about a couple of different possibilities, but said he would wait for his mother and Becca to come up with some suggestions as well, and then they would make their decision.

Finally, after a couple days of thinking about three or four different songs, they all agreed that there was no need for Jimmy to sing, and chose *Under The Double Eagle* for him to play on the piano. He could really make the piano talk when he played that. The three of them thought it definitely was a good choice.

But it wasn't even Thanksgiving yet, so there was plenty of time before his performance. Elizabeth had already decided that they would spend Thanksgiving with her parents. So she and the kids were looking forward to that. They had also asked Mary Ann to spend the holiday with them.

♫ *Chapter Twenty-Eight*

O n the Wednesday before Thanksgiving Day, after Jimmy got home from school, they all went to Elizabeth's parents. Mary Ann drove them there. Not only had Elizabeth invited her for the holiday, but Annette had asked her as well. She told Mary Ann that she was like a part of the family, had to come, that they wouldn't take no for an answer.

Of course Tommy was there, but Amy and John were away at college. They would be home for Christmas, though. Two trips so close together would've been out of the question, just too costly.

Annette and Troy Bolin's house wasn't very big. There were three bedrooms, but they were small. A cot and a fold-away bed would provide a place for everyone to sleep, though. And of course if it wasn't too cold, some of them could sleep out on the screened-in porch.

Annette outdid herself in the kitchen during the holidays. She cooked a turkey, a ham, all kinds of vegetables and two or three desserts. She liked to cook, and was very good at it. But her real pleasure came in seeing people eat the food with gusto, enjoying every bite. Elizabeth had always said that her mother was the best cook anywhere, and she believed that Mary Ann was a very close runner-up.

It was the first get-together for the family since the week before school had begun back in September. And everyone enjoyed it; the entire week-end was a lot of fun. Besides feasting on Annette's good cooking, they all went fishing on Saturday. On Sunday, they went to church. Jimmy and Becca had only been to church a few times before, and that was when they visited their grandparents. Jimmy joined in the singing as if he were a regular. He knew the words to some of the songs because his mother, or his grandmother, often sang gospel songs at home and Jimmy always learned the lyrics quickly.

On Sunday afternoon, Elizabeth, Mary Ann and the children drove back home. Annette had tears in her eyes when she hugged all of them, saying, "Y'all be careful now, and we'll see you at Jimmy's Christmas program. I'm really looking forward to that; I know it's going to be special."

Elizabeth also had tears in her eyes as they left, but it was time now to get back home and get down to business. Tomorrow, after getting Jimmy off to school, she would ask Mary Ann to take her into town again to look for a job.

She had almost forgotten about Louise Powell's scheduled arrival the next day, but remembered as they were driving home. And she was pleased when, at about nine o'clock on Monday morning, Louise drove up in her green 1949 Plymouth. It made Elizabeth start thinking again about trying to buy a car sometime soon.

She helped Louise bring her things into the house and get her settled in her bedroom. Then she asked Becca if she wanted to stay with Louise while she and Mary Ann went into town or if she wanted to go with them. Becca was almost apologetic when she said that she wanted to go with them. She told Louise that she would stay with her the next time. Louise smiled at Becca and told her that she would be looking forward to that. Elizabeth and Louise both agreed that it was probably for the best, that it would just take a little time for Becca to get used to her.

Elizabeth told Louise to get her room situated the way she wanted it, go for a walk or just relax and take it easy while they were gone. She told her that they wouldn't be gone too long, that she planned to go to only a couple of doctor's offices and put in her application. It had been Dr. Jones, Edward's doctor, who suggested that Elizabeth might find work as a receptionist or file clerk in a doctor's office. He had given her the name of two doctors in Gillette who might have an opening.

Mary Ann came by to pick up Elizabeth and Becca and they headed into Gillette. The doctor's offices were easy to find and Elizabeth was disappointed when, at the first office, she was told that they didn't have any openings. She was asked, though, to complete an application and told they would keep it on file. She completed the application but was not very optimistic about getting a job there.

When she was told at the next doctor's office that they would have an opening for a receptionist in a couple of weeks, Elizabeth was thrilled. The woman who now had that job would be leaving. She completed the application and was then interviewed by the doctor. His name was Dr. Samuel Parker, a man who appeared to be about forty or forty-five years old, very tall and slender, with sandy-blond hair and penetrating blue eyes. It was a pleasant surprise to find that he was friendly and not at all intimidating. Elizabeth's opinion of doctors had always been that they had a superior air about them. She relaxed and felt quite comfortable during the interview, and hoped that she was making a good impression.

Dr. Parker shook Elizabeth's hand after the interview and told her that he or someone from his office would contact her in a couple of days. He said there were two other women scheduled for an interview later that day, and that he would make his choice within the week.

Elizabeth was feeling great as she walked out to the truck, where Mary Ann and Becca were waiting. She was smiling like a Cheshire cat as she opened the door and got in. Mary Ann knew that was a good sign and said, "Well, did you get it?" Elizabeth told her she hadn't actually got the job, but was very hopeful that she would, and then told her all about Dr. Parker and the interview, and how well she thought it went.

On Thursday of that week, Dr. Parker himself called Elizabeth to say that she had the job of receptionist in his office, but that she couldn't start until the first week of January. His present receptionist would be staying on for the first two weeks of January in order to train Elizabeth in her office duties. After he told her when to report in, she thanked him and hung up the telephone.

Elizabeth was absolutely ecstatic after the telephone call, and immediately ran outside where Louise was playing with Becca and told them that she had the job. Becca began jumping up and down, saying, "Oh, Mommy, you did it, you did it," and gave Elizabeth a big hug. Louise congratulated her and said that would be a terrific start for the New Year.

She went back into the house and called Mary Ann, who told her that they should celebrate. After asking what kind of celebration she had in mind, Mary Ann said, "Oh, well, nothing that spectacular, just a nice supper at a restaurant in Gillette. We can all go after Jimmy gets home from school. How does that sound? It'll be my treat, okay?"

"It's a wonderful idea, Mary Ann, but it's not going to be your treat. I'll treat and that's final. All I ask from you is that you drive us to the restaurant. Now, since that's all settled, I'll hang up and get some things done around here. Why don't you come by about four thirty this afternoon? Does that sound all right?"

"Well, okay, but I wish you'd let me treat. It's your new job that we'll be celebratin', but I'm not gonna argue with you this time. So I'll see you then."

Elizabeth had no intention of leaving Louise at home while they went out to eat, but she knew the restaurants wouldn't allow her to eat with them in the main dining area. So she made up her mind that they would just go to a drive-in. She certainly couldn't be refused service in one of those places. A minor little problem, though, would be how all five of them could ride comfortably in the cab of Mary Ann's pick-up, but somehow they would manage.

At first, Louise was unwilling to go with them to eat, said that she didn't want to cause any problems. But Elizabeth, with Mary

Ann's help, finally convinced her that there would be no problems, and she reluctantly agreed to go.

Even the seating arrangement in the truck worked out okay. The seat was big enough for the three adults with Jimmy sitting on Elizabeth's lap, and Becca on Louise's lap. And of course Mary Ann drove. But after they got their food, they realized that all of them trying to eat in the truck wouldn't be easy. So they went to the park with their food and sat on park benches. It was dark by the time they finished and headed for home.

♪ Chapter Twenty-Nine

The family was eager for Jimmy's Christmas performance, excited too. It was his first time to perform before a large audience. There were several acts before it was his turn. When he was introduced, Jimmy took a little bow and was helped onto the piano stool by the school principal. He didn't appear to be nervous, and played *Under The Double Eagle* perfectly. The crowd seemed stunned; clearly, they weren't expecting that kind of talent in such a tiny little person. At the end, there was a standing ovation, the applause deafening. He slid off the stool, smiled and took another bow. The principal walked over to Jimmy and asked if he could play something else, that the audience would sure like to hear another song.

Of course Jimmy was agreeable to that. He chose *Ode to Joy,* the well known piece from Beethoven's Ninth Symphony. Before beginning, Jimmy told the people what he was about to play. Then he told them that Beethoven had first played a concert for the public when he was either six or seven years old. Again, as he finished playing, the audience stood and applauded for what seemed like a couple of minutes. There were a few of those high-pitched, piercing whistles, too; spirited and enthusiastic, and probably heard all the way out to the school parking lot. Once again Jimmy bowed, smiled broadly, then waved and walked off the stage.

Elizabeth's mother and daddy, along with her brother Tommy, had come for the program. They bragged and bragged on Jimmy, and wondered how he could play like he did in front of all those people. After chatting a while with Mary Ann and Elizabeth, they left to go back home. Annette reminded them that they would all be together again for Christmas, only a little more than a week away.

As they were leaving, Mary Ann said to Jimmy, "You did great, kiddo, you did great." Then she told him that tears had come to her eyes as he played Ode to Joy. Jimmy gave her a big smile and said that was what music should do, make people cry, laugh, dance or maybe shout. Then he said, "It should just make you emote in some way."

Mary Ann started laughing, and said, "Now Jimbo, you shouldn't be using those fancy words that your poor ol' Mimi doesn't even know."

"Aww, Mimi, you know what emote means; showing some emotion, that's all. I know you're just playin' with me." He smiled and said, "You do that to me all the time, but it's okay … I kinda like it."

"Well, yeah, I do kid you a lot, but you and I both know that your vocabulary is much, much better than mine. You know all kinds of words that I don't know, but you keep right on usin' 'em, you hear? Maybe we'll learn somethin' from you. I may be just a little ticked-off, though, that my favorite boy in the whole wide world is so much smarter than me." Mary Ann grinned, told him that of course she was kidding, and that she was very proud of him for being so smart. She was thinking to herself that he truly was an exceptional child. He not only was smart as a whip, but he was talented, funny, handsome, and just as sweet and lovable as he could be. Everybody loved Jimmy.

Becca was so excited, telling Jimmy that his playing sounded really, really good, and that she wished she could play a piano. But when Jimmy asked her if she wanted him to teach her, Becca replied, "No, Jimmy, I don't think I could learn to play. And besides, there are other things that I'm going to learn how to do when I get older. I may become a baseball player or a magician when I grow up; I don't know yet." Becca was serious, too, never thinking for a minute that becoming a professional baseball player might be an impossible dream for a girl. And certainly no one wanted to disillusion her. Then she took Jimmy's hand and held it as they all walked back to Mary Ann's truck.

Elizabeth began her shopping that week before Christmas, and for the first time she left the kids with Louise. All the gifts stayed in Mary Ann's truck. She would keep them hidden at her house to be sure that Becca and Jimmy didn't see them.

A few days before Christmas, Elizabeth mailed a package to Edward. She sent him home-made cookies, brownies, candy bars, chewing gum, writing paper, envelopes, a fountain pen and a few pencils. She also sent him a deck of playing cards and a box of dominoes. She saw no reason why those things wouldn't be allowed, and hoped he would get some enjoyment from them.

Recently, Elizabeth had asked Dr. Jones if he had had any news from Edward's doctor at the mental hospital, but he hadn't. He had given Elizabeth a telephone number where she could call and perhaps get some information about Edward's condition. He said they might not tell her much, but that it was worth a try to give them a call. When she made the telephone call, she was told that Edward was doing just fine. But when she asked if he might be coming home soon, Elizabeth was told "probably not for some time." That was about all she could get out of them.

In the package she sent Edward, Elizabeth had Jimmy write a little note and Becca sent him a picture out of her coloring book that she had colored. The children never talked about him, but Elizabeth tried to keep them posted if and when she had anything to tell them. She really thought that they were happier since he'd been away, and she felt badly about that. But the truth of the matter was that she herself was much happier too. Their home life was so tranquil, so peaceful.

Louise left the day before Christmas Eve, and that same afternoon, Elizabeth, Mary Ann, Becca and Jimmy went to Elizabeth's parents. She told Becca and Jimmy that Santa would probably leave most of their gifts at their house instead of their grandparents. She explained that Santa might not know that they would be away, but she assured them that they would get some presents from their grandparents, from Amy, John and Tommy, as well. That was fine with them; they were just anxious to go. They knew that Tommy would play games with them and that their Papa would let them ride the horse. Jimmy would ride by himself with his grandfather walking alongside the horse, but Becca only got to ride with her grandfather or Tommy because she was too little to ride all by herself.

The Christmas holidays were wonderful. Mary Ann left the day after Christmas; she had to get back home. She told Elizabeth that she'd be back to get her and the children when they were ready, but Elizabeth's parents said that they would drive them home. The plan was for them to stay until New Year's Eve, then go home and get things ready for Jimmy to go back to school. And Elizabeth had to get herself ready to start the new job. She was really looking forward to that.

Elizabeth hadn't seen her sister Amy, or her brother John, in several months because they had been away at college. And now she was amazed; they both seemed so grown up and mature, and very sophisticated. Gone were the days of arguments and disagreements between the two sisters. When Elizabeth told Amy that she needed to buy some new clothes for work, Amy insisted that they go into town together to shop. She wanted to help her pick out the new things.

They did that, just the two of them, and had so much fun. And it was a new experience for Elizabeth. She had left Becca and Jimmy with her parents. As much as she loved them, and delighted in their presence, she had to admit that a little time away from them now and then was probably good for her. It might be good for them, too. And that would be happening a lot now that she would be going off to work every day.

Elizabeth's mother and daddy drove Elizabeth and the children home on New Year's Eve. Becca and Jimmy didn't want to leave their uncle Tommy, and began crying when it was time to go. It looked as if Tommy was going to cry too, but he didn't. He just told them that he'd be seeing them before long. The children were much closer to Tommy than they were to Amy and John; they hadn't been around them very much. But Elizabeth knew that she wouldn't see Amy and John again for some time since they would be going back to college. And that made her sad. Of course she would see her mother and daddy and Tommy much more often. She could hardly wait until she had a car; she planned to visit them at least every couple of week-ends.

Finally she was able to appease Becca and Jimmy a little by reminding them that they would have presents from Santa Claus when they got home. And the look on their faces when they saw what was in their yard was priceless. They were so surprised, and absolutely tickled pink when they saw a brand new swing set out in the yard, along with a slide and a seesaw. Rushing to get out of the truck, they ran and began playing immediately. Elizabeth suggested that they should first go into the house and see if Santa had left some things inside for them. But it was just too hard to pull them away, so Elizabeth and her parents stayed with them in the yard for a while, swinging them and helping them on the slide. Even though Becca was a couple of years younger, her weight was about the same as Jimmy's; that made them a pretty even match for the seesaw.

Mary Ann had told Elizabeth that she was buying the playground equipment for Becca and Jimmy, but wanted them to think Santa Claus had brought it to them. She'd had a friend set everything up in the yard so it would be ready when the children arrived. Elizabeth had told Mary Ann that it was too big of an expense, buying all those things, but Mary Ann said she wanted to do it and that the cost didn't matter.

After a couple of hours, Annette and Troy said they had to be going, but first managed to get the kids to go into the house for a snack before they left. Of course they wanted to see the reaction when they saw the rest of the toys and things Santa had brought them.

Becca's things were in one corner of the room with a big sign that said, "For Becca" and Jimmy's were in another corner with his name.

Becca had a tricycle, a baby doll and a little Donald Duck wind-up toy, along with a couple of books. Jimmy had a small trampoline and an electric train set. He also had a new dictionary and two other books, *Treasure Island,* and a Hardy Boys one titled, *The Wailing Siren Mystery.* Of course both books were written for older children, but Jimmy read far, far above his grade level. And he had asked for both those books.

Becca began to ride her tricycle, but there wasn't much room, so her Papa took her outside to ride it for a little while. Jimmy couldn't decide what he wanted to play with first, the trampoline or the train set, or if he just wanted to read for a while. He finally decided to play on the trampoline, but his mother suggested that they put it out on the porch for now, and later it could go out in the yard when the weather was nice. He agreed, but decided to first set up the train and train tracks; for that he needed a little help from his mother.

At last, as the children played, Elizabeth and her parents sat down and talked for a while. But Annette and Troy soon had to leave. After hugs and kisses from the children, they wished Elizabeth well on her new job, and left.

🎵 Chapter Thirty

The New Year was going to be a good one. Elizabeth got settled into her job, and things went so smoothly that she was worried it wasn't real, that maybe she was dreaming all of it. But no, it was very real and she was enjoying herself more than she had in years.

Jimmy was back in school. He told his mother that the kids who had seen him play the piano at the Christmas program said he really did a good job; they hadn't known that he could play. One of the boys, who said his older sister could play a piano, told Jimmy that she certainly couldn't play it the way he did.

Becca was happily spending her days with Louise, who was more than Elizabeth had even hoped for. She was wonderful with the children, also was a good cook and housekeeper. The household had never run more smoothly. Louise was truly a god-send.

Elizabeth had hoped that Edward might write a letter and let her know how he was doing, but she heard nothing. She did write him a short note once in a while, but was just about running out of things to say.

One Saturday morning, only a couple of weeks before school was out, Elizabeth left Becca and Jimmy with Louise and rode into Gillette with Mary Ann. They went directly to a new-car dealership; at last, she was going to buy a car. She had told Mary Ann a few days before what she wanted to do, but had told no one else. She was so excited; it had been hard to keep quiet about her plan.

After looking at the cars, she finally chose a dark blue 1951 Chevrolet Bel Air hardtop. Oh, how she loved the look and smell of that car! The salesman took Elizabeth and Mary Ann for a ride, and then he had Elizabeth drive it. Afterward, her mind was made up. There was no haggling over the price; she paid for the car in cash: $1,780.00.

She had been saving that money for quite sometime, with the intention of one day buying a new car. Some of it had come from Edward's savings account, and a big part was saved from the salary he was paid after the accident. Those checks that were originally sent to Edward's father as the "next of kin" had been significant. Of course after Elizabeth retained a lawyer, the checks had been given to her, and rightfully so. Now, she was using that money, at least some of it, to buy a brand-new car. She could hardly believe it was finally happening.

Elizabeth had thought long and hard before making the decision to buy a new car, but finally decided that it was now or never. There was a terrible conflict going on in Korea. The United States had become involved in 1950 when they intervened on behalf of South Korea who was being attacked by North Korea. Even though Elizabeth knew no military people who had been sent there, she certainly was sympathetic to those families whose loved ones were over there fighting and being killed.

Of course, the "conflict" had many people worried, especially those with husbands, brothers or fathers being sent over there to fight. And naturally, there was a real fear that communism would spread. But the so-called "limited war" wasn't really talked about much among Elizabeth's friends and acquaintances. And since she wasn't directly affected by the war, and she had the money to pay for a car, she was going to go ahead and buy it. She knew that it just might not be possible later on, especially after Edward came home.

Actually, Jimmy seemed to be the only one who knew much about the Korean conflict, and sometimes would talk about it. He said that North Korea wanted to control South Korea and force them to become communists. Finally, in 1953, a cease-fire had been declared, but sadly thousands and thousands of American soldiers had lost their lives by that time.

At last, after completing all the paperwork for the car purchase, Elizabeth got into her new Chevrolet and headed for home. Mary Ann followed in her truck.

When Elizabeth pulled up in front of their house, Louise and the children were out in the yard, playing. At first they had no idea who was in the car; when Elizabeth stepped out of the driver's side, Jimmy and Becca began hollering, "Mommy, Mommy, is that your car?" They ran to Elizabeth, laughing and yelling, "Can we see it inside? Can we go for a ride; can we, can we?"

Elizabeth said okay, and asked Louise if she'd like to go, but she declined. She said that she'd get a chance some other time to ride in it. As Louise started back into the house, Elizabeth told her that they would be back shortly. She put Becca and Jimmy into the front passenger seat, and they took off for their ride. Jimmy had all kinds of questions for Elizabeth: what was the horse-power, how much gas did it hold, where did she buy it, how much did it cost? She finally shushed him, and said that he didn't need an answer right now to all those questions. He just gave her a big smile, and said, "Maybe later."

And he probably wouldn't forget to ask the same questions at some time in the future. After all, Jimmy was curious about almost everything. And if he couldn't get someone to answer his questions, he'd try to find the answers in a book. He never ceased to amaze Elizabeth, or anyone else who was around him for any length of time.

School was out at the end of May, and Becca was so happy to have Jimmy at home with her. He really liked baseball now, and listened to a lot of the professional games on the radio. The 1951 season had barely begun (in April) when Jimmy had predicted a World Series win that year for the New York Yankees. Mary Ann was a baseball fan too, and she told Jimmy not to count his chickens before they hatched. She believed it was the year for the New York Giants in the National League. Jimmy just gave her his big smile, and said, "You'll see, Mimi, you'll see." Of course it would be months before time for the World Series.

In the month of July, Jimmy and Becca spent two weeks with their grandparents. Even though it would mean being alone, Elizabeth suggested that Louise take time off and do something for herself. Louise declined, saying she would rather stay and cook for Elizabeth and take care of the house. Of course Elizabeth was grateful; she didn't relish the idea of being alone.

♫ Chapter Thirty-One

The summer passed quickly and once again it was time for Jimmy to start school. But instead of beginning the second grade, he was moved up to third. Elizabeth was called in to discuss the matter. Although Jimmy was thrilled about it, Elizabeth had to give it serious thought because of his age and his size. She was afraid it would be a difficult adjustment for him, socially at least.

Jimmy assured his mother that he would be fine. He didn't think that there would be any problems, and he was right; Elizabeth had worried unnecessarily. Jimmy seemed to fare really well; flourished, as a matter of fact. He made a lot of new friends, and would come home every day talking about things at school. Clearly, adapting was easy for Jimmy. Being smaller than most of his classmates made no difference to him, and emotionally he was probably more mature, in spite of his age.

Fortunately, Becca didn't take Jimmy's return to school too hard. She spent her days with Louise, whom she loved. Louise played with her, took her for rides in the car, sometimes going to the park in Gillette. And since it was understood by the merchants in town that Louise was just taking care of the white child, she was permitted to take Becca into the drugstore for an ice cream cone or a soda. But they were always at home in time to wait for Jimmy at the bus stop every afternoon.

Elizabeth couldn't remember ever being so happy. She loved her job, had met some real nice people, patients of Dr. Parker. The office staff had been wonderful to her, and she had become very fond of them.

There were a couple of male patients who had flirted with Elizabeth. She was nice and friendly to them, but didn't flirt back. One of them had asked her out, but she told him that she was married. One thing was for sure: she definitely was flattered by the attention. Maybe one of these days, probably a year or two, after she divorced Edward, she would be able to date if she chose. However, right now she couldn't spend time thinking about such possibilities. She still didn't know what would happen with Edward. She was sure, though, that she would make no effort to divorce him until he was back home and on his feet again. And there was no telling just how long that would take.

One evening when she got home from work, Elizabeth was surprised to find that Jimmy was quieter than usual and appeared to have something on his mind, something that was troubling him. After she had changed from her work clothes and chatted with Louise and Becca for a while, she went into the living room where Jimmy was playing the piano and asked him if something was wrong.

It looked as if he might cry, but straightened up like a little man, frowned a bit and said, almost in a whisper, "Yes Mommy, something's wrong. But I would rather wait and tell you when Becca and Miss Louise can't hear me." Then he tried to smile and said, "Mommy, I think saying Miss Louise is too long; is it all right if I call her Miss Lou?"

Elizabeth walked over to the piano stool, hugged Jimmy and said, "Oh, sweetheart, I'm sure it would be all right. Let's go in the kitchen and ask her. After that, we'll go out in the back yard, just you and me, and talk." Then she helped him from the piano stool, and holding his hand they walked together into the kitchen.

Louise was getting ready to put supper on the table and Becca was chattering away, following her back and forth from the stove to the table. Elizabeth let go of Jimmy's hand, walked over and picked up Becca and said, "Hey, my precious, are you helping Miss Louise?"

Becca giggled and said, "No, Mommy, I'm telling her a story and I haven't finished it yet. Can I please finish it before we eat supper?"

"Well, I think that might be okay since I was going to ask Miss Louise if we could postpone supper for a little while. Jimmy and I would first like to go out in the yard and talk about something; it shouldn't take too long. Is that okay with you, Louise, and you, Becca?"

Louise said that would be fine, but Becca decided she wanted to go with them. Elizabeth reminded her that she had to finish telling her story, and said they'd only be gone for a few minutes. "But first, Louise," Elizabeth said, "Jimmy would like to ask you something. Go ahead, Jimmy, ask her."

Jimmy looked up at Louise and said, "I just wanted to ask if I can call you Miss Lou instead of Miss Louise; that name is too long. Would that be okay?"

Louise gave him a big smile and said, "Yes, Jimmy, that would be just fine. As a matter of fact, I think I just might like that even better. I'm glad you thought of it. And how about you, Becca, would you like to call me that, too?"

"Yes ma'am," said Becca.

"Okay, now that that's been settled, we'll be back in just a bit," Elizabeth said, as she and Jimmy walked out the back door.

They sat down on the trampoline and Jimmy began, "Well, in school I sit by a girl named Jane. She's older than me, but only a little bit taller, and one day she told me that she liked me and asked if I liked her. I told her that I did, and she ran away, smiling. I hadn't seen her smile before; she usually looks sort of sad. Since that day, she's talked to me a bunch of times, and today in the classroom all at once I knew that her mother was going to die. I don't know how I knew; it suddenly was in my head. Or I guess I should say it was in my brain. I asked Jane at recess if her mother was sick, and she said, 'Yes, but how did you know, Jimmy?' I remembered what you told me about not telling anyone how at times I just know things that others don't know. So I told Jane that I was guessing because sometimes she looked so sad. But I know that her mommy is going to die, and there's nothing I can do about it, is there?"

As he sat there on the trampoline with a look of defeat, of sadness in his eyes that she seldom had seen, Elizabeth didn't know what to say, but slowly the words came. "Oh, my little hero, my sweet, wonderful boy. I know how caring, how compassionate you are and how much you would like to help Jane. Don't you think, though, that it would be best not to tell her that her mother is going to die? Maybe someone in her family has already talked to her about that possibility, or maybe she has sensed that herself. I think the best way for you to help Jane is to continue being her friend, play with her at recess and talk to her. Be very kind and remember that miracles do happen. It's possible that her mother may recover from her illness. Also, it's perfectly all right for you to tell her how sorry you are that her mother is sick, but try to be positive around her and don't let on that you've had the premonition. I know you'll be able to do that, Jimmy, won't you?"

"Yes ma'am, I think I can, but it makes me sad, and I wish I could stop her mommy from being sick and from dying."

"I know you do, Jimmy," Elizabeth said, and she pulled him to her and held him for a few minutes, sitting there in complete silence. Finally, they got up and walked back into the house.

It had been a while since Elizabeth had been faced with one of Jimmy's uncanny, mysterious predictions or the forewarning of future events. It was unsettling, to say the least. But, as she'd told herself many times, she could not, and would not discourage him or give any indication of disapproval.

She did make the decision, though, that she would try to find out more about the little girl's situation. She would discreetly make inquiries in an effort to get more information about the child's mother and her illness.

Unfortunately, Elizabeth never got the chance to obtain information about Jane's mother. Two days later when she came in from work, Jimmy told her that Jane hadn't been at school that day. Before the teacher had dismissed the class that afternoon, she told them that Jane's mother had died and that Jane would be out for a few days. She also told the class that she would buy a sympathy card and some flowers, and they could all sign their name to the card the following day.

As Jimmy was telling all this to Elizabeth, tears welled up in his eyes. She held him tightly and whispered, "It'll be okay sweetheart. I know you're sad for Jane. Do you know if she has brothers and sisters?"

He was sniffling and trying to wipe away his tears as he looked up at his mother and said, "I don't know, Mommy." Becca had come into the room, sat down beside them and began gently patting Jimmy's arm.

A few minutes later Louise came in and immediately sensed that everybody was upset about something. Elizabeth explained that the mother of Jimmy's little friend had died, and that they were all sad about that.

Louise asked Jimmy if he would like for her to teach him a new song on the piano. He looked up in surprise, "Miss Lou, can you play the piano?"

"Yes, I can play a little, Jimmy, but certainly not like you. I know a few religious and spiritual songs that my grandmother taught me many years ago. I have a piano at my home, and once in a while I play a song or two. Now, how would you like to hear one of the songs, or would you rather eat supper first?"

"No ma'am, I'd like to hear you play the piano."

As Louise walked over to the piano and sat down, Becca, Jimmy and Elizabeth followed and stood behind the piano stool. Then Louise told Jimmy that he should sit beside her so he could learn the song.

She began playing *Go Tell It On The Mountain* and Jimmy was smiling from ear to ear, enthralled, and watching every move of Louise's fingers. When she finished, Jimmy asked her to play it again. As she played the song again, she also sang the words.

Afterwards, Jimmy asked Louise if she would please write down the words to the song. She agreed to do that, saying she would have it ready for him when he got home from school the following day. He was really excited and began talking so fast that he was almost stuttering. He wanted to know if Louise would teach him all the spiritual songs she knew, if she would write down the lyrics, and did she think that he would be able to play all of them.

She laughed and said, "Okay, slow down a bit, Jimmy, or I can't understand what you're saying. Now, I don't know if I can teach you all of them, but we'll do one song at a time and see how long you want to continue. How does that sound?"

"Oh, I'll sure want to continue. I'm not gonna get tired of learning new songs. I didn't even know you could play the piano. Why didn't you tell me?"

"Well, I just haven't gotten around to it yet. I did intend to tell you, though. But I've enjoyed hearing you play so much, and you play that piano so well. I'm almost embarrassed to do my little bit of playing. But I'm glad that you like the idea of learning some spirituals. Maybe you can go to church with me some Sunday, and you'll hear the songs sung a lot better than I can sing them, and played a lot better, too. You'll have to ask your mommy about that."

"Mommy, can I go to church with Miss Lou?"

"Well, right now I see no reason why you can't, but let's talk about it some other time. We have to eat supper; I'm so hungry I could eat a horse and chase the rider."

That really tickled Jimmy and Becca; they just couldn't stop laughing, real belly laughs. Soon Louise and Elizabeth were laughing right along with them, just as hard. After finally settling down, which took a while, Becca and Jimmy washed their hands and everybody sat down at the dining room table to eat supper.

The happy mood continued, with a lot of laughing and chatting about all kinds of things. Elizabeth was glad to see that Jimmy was at least temporarily able to think of other things, and get his mind off the death of his little friend's mother. But he would be bothered by that for days, if not weeks.

Chapter Thirty-Two

October, 1952, was an exciting month for Jimmy and Mary Ann. Both of them had become avid baseball fans. At the beginning of the season that year, Jimmy said that the New York Yankees definitely would be in the World Series again. And sure enough, they were playing the Brooklyn Dodgers. He and Mary Ann listened to most of the games on the radio. Jimmy had predicted that the series would go the full seven games, and that the Yankees would be the winners. That's exactly what happened. The Yankees beat the Dodgers four games to three.

The entire year had been a happy and peaceful one for the family. But, during the first week of November when Elizabeth received a phone call from Dr. Milton Jones, she was afraid that things were about to change. Dr. Jones had been Edward's doctor before he was sent to the mental hospital. After chatting for a few minutes, asking Elizabeth how she and the kids were doing and if she liked her job, he told her that Edward would be home at the end of the week.

Dr. Jones said that he'd received a telephone call from a doctor at the mental hospital in Farmingdale. The doctor had sounded optimistic, saying that Edward had made great strides. The general consensus among the psychiatrists there was that he should be fine and have no trouble adjusting to his home-life once again. The doctor stressed, though, that he would have to take medication for the rest of his life. And of course they intended to make that point very clear to Edward. The medication was absolutely essential, and without it his irrational distrust of others and his violent tendencies would likely resurface.

After the telephone conversation, Elizabeth felt deflated; it was as if all her air had escaped. It was even difficult for her to breathe and she rushed into the bathroom and locked the door. After she'd been in there for several minutes, Louise tapped on the door and asked if she was okay. Elizabeth told her that she'd felt a little faint, but that she would be okay and would be out in a couple more minutes.

For some time Elizabeth stood there and stared at herself in the bathroom mirror, trying to breathe normally. She was thinking, *Oh, dear Lord, You have to help me out. How in the world will I be able to deal with Edward once again being in this house?*

At last, after splashing water on her face and trying to straighten her hair a little, she walked back into the living room where Louise was reading a story to Becca and Jimmy. The children didn't seem at all concerned about Elizabeth being in the bathroom so long, but Louise gave her a questioning look, wanting to know if she was all right. Elizabeth smiled at her, saying, "Am I interrupting a good story? I'm just going to sit down here with you all and listen for a while, if it's okay."

"Sure, Mommy, it's okay," Jimmy told her, as he turned back toward Louise, waiting for her to continue reading.

Elizabeth just sat there, thinking, *what do I do now?* She needed to tell the children that their daddy was coming home. Also, she would have to talk to Louise about what to expect when Edward did arrive.

She decided to talk to them later when everybody was ready for bed. So she sat there for the next thirty minutes or so and tried listening to the story Louise was reading to Becca and Jimmy. Although if asked, she would be unable to say what the story was about, or even the name of it.

The following morning when she arrived at work, Elizabeth asked for Friday off, explaining that it was for "personal reasons." She hadn't missed a day of work so far, and hadn't even been late one time. So there was no problem with her taking the time off.

She wanted to be at home on Friday when Edward arrived. Dr. Jones had told Elizabeth that he would drive Edward out to their house when he arrived in Gillette. One of Clarence Johnson's employees would drive to Farmingdale to get Edward. And before going on home, Edward would stop and visit with his daddy for a while.

Clarence Johnson himself was in poor health, but apparently had managed to keep in touch with the hospital and had been apprised of his son's progress. At least that appeared to be the case, since he knew when Edward was being released and had sent someone to pick him up at the hospital.

On that Monday night of Dr. Jones' call, and after Becca and Jimmy were ready for bed, Elizabeth had talked to them about their daddy coming home. Neither seemed happy about it, nor did they appear unhappy. They were just stoic, without emotion. But Elizabeth was pretty sure she knew what they were thinking.

After Becca and Jimmy were asleep, Elizabeth had knocked on Louise's bedroom door and asked if she could talk to her for a few minutes.

"Of course, Mrs. Johnson, come on in," Louise replied.

Standing in the doorway, Elizabeth said, "Actually, I'd rather you come into the living room if that's okay. We'll be more comfortable there on the sofa."

"Well, certainly, just let me get my housecoat and I'll be right there."

As soon as they were both seated on the sofa, Elizabeth began by saying, "As you know, Louise, my husband will be home on Friday. You know, of course, that he's been in a mental hospital for more than a year. He was diagnosed as having a nervous breakdown. According to his doctor in Gillette, Edward will have to take medication for the rest of his life to control his moods and behavior. And that makes me think that his condition was something more than simply a nervous breakdown.

"I don't think the children are looking forward to Edward's return. And frankly, neither am I, although I would rather you didn't mention that to anyone." Louise said nothing, but gave a slight nod.

Elizabeth continued talking, "Edward was an angry, disagreeable and controlling man almost from the day we were married. However, he didn't give that impression before the marriage. I was only sixteen years old, innocent and naïve. I wasn't in love with Edward, but I did like him, and expected married life to be great. Oh, what a disappointment! Edward was abusive to me and the children, particularly to Jimmy. The only attention he gave Jimmy was when he spanked him.

"Also, Louise, I know that Edward is a bigot and even if medicine keeps him calmer and able to control his temper, he'll still be furious when he sees you here. Now, I do intend to make sure that he keeps his mouth shut, and his thoughts to himself. I'll let him know right off the bat that he'll be out of here in the blink of an eye if he treats you badly. And the fact that he's not well will make no difference to me. He'll know soon enough that I'm not the meek, submissive, obedient little wife I once was, and that I won't put up with any of his nonsense.

"I don't want you to leave, Louise. You've been wonderful, great with the children and a good housekeeper and cook. I can't imagine now what we would do without you.

"I don't think there's any reason to fear Edward; I doubt that he'll be able to do much of anything physically. He'll be frail and probably can't get around very well. The only thing he'll be capable of is verbal abuse. But if he does talk to you ugly, if he calls you names or anything like that, I want you to tell me.

"There's no way of knowing how long it will take for him to regain his strength and be able to walk and do things for himself. But once that happens, and when he returns to work, I'm going to divorce him. I know that I'll get a lot of criticism and people will not approve, but that won't stop me. My mind is made up. Even if Edward has had a complete turn-around, which I seriously doubt, it will have no bearing on my decision to leave him. So, what do you think, Louise, will you stay? Oh, I do hope you will!"

"Well, Mrs. Johnson, I'll try it for a while, but he sounds like the kind of person I wouldn't be able to tolerate. We'll have to wait and see how it all turns out. This much I can say: I won't just walk away one day without letting you know in advance. I'm afraid, though, that I can't agree to anything more than that right now."

"That's good enough for me, Louise. That's all I need to hear. I guess I better get to bed now. See you in the morning. Good night."

"Night, Mrs. Johnson. I know this is all very hard for you, and I'm certainly gonna pray about it." Then Louise walked to her room and Elizabeth to hers.

Friday came too soon as far as Elizabeth was concerned. She was more than a little nervous. At three-thirty in the afternoon, Dr. Jones drove up with Edward. Elizabeth had told Becca and Jimmy to greet their daddy and to try and remember that he had been sick, and maybe now he would be an entirely different person. She explained that only time would prove or disprove the truth of that, and asked them to be patient.

Dr. Jones helped Edward out of the car and when Elizabeth got a good look at him, she was shocked. He was as thin as a broomstick and looked so fragile that he was almost unrecognizable. He didn't look at all like the man she had married more than eight years ago. He could barely walk and appeared to hold on tightly to Dr. Jones' arm as they proceeded up the walkway to the house.

Her anxiety was probably revealed in her eyes, as well as her actions. Elizabeth's hands shook and she shivered as if she were cold. Her mouth was dry, but she managed to walk to the door and greet Dr. Jones and Edward with a smile and a pleasant, "Hello there."

"Elizabeth, how are you?" Dr. Jones asked. Edward made no effort to speak, and Dr. Jones continued talking. "Edward is better now, Elizabeth, and I'm sure he'll improve even more when he begins eating right and gets some physical therapy. It's just going to take more time to get him back on his feet again. We'll have a therapist come out here maybe three days a week for a while to help him walk a little better. He's going to be fine after a while, I feel sure."

As Edward and Dr. Jones entered the living room, Becca and Jimmy shyly walked toward their daddy and Jimmy said, "Hi Daddy, you were gone a long time." It was a surprise to Elizabeth when Edward, with some difficulty, leaned down and hugged Jimmy, then Becca, who was standing right next to him. Both children were trying their best to smile.

Edward said, "I'm glad to see you two after all this time. Looks like you've grown some, especially you, Becca. Jimbo, she's almost as tall as you are. What do you think of that, huh? Tell me what y'all been doin'? How's school?"

Jimmy tried to act normal, smiled and said, "School's just fine, Daddy; I like it a lot. My teacher is Mrs. Phillips, and she says that I'm the best speller in her class." Then, looking at Becca, he added, "Becca's gonna start to school next year, aren't you, Bec?" Becca just nodded, didn't say anything.

Edward tried to hide it, but obviously there was disappointment in the way his children were reacting to his return home. It certainly was not a very exuberant welcome.

Suddenly, Edward looked over at the dining room where Louise was ironing. She had set the ironing board up in there because it was the only room where there was plenty of space. Edward stiffened and glared at Louise for a minute. Then he looked at Elizabeth and asked, "Who is she, and what's she doing in my house?"

Without hesitation, Elizabeth replied, "That's Louise Powell, and she stays with the children while I'm at work. She cooks, cleans house and takes care of all of us. She has been a welcome addition to our family."

"What do you mean, an addition to our family? She's a nigger; she's not a part of my family. I want her out of here. Tell her to get her things together and get out of my house, now."

Elizabeth turned red as a beet and was shaking like a leaf. She was furious, and didn't waste any time getting right to the point. "I will not ask her to leave, Edward. She's a kind, caring and generous person. She loves Becca and Jimmy and they love her. And I will not stand for you calling her names or mistreating her in any way. Do you understand that, Edward?"

For a few seconds, Edward made no reply. Then, with a hint of his old bitter and rancorous self, he began what at one time would have been a shameful outburst. Trying hard to exercise the control he had once had, and in the most angry and threatening tone he could muster, he said, "You listen to me, Elizabeth, and listen good! I'm still the head of this house and you won't tell me what I can or cannot do. I won't allow a nigger to stay here, and if you mouth off at me anymore you won't stay here either. This is my house and everything in it belongs to me. Now, you just keep that in mind, keep your mouth shut and do as I say. Get that woman out of my house now."

Even though it was a weak and feeble display, it appeared to have exerted him, drained him of all his strength. Clearly, he was no longer able to maintain that role of the loud-mouthed, mean-spirited bully. There was no energy, no vigor, no zip left in him. Edward was a mere shell of his old self, which didn't mean, of course, that one day he wouldn't regain all that he'd lost.

Elizabeth realized that his weakness and frailty had only slowed Edward temporarily. But she knew now was the time to show him that his verbal attack, his attempt to resume his dominant role, didn't scare her one bit. She was not going to allow him to intimidate her or scare her into submission. Truth of the matter was that she no longer feared Edward Johnson in any way whatsoever.

Whether her next move was real bravado or just an uncontrollable reaction, she wasn't sure, but Elizabeth was suddenly enraged. She screamed at Edward, "You can no longer intimidate me, control and abuse me, Edward Johnson. And this may be your house, or at least your daddy's house, but I am still your wife, Becca and Jimmy are your children, and you cannot and will not throw us out. Nor will you throw Louise out. Is that clear?"

Elizabeth had forgotten that Dr. Jones was still in the house, and at first was calmed a bit when he chose to put in his two cents worth. He said, "Look Edward, and you too, Elizabeth, this is no way to begin a new start. Please don't let this go any further; it won't solve anything.

"Edward, Elizabeth has a job now, and she has to have someone here to care for the children. There is absolutely nothing wrong with having Louise here. As a matter of fact, her presence could prove to be a help to you as well."

She'd heard enough, and before Dr. Jones could say anything more, Elizabeth politely interrupted him, saying, "Dr. Jones, thank you for trying to inject some reason into this argument, but I'm adamant about my position. I'm afraid there's no room for compromise. You may not agree, but I feel very strongly about this. Edward will no longer mistreat me or his children, nor will he mistreat Louise. She is a good woman, a hard-working woman, and the children and I have welcomed her into this house. And this may sound a bit melodramatic, but so be it. The only way Edward Johnson will remove Louise from this house will be over my dead body. Now then, Dr. Jones, thank you for everything. I think I'll be able to manage this situation, so please feel free to leave now and get back to your work."

Elizabeth walked over and opened the front door; she held it while Dr. Jones slowly walked out. She followed him to his car and said, "I'm sorry if I appeared rude, Dr. Jones, but I will do whatever is necessary to keep my husband from ever again abusing me, his children or anyone else, and that includes Louise Powell. You can report me to the authorities if you wish, but I'm telling you here and now that I will kill Edward Johnson if he lifts a hand to do harm to anyone in this house.

"If Edward is willing to behave like a human being should, I'll help him in any way that I can to return to normalcy and good health. I have no idea how long that will take, but once he has fully recovered I intend to divorce him. And I will retain a lawyer to see that my children and I can continue living in this house just as long as we wish. Edward will be the one who'll have to leave, not me and my children."

As he got into his car, Dr. Jones said, "Elizabeth, please don't do anything that you'll later regret."

"If things get out of hand, if I have to resort to desperate measures, Dr. Jones, be assured that I won't regret it. Thank you, doctor. Bye, now."

Back inside the house, Elizabeth saw that Louise was still ironing clothes, and Edward was sitting on the sofa, smoking a cigarette, looking pale and exhausted. Becca and Jimmy were no where to be seen. She walked over to Louise and said, "Where are Becca and Jimmy?"

"Oh, they're fine, Mrs. Johnson. They went out in the back yard to play."

Elizabeth walked over to the sofa and sat down, just a short distance from Edward. In a calm, almost soothing voice, she said, "Edward, I don't want to argue with you, but I want you to understand that I will no longer be subjected to your abuse, neither physical nor verbal. I want you to get well, and I'll help in any way that I can if you'll just be reasonable and behave decently.

"But please understand, Edward, Louise is going to stay right here and continue to do her job. I'm sure she'll cook for you and do anything she can to help you get well if you'll just let her. Something you must accept, though, is that you cannot call her derogatory names or mistreat her in any way. I won't stand for it, Edward.

"It's not my intention to try and diminish your manhood, and I don't want to 'wear the pants' in the family, but if being independent and having a mind of my own is called that, then I'll wear them proudly.

"Remember, I will do whatever is necessary to keep you from mistreating any of us. And that means you won't call Louise names, and you won't hit Becca or Jimmy simply because you're angry and things aren't going your way. That's all I have to say, Edward."

Elizabeth turned and started to walk away, then looked back and said, "No, in fact that's not all. I beg you to believe me when I say that I'm as serious about this as I've ever been about anything in my life. I can kill you if I have to, Edward. And should you doubt my sincerity and my ability to follow through on that threat, just try me." Edward sat there, white as a sheet, trembling and no doubt humiliated, but he didn't say a word.

Elizabeth got up and walked out to the backyard and played a while with Becca and Jimmy. It was almost dark when Louise came to the back door and told them that supper was ready.

The events of the day had left all of them a little tense, and soon after supper they were ready to go to bed. Elizabeth had moved some of her things out of her bedroom and fixed it for Edward. She planned to sleep on a pallet in the children's bedroom, and Edward would have her room all to himself.

Chapter Thirty-Three

For the first few weeks after his return, Edward took his medication regularly, ate the food Louise served him and didn't get mad or even use any curse words. It was a pleasant surprise for everyone.

He even agreed to go with Elizabeth and the children to Annette and Troy Bolin's for the Thanksgiving and Christmas holidays. He didn't talk much around them, and he didn't become angry or appear agitated at any time. When other members of the family got into a debate over some subject, Edward remained quiet, contributed nothing. He would have behaved much differently in the past.

Elizabeth had been extremely pleased when he hadn't gotten upset or expressed disapproval about her purchase of the new car. As a matter of fact, he seemed to like the car, and didn't even criticize her driving as they traveled to her parents' home. She was shocked, could hardly believe it.

Then as the New Year began, Elizabeth had a strange feeling that things were going too well, just too good to be true. But she tried not to think that way, didn't want to put a hex on their somewhat stable life.

Louise seemed contented and clearly loved Becca and Jimmy, and they absolutely adored her. And so far Edward had treated her, if not with courtesy and kindness, at least without contempt and scorn. It was a relationship with no blatant rancor on the part of either.

Jimmy loved school, had some interesting story to tell almost every day when he came home. He talked a lot about his little friend, Jane, and said he wished she lived closer so they could play together when school was out. Elizabeth said that maybe it would be possible for her to visit once in a while, and told him that if Jane's father would allow her to come and spend the day, then she would drive to her house and pick her up.

When May rolled around and it was time for school to be out, Jimmy told Jane what his mother had said about visiting during the summer. She seemed pleased when he told her that, but after a brief hesitation, said that her daddy was thinking about moving them to another town. So Jimmy gave her their telephone number, and Jane said she'd call and tell him if they moved.

It turned out that Jane did move that summer and after hearing about it, Jimmy seemed a little sad for the next few days. But soon after that, a new family moved into what had been old Mr. Clancy's house. Mr. Clancy had died a couple of months before. The house was a little more than a mile away, but when Elizabeth found out that there were children in the family, she, Becca and Jimmy walked down there one Saturday and introduced themselves. Elizabeth took a plate of brownies she'd baked that morning.

When they knocked and the door was opened, a young boy and girl stood there. The girl, who was probably nine or ten, said, "Are you our neighbors? Our mother's in the back yard planting some flowers." The boy, who was bigger than Jimmy, but looked to be about the same age, was grinning at Jimmy and Becca, and kind of waved his hand at Jimmy, as if in a friendly hello.

Elizabeth said to the children, "I'm Elizabeth Johnson and this is Becca and Jimmy. We live about a mile down the road and just wanted to stop by and say hello. You just moved in about a week ago, didn't you?"

"Yes ma'am," the little girl said politely. Then, "My name's Carolyn and this is my brother, Billy. He's seven and I'm ten. Do you want me to go get my mother?"

"Yes, Carolyn, if you don't mind. Tell her we'll only keep her a couple of minutes. I'd just like for her to know how happy we are to have you all as our new neighbors."

It seemed less than a minute before Carolyn had returned with her mother. They came around the side of the house through the yard. As the young boy, Billy, saw her, he came out of the house and walked over to his mother.

The woman greeted Elizabeth warmly, as if she were a long lost friend. She was smiling broadly as she reached for Elizabeth's hand, but then realized she still had on gloves, took them off and shook Elizabeth's hand, saying, "Well, hello there. Carolyn tells me that you all are our neighbors. I'm so happy to meet you. I'm Peggy Sue Higginbotham, and you've already met Carolyn and Billy. My husband, Cliff, is still asleep. He works the graveyard shift at the Paper Mill in Gillette. Y'all come on in the house."

"Oh, Peggy Sue, we can't stay. We just wanted to come by and welcome you, and bring you a plate of brownies; I baked them this morning." She smiled and said, "I'm Elizabeth Johnson and these are my children, Becca and Jimmy. We live in that brick house that's about a mile down the road on the left side. I think you've met our nearest neighbor, Mary Ann Butler.

"Mary Ann is the one who told us about you moving in. We don't want to keep you though, so we'll get on back to the house. I hope all of you can come visit us real soon."

"Oh, I hope we can, too, and y'all come back any time you get a chance. I wish you didn't have to hurry off," Peggy Sue said. "Yes, we did meet Mary Ann; she seems like such a nice lady." Peggy Sue smiled, and added, "I think we're really going to like it here. Thank you so much for the brownies; that was very nice of you."

The kids had begun running around in the yard, laughing and having a good time. Elizabeth called out, "Okay, kids, we have to go now. Maybe you can come back and play another time, or Billy and Carolyn can come down to our house."

Billy walked over to Elizabeth and said, "Ma'am, would it be all right if I show Becca and Jimmy my horse before you go?"

"Of course, Billy. I'd like to see him, too. I love horses, rode a lot when I was a kid. My parents still have horses and Becca and Jimmy get to ride when we go there for a visit."

Elizabeth and Peggy Sue followed the children around to the back of the house. Carolyn opened a gate and they all walked down a short path to the barn.

Billy began whistling and calling, "Come on, Tiny, come on out."

A Shetland pony suddenly appeared, and the name *Tiny* suited him perfectly. The pony was three, maybe three and a half feet tall. He was the cutest little thing. Jimmy and Becca were googly-eyed, staring at the little horse with absolute glee.

Elizabeth had grown up around horses and of course Becca and Jimmy had been around them when they were at their grandparents' farm. But this was the first time Elizabeth or the children had seen a Shetland.

Jimmy was transfixed, but finally looked up at Elizabeth and said, "Oh, Mommy, can I ride him, please?" Then he turned and gave a pleading look at Peggy Sue, but didn't say anything.

As Elizabeth started to respond, Peggy Sue said, "Tiny is real tame; Billy rides him all the time. So if it's okay with you, Elizabeth, it's certainly okay with me for Jimmy to ride, and Becca, too."

"Is there no problem with them riding bareback; Tiny won't mind?" Elizabeth wanted to be sure that the little horse wouldn't object to having a stranger on his back. Then she said, "That would be wonderful if they could ride for just a couple of minutes."

"Oh, sure, it's perfectly safe to ride him bareback, but it'll just take a minute to get him all saddled up," Peggy Sue said, as she headed inside the barn. The pony followed, and so did Carolyn and Billy.

Elizabeth, Becca and Jimmy waited until they returned with Tiny, saddled, and ready to ride. Peggy Sue sat Jimmy up on the pony, and began leading him around the barnyard. She told him that the next time he could ride all by himself. Jimmy was so excited that it probably was a good idea for Peggy Sue to lead the horse. He might have fallen off in his unrestrained joy and exuberance.

After Jimmy rode around the barnyard a couple of times, Peggy Sue asked Becca if she wanted to ride, and of course she did. She was as thrilled about it as Jimmy.

At last, Elizabeth, Jimmy and Becca headed for home. They thanked Peggy Sue for the pony ride, and Jimmy asked if Carolyn and Billy could come down to their house and play. Peggy Sue said they couldn't go today because they had to go into town a little later.

When Jimmy appeared to be disappointed, Peggy Sue assured him that they would be able to come down and play before too long, maybe sometime during the week. That pleased Jimmy, and he was practically jumping with joy all the way home.

Becca didn't seem as happy as Jimmy about having new kids as neighbors. Elizabeth guessed that she might be afraid Jimmy would want to spend his free time with Billy and wouldn't be around to play with her as much. But of course Jimmy would want Becca to tag along, wherever he was. He adored his little sister.

Although Becca might soon be taller than Jimmy, she would still be his "little" sister. And it didn't seem to bother him at all that he wasn't growing very fast. Elizabeth remembered Jimmy telling her one time that some great men in history had been small in stature, and then named a few: John Keats, the poet; Max Linder, a silent film actor; Fiorello LaGuardia, who had once been the mayor of New York City; and Andrew Carnegie, a steel industry businessman and millionaire.

When he told her this, Elizabeth had playfully asked, "Who are you trying to impress, my sensational, sensible, super son? I already know you are amazing, that you're the brightest star in the solar system." And then more seriously, with tears in her eyes Elizabeth had said, "I'm so proud of you, sweetheart, and I love you more than life itself."

"Mommy, please don't cry about it. By the way, your alliteration with the *Esses* was a terrific tangle of tantalizing and tasteful teasing." Jimmy had barely managed to get that sentence out of his mouth before he burst out laughing. Elizabeth began laughing, too, and the more they tried to stop, the harder they laughed, side-splitting howls.

At last, after the laughing had slowed to a little snickering, Jimmy said, "That was fun, wasn't it, Mommy?"

"Ya darn tootin'," she said, and the laughing had started all over again.

That summer, Elizabeth thanked her lucky stars for Peggy Sue Higginbotham and her family. Since Peggy Sue was at home every day she invited Becca and Jimmy down to play with Carolyn and Billy a lot during that summer. Louise would walk them down, then Peggy Sue would later walk them back home.

And every once in a while, Mary Ann would take all four kids into town for an ice cream cone, and sometime they would go to the park and play there for a while. It was a fun summer for Becca and Jimmy.

Chapter Thirty-Four

Elizabeth's earlier thoughts that things had been going too well and wouldn't last forever, persisted. She didn't have any special abilities to see things in the future as her son sometimes could, but she did have a nagging feeling that something was about to happen, something that would disrupt their present peaceful existence. And she just couldn't shake that notion.

At the beginning of the school year in 1953, Becca, then six years old, entered the first grade. Jimmy was eight and in the fourth. They were at the same school, and Jimmy promised to look after Becca; he said they could even eat lunch together every day.

Elizabeth stayed home from work on the first day of school to help lessen any fears Becca might have. She helped her get dressed and ready to go after she and Jimmy had their breakfast. And Becca looked so cute in her little blue dress and Mary Jane shoes. She was excited and happy to be going off to school. Elizabeth waited with her and Jimmy at the bus stop, but told them she wouldn't be able to do that anymore because she'd have to leave for work before the bus came. But Louise said that she'd wait with them every morning, and of course be there when they returned every afternoon.

It turned out that Becca really liked school, and especially liked her teacher, Mrs. Thompson. Becca wasn't quite as outgoing as Jimmy, but still was able to make some friends right away.

Work was going well for Elizabeth, the kids were doing really well, and Louise had settled into a fairly comfortable routine with Edward. He was still at home every day, not yet ready to return to work. However, he'd gotten much stronger and gained perhaps twenty-five or thirty pounds. After the physical therapy stopped, Edward continued doing some of the exercises the therapist had recommended. He was walking a lot better now, still using a cane, but had only a slight limp.

Elizabeth recently had bought a little black and white television set that she felt would be a lot of company for Edward, and it was. He loved it, thought it was the greatest invention of all time, and the children loved it, too. It was an Admiral 17 inch set that she knew they couldn't afford, but had gone ahead and bought it anyway. An antenna was installed on the roof and still they were able to get only two channels. But folks thought that more towns and cities would soon have television stations.

One of the shows Edward liked was a comedy called *I Love Lucy*, with Lucille Ball and Desi Arnaz. Becca and Jimmy really liked it, too. They would get so tickled when that show was on. Another favorite of Jimmy's was *Your Hit Parade*. Edward liked that one, as well. There were several singers who appeared on the show each week: Snooky Lanson, Dorothy Collins, Giselle MacKenzie and others would sing what was most popular that week. Sometimes Jimmy already knew the songs. If he didn't, he would learn the lyrics of those he really liked and soon be singing and playing them.

At last, during the second week of November, Edward was able to return to work, but only part time. The doctor had restricted him to only four hours a day, for maybe one month; if he did well, then he could go full time. It had been a long time coming, and Edward was pleased. Elizabeth knew his struggle had been a difficult one.

She wasn't at all surprised that the Paper Mill took him back on as an electrician. She'd been told by several people that Edward had been well liked at the Mill, and that he was an exceptionally good worker. Apparently that had been true even during the times when he'd been on his worst behavior in his own home:

drinking excessively, throwing fits, whipping the children, ranting and raving. Elizabeth didn't like to think about those days; they were best forgotten. Of course she hoped that Edward was now a changed man, but she had her doubts. In the long run, however, it would make absolutely no difference in her decision to leave him.

Elizabeth was still sleeping in the children's room and had no intention of resuming an intimate relationship with Edward. He had tried a few times to broach the subject with her but she told him she wasn't interested, that it could never happen again. He became a bit irritated and asked her what he was supposed to do if she would have nothing to do with him. She told him to do whatever he wanted, and then asked how he had solved that problem in the hospital for more than a year and a half. Edward had walked away, not responding.

Elizabeth had only heard him curse a few times since he'd been home from the hospital, and he'd made no attempt to spank Becca or Jimmy. But he'd yelled at them plenty of times. That, to some degree, could be overlooked when he was feeling so bad and they got on his nerves. The surprise had been that he continued to be quite civil to Louise.

Then one day, a couple of weeks after Edward had returned to work, Elizabeth received a telephone call from his workplace, telling her that he'd been injured in an accident, and had been taken to Gillette General Hospital. The call had first been made to Elizabeth's home, and after determining that it was an emergency, Louise had given the caller Elizabeth's office number.

Her office wasn't far from the hospital, and after telling Dr. Parker about the accident he told her to go on over to the hospital right away. Dr. Parker was a wonderful boss, and had treated Elizabeth so well since she'd been working there.

The person who called didn't say what Edward's injuries were, acted as if he didn't know, and maybe he didn't. He just said there had been an accident and that Edward was being treated at the hospital. Elizabeth knew that working with electricity could sometimes be dangerous, and she hoped that he hadn't been electrocuted.

After arriving at the hospital, she nervously walked to the Information Desk and asked where she could find Edward Johnson. After learning that, she stopped by the Nurses Station, identified herself, and inquired about Edward's condition. She was then introduced to a Dr. Burton who was sitting there doing some paper work. He was the doctor who had treated Edward upon his arrival in the Emergency Room.

Dr. Burton didn't know all the details of the accident, but was told by the ambulance attendant as much as he himself knew. Edward apparently had gone into an electrical box looking for loose wires after being told someone had been shocked. As he had stuck a screwdriver in to tighten wires, somehow he accidentally touched metal; this caused an electrical arc flash. There was a very bright light and a deafening explosion as the radiant energy from the electrical equipment spread.

Edward received severe burns and quite a gash on his forehead as he fell. Other workers were somehow able to help him, and an ambulance arrived within a very few minutes. Another worker received minor burns, and there was extensive damage to equipment, tools and the surrounding work area.

Dr. Burton said Edward had sustained what at the moment he was calling moderate third-degree burns on one arm. The burns on his other arm and his torso were not as deep, and could be classified as second-degree. But he said that they were still bad enough to cause a great deal of pain, as well as scarring, and would take some time to heal.

The doctor told Elizabeth they had Edward on an IV line to replace lost fluids, and that a tube had been inserted into his throat to help him breathe. The burns had been cleaned and the dead tissue surgically removed. Then antibiotic cream was put on the burns and they were lightly covered with sterile bandages. And naturally he had to have pain medication and antibiotics.

Dr. Burton explained that they would need to change the bandages frequently and carefully monitor the burns to watch for infection. He concluded by saying that there might be some damage to his eyes or even some loss of hearing. It would be several days before the extent of his injuries could be fully determined. And then he remembered to tell Elizabeth that the gash in Edward's head had required quite a few stitches, and that he had a mild concussion.

Elizabeth looked in on Edward for a few minutes; he had been heavily sedated. A little later, as she left the hospital, it was pouring rain. With her office being only two blocks from the hospital, she'd chosen to walk there, thinking it might be difficult to find a parking space. Unfortunately, at the time, she hadn't considered that a storm might be brewing, even though it had been thundering and looking rainy most of the day.

She began running as fast as she could, and was panting after a few hundred yards. Already drenched, she chose to walk the rest of the way, and reached the office looking wet and wilted. Dr. Parker's nurse, Karen, saw her and said, "Good gracious Elizabeth, you must have walked to the hospital. Why didn't you take your car? You're soaking wet, girl. You better go home and get on some dry clothes. First though, tell us what happened with Edward; is he all right?"

Elizabeth just wasn't in the mood to talk, but told Karen and the others what she'd found out about Edward's accident. Then she decided to take Karen's advice and go on home. Dr. Parker had already left, and since it was near quitting time, she didn't think twice about leaving a bit early.

She got an old towel from the trunk of the car and laid it on the seat to protect it from her wet clothes. She liked to keep the car spic and span, in tip-top shape. As she drove home, Elizabeth was thinking that fate had once again dealt her a bad blow. Then she started to feel guilty; after all, it wasn't her lying injured in a hospital bed. Edward was the one who had been dealt the bad blow, and of course she felt sorry for him. But he seemed destined to have bad luck for the rest of his life, and she couldn't help thinking that *one's actions inevitably lead to consequences.* That old adage, "you reap what you sow" seemed to apply to Edward's life.

However, it was important that she not judge Edward, and do whatever she could to help him. Even though her plans would once again go by the wayside, she had to deal with the matter at hand. She was sure that eventually things would work out okay.

Edward remained in the hospital through the Christmas holidays. Elizabeth and the children went to her parents' house where she was able to relax for a few days. It was reinvigorating, as well.

Amy had graduated from college and had a job at a law firm in Garden City. John had another year in college, had changed his major several times, and still didn't know what he was going to do after he graduated. They were both at home for the holidays, and of course Tommy was there, too. As always, the visit was so much fun for Becca and Jimmy; they loved going to their grandparents' house. And now that Elizabeth had a car, she'd been able to take them for a visit quite often.

Mary Ann had been away during Christmas time, and was sorely missed by all of Elizabeth's family. She had taken a trip to New York City with an old friend whom she'd recently been in touch with. It was her first time in the big city, and afterward just couldn't stop talking about it. She had Becca and Jimmy wanting to go there after telling them about all the things she saw. Jimmy was particularly interested in the Empire State Building, and asked Mary Ann all kinds of questions.

But what Elizabeth wanted to talk about was Mary Ann's old friend, Kevin. Mary Ann got a real kick out of that; she knew Elizabeth was hoping that it was the beginning of a romance, which was not the case. It took her a while to convince Elizabeth that there was absolutely nothing romantic about the relationship, that she had grown up with Kevin and he had always been like a brother, still was.

Chapter Thirty-Five

In January of the New Year, 1954, the weather suddenly turned real cold. The winter up to that point had been quite mild, which was pretty typical for the winter months. The cold spell lasted a while and on the day Edward was released from the hospital, the last week in February, it even snowed a little bit. There was enough for the children to build a very skinny little snowman. By the following day, though, the snow was almost gone. Still, it was colder than a witch's you-know-what.

Edward wasn't in the best of shape, but the burns were healing, and Dr. Jones thought he would do okay at home. His health insurance was paying for a nurse to come by every other day to change his bandages and help him bathe. The scarring was going to be bad, at least on the one arm. He was still in pain and taking a lot of medication. And even though he was able to sit up for short periods, he spent much of his time in bed. Physical therapy would be needed to help him use his arms again; that would come later.

According to Dr. Burton, who had treated Edward after the accident, it probably would be quite a long time before Edward could return to work. But fortunately, because he had been injured there, Edward was able to collect what was called Workmen's Compensation, a law that had been enacted a few years before, to protect employees injured on the job. It paid only a percentage of his salary, but that, in addition to what Elizabeth brought home from her job, was enough to manage okay. Finances were not the most serious problem at the moment. The problem was that Edward seemed to be so discontented; miserable, in fact. And he was losing his temper with some regularity.

Elizabeth was concerned that he would throw a fit and jump on the children, or even Louise, about something or other. Oh, how she hoped that wouldn't happen!

One Sunday, Louise's day off, she asked Elizabeth if she could take Becca and Jimmy with her for the day, that they would first go to church and then she would "show them off" to some of her neighbors. Jimmy begged his mother to say okay, and finally she agreed, after assurance from Louise that being with them all week didn't wear her out, that she still wanted to spend the day with them. And of course, Jimmy and Becca were thrilled.

Louise had taught Jimmy two or three more songs, some of them old spirituals, but he still wanted to hear more and knew that Louise's church would be the place for that. He could now play, and sing, *Swing Low, Sweet Chariot* and *Were You There When They Crucified My Lord*. He did a great job, too; Louise could hardly believe how quickly he'd learned the songs. And she had been moved to tears the first time she heard him play and sing *How Great Thou Art*.

When Louise, Becca and Jimmy returned home that evening, Jimmy was anxious to tell his mother what happened at church, but didn't want to do it right away. He was afraid his daddy would hear, get mad and start yelling and cursing. Edward didn't know they were going to Louise's church; he wouldn't have liked that at all. And Jimmy certainly didn't want to say anything in his presence that would set him off.

When Elizabeth asked them if they'd had fun, Jimmy tried to be humorous and said, "Yes, Mommy, we had as much fun as a tumblebug in a pile of ....."

"*Jimmy Johnson!* Don't you dare say that," interrupted Elizabeth, and turned away to hide her smile.

"But, Mommy, you didn't let me finish. I was only going to say 'a pile of dung'; is that a bad word?"

"Well, no, it's not really a bad word, but neither is it a pleasant one. I'm sorry, though, that I jumped the gun."

"That's okay." Then he laughed and said, "You know I wouldn't say that word. But we really did have fun today, and I'll tell you all about it a little later. I think Miss Lou and Becca had as much fun as I did."

Becca said, "And Mommy, Miss Lou took us to the grocery store and bought our lunch. She fixed us ham and cheese sandwiches, Fritos, Dr. Pepper and oatmeal cookies. And you know what? We played with some kids that lived next to her house. We played jump rope and hopscotch; it was fun."

"Oh, I bet it was; sounds like a yummy lunch, too. Maybe some day you can do that again. Right now, though, you and Jimmy should go in the bedroom and say hello to your daddy. But don't wake him if he's sleeping," Elizabeth said, and off they went.

They were back in the living room right away, telling Elizabeth that their daddy was asleep. Then Jimmy said, rather quietly, "Now, Mommy, I can tell you about the service at Miss Lou's church; you should have been there. There was a lady who played the piano, and she could play much better than me. I've never heard singing like that; it was really, really good. After the service, Miss Lou introduced us and told her that I could play the piano, too. Her name was Mrs. Williams; she was nice and smelled like baby powder.

He hesitated a few seconds, chuckled a bit and said, "Do you remember that one time when I told Mimi that people should 'emote' when they listened to good music? Remember that?"

"Yes, I do remember."

Jimmy grinned from ear to ear and said, "Well, the people in Miss Lou's church were emoting all over the place. I never saw anything like that before. They sang, and I mean they could really sing. They were clapping, keeping time to the music and swaying back and forth. During the preacher's sermon, they said 'amen' a lot and some words I didn't understand. But I especially liked the music, the playing and singing. I think maybe Becca was at first just a little bit scared, weren't you, Bec?"

"No, Jimmy, I wasn't scared. It surprised me, that's all," Becca said.

As Elizabeth was telling them how glad she was that they'd had a fun day, Louise came out of her room and asked, "Did the children tell you about our day?"

"They sure did, Louise; sounds like a great time was had by all. It was a new experience for Becca and Jimmy, and was certainly nice of you to take them. Jimmy loved the service, and I'm sure he'll soon be after you to teach him some of the songs he heard today."

"Yes, I think so, and I'll be happy to teach him," Louise said. "I'm so glad they had a good time. They're fine children, respectful of others and well-behaved."

♫ Chapter Thirty-Six

Jimmy celebrated his tenth birthday in February of 1955. Louise had baked him a chocolate cake and there it was on the table when he got home from school, with ten candles. Mary Ann came down after supper and brought him a couple of books he'd asked for. Louise gave him a fancy checkerboard and a box of checkers. Elizabeth gave him a brand new five-dollar bill, had it wrapped up in a little box, and told him to buy whatever he wanted with it. She knew, though, that he had been saving every penny he got; he wanted to buy a bicycle.

Edward gave Jimmy two one-dollar bills, and Becca was as happy as a lark when she gave him a Monopoly set and a funny little card. She and her mother had gone shopping together to get the present and card.

Jimmy was thrilled with all his gifts and seemed especially pleased about getting the money. He told everyone that he was saving it and one day would have enough to buy a bicycle from Sears and Roebuck for $19.95.

His grandmother called to wish him a happy birthday, and said they would come to see him over the weekend.

Edward sat in the living room with everybody and even though he didn't sing along, seemed to enjoy hearing everyone else sing *Happy Birthday* to Jimmy. But the party had to be called to a halt early so that Becca and Jimmy could get to bed; they had to go to school the next day.

One evening after Elizabeth got home from work, a couple of weeks after his birthday, Jimmy told his mother that he wanted to talk to her, alone. She took him into his bedroom and closed the door. He began talking rapidly, which he usually did when he was real excited or anxious about something.

"Mommy, I have a friend at school, his name is Wayne. And when we were playing at recess, he said he had a rock in his shoe. He sat down on the ground and took it off so he could get the rock out. I had noticed his shoes before, all raggedy looking, and when he tried to shake out the rock I saw the bottom and there was a big hole. Before he put it back on, he pulled out something that looked like part of a paper sack, then refolded it and placed it back in the shoe, to help cover the hole, I guess.

"I didn't say anything, but another boy saw it and began a singsong or a chant, I guess it was: 'Wayne's got a holey shoe, Wayne's got a holey shoe,' laughed, and ran off.

"Wayne was embarrassed, I could tell, but he just put his shoe back on, tied it, then got up and said, 'throw me the ball, Jimbo.' And he threw that ball harder than I'd ever seen, trying to hit the boy, but missed.

"I want to give the money I've saved to Wayne's mother so she can buy him new shoes. But I don't want them to know where it came from. See, I don't think he wants charity and he doesn't want people feeling sorry for him either. He lives in Gillette with his mother and little brother. His daddy's in jail for stealing, he told me. Mommy, can we give his mother the money without them knowing where it came from?"

Elizabeth hugged Jimmy close to her and just held him there for a while. Finally she said, "Oh, my precious Jimmy, you are such a wonderful boy, so giving and loving. But do you really want to give up the money you've been saving for a bicycle? It might take you a long time to save that much again. You need to give it some more thought, okay? If you decide that's what you really want to do, then we'll figure out the best way to do it so that Wayne and his family won't know where the money came from. Now, just sleep on it and tell me tomorrow what you've decided. Will you do that for me?"

"Okay, but I already know what my decision will be." Elizabeth thought she knew what it would be, too.

The following morning, just before Elizabeth left for work, Jimmy told her that his mind was made up; he wanted Wayne's family to have his money and he gave her his $16.87. She told him that she would figure out some way to get the money to Wayne's family.

On Elizabeth's lunch break, she went to a public telephone booth and called Jimmy's school. She spoke with the office secretary and left a message for Jimmy's teacher, saying she would stop by the following morning to speak with her for a few minutes. She'd decided that the best thing to do was buy a money order, give it to the teacher and have her mail it to Wayne's family, anonymously. She added $8.13 to the $16.87, went to the post office and bought a money order for $25.00.

It made her sad that Jimmy was giving up his bicycle money, but she also was very proud of him. She'd try to figure out a way to get that bicycle before too long. There was still a little money in Edward's savings account, although not enough to fritter away. She had to be a bit more frugal now, but was thinking, *where there's a will, there's a way.*

The following morning Elizabeth found Jimmy's teacher, Mrs. Robinson, in her classroom grading papers before class started. After Elizabeth explained things to her, Mrs. Robinson agreed to send the money directly to Wayne's home, and to send a note saying something like "Santa was a bit late getting to your house, so use this money to buy your children some things they might need."

"Do you think it will be okay to send a note like that?" Mrs. Robinson asked.

"Of course. As a matter of fact, that's a good idea,' said Elizabeth. "I was wondering, Mrs. Robinson, if you've met Wayne's mother? Do you know anything about the family?"

"Yes, she came by the school a few days ago to pick up Wayne. She seemed real nice. I don't want to gossip, but apparently Wayne's daddy is in jail for stealing money from the garage where he worked. I don't know how long he'll be there, but clearly Wayne's mother was embarrassed and ashamed at having to disclose that information. There's only one other child besides Wayne, a little boy about four or five.

"Mrs. Johnson, I just want to say that this generous gesture of Jimmy's is extraordinary, very unusual for a child that age. Clearly, Jimmy doesn't have a selfish bone in his body; he's wonderful. And he's so smart, too, but has never lorded that over the other kids. He's nice to everybody, and it's impossible not to love him. He never loses his temper or gets upset, a truly remarkable child."

"You're right, Mrs. Robinson. I, too, think that he's remarkable. Oh, and before I go, I need to remind you that Jimmy doesn't want anyone to know that he's done this. It's to be kept a secret, okay?"

"Certainly; I won't say a word to anyone, not even to the school principal. You have my word."

"That's fine, Mrs. Robinson. Thank you so much; I'll be going now." Elizabeth walked to her car and headed back to the office. She was so proud of her son, thinking how true Mrs. Robinson's words were, that Jimmy was "remarkable."

Jimmy was so happy when Elizabeth told him that the money was being sent to Wayne's family, and asked, "Do you think his mother will buy him new shoes?"

"I think she probably will, Jimmy. Unless, of course, there are other things that are needed more. But if she doesn't, one day maybe you can figure out how to get his shoe size and we'll buy some for him. How's that?"

"Okay, that'll be perfect."

A couple of weeks later, Jimmy ran to his mother's car as she was driving up after work, and said, "Mommy, guess what? Wayne has new shoes and he wore a new pair of pants and a new shirt, too. Isn't that good news? And he looked happier than he usually looks, but didn't say a word about the new things. I bet with those old shoes his feet really got cold, and wet too, when the weather was bad. I prayed hard that his mother would buy him new ones with some of that money, so my prayers were answered, weren't they?"

"Yes, they were, Jimmy, they certainly were."

♫ Chapter Thirty-Seven

I n May of 1955, Becca turned eight and Elizabeth decided to have a party for her on the Saturday following her birthday. Billy and Carolyn Higginbotham, who lived down the road from the Johnsons, were invited. Two little girls from Becca's class came; their parents drove them there. Elizabeth drove them home later in the afternoon.

Becca's grandparents came early that morning and spent the day. They brought Becca two cute little dresses and a little play-stove and dinnerware set; Becca loved that. Recently she had started begging Louise to let her help with the cooking, but she was too little for anything like that. She got several other gifts: a set of jacks, barrettes for her hair, a little doll that cried, as well as some paper dolls.

The party was a big success, with cake and ice cream after the presents were opened. The children played out in the yard for a while, mostly on the swing and sliding board. Then Elizabeth dropped Billy and Carolyn off at their house, and drove Becca's two little friends home.

School was out a couple of weeks later, and Jimmy and Becca worried Louise every day to take them to the creek to fish. Mary Ann had bought fishing poles for them the summer before and had taken them fishing a couple of times. If Louise or Mary Ann would have agreed to go with them, they'd be down at that creek every day. But since that wasn't going to happen, they had to find other things to occupy their time.

Jimmy and Billy Higginbotham had become real buddies, and they visited back and forth a lot during that summer. But one day when both Becca and Jimmy were down there playing, climbing trees, Jimmy fell out of a tree, breaking his arm.

Peggy Sue, Billy's mother, immediately telephoned Louise and asked her to call and tell Elizabeth. She said she would take Jimmy to the Emergency Room at the hospital in Gillette, and that Elizabeth should meet them there.

It was rare for her children to get sick, maybe a little cold now and then. Neither had ever broken a bone, so naturally the telephone call telling Elizabeth that Jimmy had broken his arm really scared her, and she rushed right over to the hospital.

By the time Elizabeth arrived, the doctor had set Jimmy's arm and had it in a cast. Jimmy was crying, and she hugged him and tried to reassure him, telling him he'd soon be as good as new. He complained that his arm was hurting. Of course he'd been given medicine that would help relieve the pain. When the doctor turned away from Jimmy for a second and then turned back to look at him, he was wearing a big rubber clown's nose. That made Jimmy laugh, and his crying stopped for a little while.

After the doctor was finished, Elizabeth thanked Peggy Sue and put Jimmy in her car and drove home. He fell asleep on the way, but woke up as she started to carry him into the house. He started crying again when he looked at the cast on his arm.

Louise had picked Becca up from Peggy Sue's house after getting the call about Jimmy. And when Becca saw Elizabeth drive up, she ran out and began talking to him, saying, "It's okay, Jimmy; don't cry, you're gonna be okay," and patted his leg as they went in the house.

It was Edward's opportunity once again to act like a complete fool. The minute he saw Jimmy crying he began to taunt him. He told him that only sissies cried like that, and continued to harass him until Elizabeth had had enough. She told him to please shut up, that he ought to be ashamed of himself. She said that he, of all people, should be a little more understanding when he saw someone hurt, and especially when it was his very own child.

Jimmy, however, didn't seem to pay any attention to Edward, and when Elizabeth asked Louise to bring him a bowl of ice cream, he even smiled. Shortly afterward, he fell asleep on the sofa. Becca sat right there beside him until he woke up. Then she began asking him silly little riddles, and before long they were both laughing.

It was a few days, though, before Jimmy felt like playing. But he healed quickly and the cast was removed after six weeks. By that time he had decided that climbing trees was not for him.

Elizabeth started to think that each year was passing by faster and faster. In September, Jimmy started sixth grade, Becca third. During the summer Jimmy had learned the names of all the presidents, in the order they had been inaugurated. After school began, at night after they finished their homework, Jimmy spent time teaching them to Becca.

Louise was real good about getting both Becca and Jimmy to do their homework after they got home from school, usually before they were allowed to go out and play. Becca had very little homework, but Jimmy always seemed to have a lot. And it turned out that he had an advantage when his class began studying about the U.S. presidents, since he already knew all of them. He also knew their vice presidents.

Jimmy's ability to recall almost everything he read, as well as images he saw, was incredible. Elizabeth believed that he had a photographic memory, which apparently really did exist in a few children, but was very, very rare.

Not only was Jimmy's class studying the presidents, but one of the assignments was to find out some unusual fact about one of them. He was so excited because he already knew an unusual fact, one that he thought was hilarious. He said that William Howard Taft, the 27th president, was so fat that he got stuck in the bathtub at the White House, and that a special tub had to be brought in for him to use. He shared that amusing fact frequently, and laughed harder each time.

Even though things were difficult with Edward, there was real sympathy for him when his daddy died just two days before Christmas. Clarence Johnson had been in poor health for quite a while, but Edward had kept in touch by calling him on the telephone now and then. Of course he hadn't been able to visit him for some time. The death of Mr. Johnson was hard for Edward, and for a few days he was quieter and more subdued. But it certainly didn't affect him in the way his mother's death had. One of Mr. Johnson's employees came and drove Edward to the funeral.

The farm and all of Clarence Johnson's assets were left to Edward, but it would be sometime before he was well enough to manage things. The foreman, who ran things at the farm, said he would stay on as long as he was needed.

Shortly into the New Year, Elizabeth consulted a lawyer about starting the divorce proceedings. The lawyer made it sound like a simple matter, saying there should be no problems. He told her that the house they were living in would become hers, and that she would probably get a sizeable monetary settlement. The amount, of course, would depend on what Edward's assets amounted to now that his daddy had left everything to him. It had been rumored that Mr. Johnson was worth a lot of money, although Elizabeth had no idea if that was true. She did know that there was a lot of property and the farm was a big operation, so that probably brought in quite a bit of money each year.

Elizabeth wasn't greedy, but naturally she would be glad to receive any sum of money that might be coming her way as a part of the divorce settlement. She could put the money away for her children's college education. She wanted both Jimmy and Becca to go to college if that was at all possible. And that would take a lot of money.

But she would take one day at a time, one step at a time. Life was just too precious to spend it worrying. She knew what her responsibilities and obligations were, and she intended to do her darndest to fulfill them. She lived for her children; they were her life, her love, and she would not waver in her determination and dedication to take care of them, come hell or high water. The divorce settlement would definitely make things a lot easier. She still believed that her prayers would be answered, that things were going to work out well, just as she had hoped and prayed.

♪ Chapter Thirty Eight

Edward's physical condition had improved greatly. He was able to use his arms more and more, even though he had little or no sensation in most of the fingers on his left hand. The doctors were now saying that the severe burns had destroyed the nerve endings and that he would not have feeling ever again in those fingers.

They also told Edward it was unlikely that he would be able to resume his job as an electrician, but assured him that he'd be able to do other kinds of work.

Upon hearing that discouraging news from the doctors, Edward became angry and upset. He started snapping at the kids more, and he was critical of Louise, but he didn't call her names or use racial epithets.

He was taking several different kinds of medication: something for pain, antibiotics, and the medicine that was prescribed for him at the mental hospital. He had been told by his doctors that he shouldn't drink alcohol while taking that medicine and he hadn't done so, as far as anyone knew.

Then one day Louise overheard him talking to someone on the telephone about bringing him some beer. An hour or so later, a man arrived with a crate that was filled with at least a couple cases of beer. Edward told the man to put it in the kitchen, then paid him and he left.

That was the beginning of a living hell for Louise, Elizabeth, Becca and Jimmy. Edward drank beer constantly, hardly eating at all. He would sit in front of the television and yell or curse at someone on the screen. At other times, he paced back and forth across the living room floor, cursing people he knew and some he didn't know.

He never answered the telephone, but when it rang, he would start screaming profanities. If it was Elizabeth who answered it, he would accuse her of talking to a boyfriend. He would make remarks like, "Just let me get my hands on that so-and-so, I'll kill him," or "That S.O.B. will wish he'd never been born."

Sometimes Elizabeth would try to reason with him, and occasionally that would calm him, but not always. She, Louise and the kids would usually go into their own rooms and try to tune him out. Some of his remarks were completely "off the wall," made no sense whatsoever. Louise believed he was insane, and told Elizabeth that she was afraid of him.

Elizabeth called Dr. Milton Jones, who had been the family doctor for a number of years. She told him that they just couldn't put up with Edward's behavior much longer, and asked for his advice. She told the doctor that she believed Edward had stopped taking the medicine that was supposed to help control his moods, even though he claimed to be taking all the medicine he'd been prescribed.

Dr. Jones came out to the house one day to talk to Edward. He tried to convince him how important it was for him to take all his medication, and that he shouldn't be drinking alcohol with any of it. He said that the combination could kill him. He pleaded with Edward to behave himself, that he shouldn't take his anger and frustration out on Louise and the family.

Edward promised Dr. Jones that he would really make an effort to do better, that he would take his medication, but that he wasn't going to give up the beer. He said that it didn't matter one iota if it killed him, that he really didn't have a reason for living anyway.

Everyone tried to avoid Edward, particularly Jimmy. Most of the time he seemed ill-at-ease and uncomfortable around his daddy. He told Elizabeth that he wished he would go away and never come back. Of course that was what all of them wished, even though they didn't say it out loud.

After again consulting the lawyer about the divorce, Elizabeth was relieved that he seemed to have a solution for the problem. He told her that she should call the sheriff the next time Edward went on a rampage, and that he probably would spend a few days in jail. He said that he'd do what he could to speed up matters concerning the divorce. He was confident that he could get some kind of order from a judge to declare a legal separation, and said that would force Edward to move out of the house.

Elizabeth was agreeable, telling the lawyer to do whatever was necessary. She felt a little better after talking with him.

Surprisingly, things improved considerably over the next several weeks, with few outbursts from Edward. He still drank a lot of beer, would call up some liquor store in Gillette when he ran out and they delivered whatever he wanted.

The lawyer called regularly to tell Elizabeth how things were progressing, assuring her that it wouldn't be long until things were settled and Edward would have to move out. He reminded her to call the sheriff when Edward threw one of his fits.

It seemed strange to Elizabeth that Edward wouldn't want to voluntarily move into his daddy's house. After all, it was now his house since Clarence Johnson's death. Surely he would be more contented there, could drink as much as he wanted and do what he pleased, without anyone interfering. He would have a housekeeper to cook and clean for him. And there would be hired hands to go buy his liquor; he could drink himself to death if he wanted to.

Becca and Jimmy had managed to do well in school in spite of all the turmoil at home. They loved school, but always looked forward to summertime. Louise took them fishing at least a couple of times a week, and they spent time playing with Billy and Carolyn

Higginbotham. They still loved the Shetland pony, but were getting too big to ride it.

Of course summer ended too quickly, as summers usually do. And it was about a week after school started when Elizabeth's attorney paid Edward a visit, with legal separation papers in hand. After that, Edward packed up his clothes and a few other things, and called a man who had worked for his daddy to come pick him up. *Too easy*, Elizabeth thought.

But it was like a heavy weight had been lifted from her, Louise and the children. There was a change in the house, a joy that was almost palpable. Jimmy began playing the piano again. Louise taught him some new songs, and often in the evening after supper was finished, everybody would gather around the piano and sing as Jimmy played. It was such a welcome change, like nothing they'd experienced for a very long time; it was heavenly.

Elizabeth didn't get her hopes up too high, but wished with every ounce of her being that Edward would stay completely out of their lives. She was afraid, though, that he would be vindictive, try to get revenge for what he might perceive as outrageous wrong-doing against him. His pride and dignity would be wounded and that would fuel his anger, resentment and bitterness.

Thankfully, there was no word from Edward for more than a year and the family settled into a comfortable routine. Becca and Jimmy were happy, made lots of friends at school and visited back and forth during the summers. Even during the school year they would invite friends to spend the night. But Elizabeth allowed them to do that only occasionally.

Jimmy's special gift of seeing things in the future had sort of waned a bit over the years. When Elizabeth had asked him about it, he said that he would rather not have that gift. He told her he was doing his best to resist, or fight it, and was happy that it didn't happen much any more.

Then one Saturday when Elizabeth had taken Becca and Jimmy into town, they stopped in a café to have lunch. At first, as they ate, Jimmy was his usual talkative, out-going self, telling about things that had happened that week at school. Suddenly, he got quiet and closed his eyes for a few seconds. Elizabeth became concerned and asked him what was wrong, thinking he might be sick.

Jimmy opened his eyes and said, "Daddy's at our house now. I think he wants to hurt Miss Lou; we have to go home, Mommy."

Elizabeth got up immediately, saying, "I'll call and see if Louise answers; there's a pay telephone right outside. Sit there, Jimmy, with Becca, and I'll be right back." She rushed out of the café, hoping and praying that Louise was safe and would answer the telephone.

She was back in a couple of minutes and before she could say anything, Jimmy asked, "Is Miss Lou okay, Mommy?"

"Yes, she's fine. But you were right, Jimmy. Your daddy went there and tried to get in, but Louise, standing right inside the front door, told him that he couldn't come in. He then began pounding on the door, but Louise knew that in his poor physical condition he couldn't break down the door. So she threatened him, saying, 'I've got a gun, Edward, and I'm not afraid to use it, so you better get in that truck and leave,' and that's exactly what he did, after a stream of obscenities.

"But I think we should be getting on home. We'll have to go to the library another day. So finish your food and let's get going."

At about the same time, both Becca and Jimmy said, "I'm finished." They got up from the table, and Elizabeth went to pay their bill.

Outside the café Jimmy asked, "Mommy, do you think that Daddy is crazy, or is he just mean? I think that he's crazy, and maybe whatever is wrong with his brain makes him mean. So I'm wondering if everybody who has something wrong with their brain can be considered crazy. But no, that can't be, 'cause just think about the people who are mentally retarded or simple-minded, they're not crazy even though something is wrong with their brain."

Elizabeth was trying to absorb what he was saying, thinking about how she could respond, when he continued, "And how about me, there is probably something abnormal about my brain, and

I'm not crazy, am I? So I guess I've answered my own question: you're not necessarily crazy just because something's wrong with your brain." He laughed, then said, "I think we should change the subject. What do you want to talk about, Bec? Got any great ideas?"

Becca said, "Jimmy, I don't think you're interested in what I want to talk about right now." She looked at Elizabeth and said, "Mommy, I was planning to ask you something while we were at lunch, so here goes. I want to get my hair cut short; can I, please? My friend, Cathy, got to go to a beauty shop and she got her hair cut real short. I wish you could see it 'cause that's exactly how I want mine. Oh, please, Mommy, will you take me to a beauty shop?"

Becca was ten years old and had begun thinking more and more about her appearance. She was growing like a weed, and just as cute as a button with her long brown hair and her sensitive blue eyes. Her complexion was fairer than Jimmy's, and she was going to be much taller, tall and willowy, Elizabeth thought. She and Jimmy were growing up much too fast to suit her. Jimmy would soon be thirteen years old; Elizabeth could hardly believe that.

She snapped out of her reverie and said to Becca, "You know what? I think getting your hair cut is an excellent idea. I'll call a beauty shop next week and make an appointment. Maybe we can get it for next Saturday; how would that be?"

"That would be great! I was afraid you'd say no 'cause --- well, I just thought you would. Now don't forget, Mommy." Becca looked at Jimmy, began laughing and said, "You can come with us and get yours cut in a D.A."

"Not me, Bec; I'm too handsome for a haircut like that, but I'll come and watch them shear you like a sheep." He patted the top of her head, and added, "They'll actually need sheep shears for all that hair." The two of them began laughing uproariously and raced to the car.

Even though Becca and Jimmy were laughing and having a good time, Elizabeth was still upset about what had happened a little while ago at their home. It had been a relief to hear Louise say that she was okay, but Elizabeth was in a hurry to get home and make sure. She just didn't trust Edward Johnson; he might have come back and tried something else. *Would she, for the rest of her life, have to worry about what Edward Johnson might or might not do,* Elizabeth thought as she hurried home.

Louise met them at the door to let them know that she was just fine, no worse off as a result of Edward's unwelcome appearance. She and Elizabeth talked for a while about what had happened, both wondering if Edward might try the same thing again.

Even though Louise didn't have a gun, Elizabeth did have one that she kept hidden. No one else knew the hiding place; she certainly didn't want Becca and Jimmy knowing. But she told Louise so that she would have access to it if ever again there was trouble with Edward or with anyone. Louise agreed with Elizabeth that the doors should be kept locked at all times. They had never before thought of doing such a thing, but there had never before been a reason to.

Thankfully, nothing more was heard from Edward, allowing them to relax a little, no longer feeling nervous and on-edge. Of course, the divorce had become final some time ago but provided no assurance that they had seen the last of Edward Johnson. He would be able to see the children if he wanted, and if *they* wanted. She had been awarded the house and child support for Becca and Jimmy until they reached the age of eighteen. She hadn't asked for alimony, but did receive a substantial settlement which she was saving for the children's college education.

Chapter Thirty-Nine

In February of 1958 Jimmy became a teen-ager, thirteen years old. His birthday fell on a Sunday and the family went to church with Louise. When Elizabeth had asked what he wanted to do for the day, that was it: "Go to Miss Lou's church and then maybe to the carnival" that was in Gillette. The carnival had been there all week, and Sunday was the last day.

Elizabeth thoroughly enjoyed the church service, and she especially enjoyed the singing. Jimmy was right about how great the piano player was, and the enthusiasm and fervor of the congregation as they sung was something to behold. If ever the Holy Spirit was present at a church service, it was there.

The pastor, Reverend Ross, and the piano player, Mrs. Williams, remembered Becca and Jimmy and greeted them with big smiles. Then Louise introduced them to Elizabeth. They chatted for a few minutes, Elizabeth telling them how much she'd enjoyed the service, the singing and piano playing. Jimmy gave Mrs. Williams a hug, and of course Becca did the same. As they all left the church, the pastor told them to come again, that they were welcome any time.

Before heading to the carnival, they went to a drive-in and had lunch. There was a big crowd at the carnival, and they were excited and eager to go on the rides and stuff themselves with cotton candy, corn dogs and lemonade. One of them might even win a prize playing some of the games. Louise seemed as thrilled to be there as Becca and Jimmy. It was fun for Elizabeth, too, but her greatest enjoyment came from seeing Becca and Jimmy have so much fun.

Late in the afternoon as they arrived at their house, Jimmy almost jumped out of his skin, and out of the car, too, even before it stopped. He saw a brand new bicycle on the front porch with several bright-colored bows placed on it. He started toward the bicycle, then turned back to Elizabeth, hugged her and said, "Mommy, thank you, thank you. That's the best birthday present you could ever get me."

He ran to the porch and first read the birthday cards: one from his mother, and one from Becca, Louise, and Mary Ann. His pleasure, his joy was indescribable. He was almost at a loss for words, at last managing to say, "Wow-wee, I got my bicycle, I got my bicycle."

He took it off the porch and began riding, at first a little wobbly, but soon picking up speed and in complete control. He'd only been on a bicycle a few times, at a birthday party he went to. One of the bigger boys had helped him keep his balance as he rode for a little while, finally being able to ride all by himself. That was Jimmy; everything seemed to be so easy for him.

The new bicycle was exactly the same as the one he'd seen in the Sears and Roebuck catalog. Elizabeth had stored the bicycle at Mary Ann's the week before, and had asked her to put it on the porch while they were gone to the carnival.

There were other presents waiting for Jimmy when he went inside: The complete set of C.S. Lewis' *Chronicles of Narnia* from Mimi; Becca gave him a forty-five of Elvis Presley's *All Shook Up;* and from Louise, a forty-five of *Purple People Eater* by Sheb Wooley and *Wake Up Little Susie* by the Everly Brothers.

Jimmy appeared to be almost as happy as on his fifth birthday when he got the piano. He didn't know which record to play first, and began *eenie, meenie, miney, moe,* trying to decide.

Louise and Elizabeth were laughing as they left Jimmy and Becca to play the records or whatever. They busily went about doing other things: Louise fixing sandwiches and Elizabeth changing her clothes, thinking about how wonderful the day had been. She was just a tiny bit sad, though, as she thought of her kids growing up, and then chided herself for that.

Summertime came and Elizabeth took a couple weeks of vacation during the month of June. She and the children went on some short road trips. They would pack a lunch, go to some scenic lake or river and fish for a while. Sometimes they just drove around, here and there, maybe to a town not far away, some place they hadn't been to before.

They also went to a drive-in movie a couple of times, saw *I Was A Teenage Frankenstein*, and another time it was *The Incredible Shrinking Man*.

In September, Becca began sixth grade and Jimmy the ninth. That would be his last year of Junior High, and he was already thinking about what high school would be like. He loved school and had lots of friends.

It was about the middle of the school year when a new girl who had just moved to Gillette enrolled in some of Jimmy's classes. Her name was Nell, and it was *love at first sight*. That was no joke; Jimmy really, really liked her and she liked him. He talked about her all the time, and one day Becca got a little huffy and said to him, "That's enough about Nell, okay? We're all tired of hearing you gush over her. You and your silly crushes! She's just a girl, and you know a lot of girls."

"But none of them are like Nell," Jimmy said, laughing and hugging Becca. Then he added, "She's almost as pretty and as nice as you, Bec, but not quite."

There wasn't much Becca could say about that, just made a funny face and a sarcastic "Ha, ha," as she walked away. She could never stay upset with Jimmy.

Late one night, after Elizabeth and everyone else in the house were sound asleep, the telephone rang. Of course, that really scared Elizabeth; she jumped out of bed and ran in the living room to answer it. It was Edward and he was so drunk that she could barely understand him. He was slurring his words and sounded as if he might be crying.

Elizabeth said, "What's wrong, Edward? This better be good …. you woke up the whole house."

"Elizabeth, I'd like to see Jimmy and Becca," Edward said. "I just want to see them for a few minutes. Can I come over for a little while?"

"For goodness sakes, Edward, it's two o'clock in the morning! Becca and Jimmy need to sleep. You know good and well that I won't allow you to come here at this time of the night. If you want to see them, call another day and we'll arrange something. Now, I have to hang up, Edward. I just hope that I'll be able to fall asleep again. Goodbye."

As Elizabeth headed back to bed, the telephone rang again. It was Edward, and his words didn't seem as slurred now. He said, "Don't you ever hang up on me like that again, and I mean it." Then he started cursing and saying hateful things; he called her a slut. And before she could say anything, he hung up the telephone.

Elizabeth was furious, thinking that if only she could get her hands on him at that moment, she would clobber Edward Johnson. She slowly walked back to her bedroom, thinking again just how spiteful and vindictive he really was. It had been almost a year since they'd heard a word from him, and now he had the nerve to pull this stupid trick. Fortunately, she was able to go back to sleep pretty quickly.

♫ Chapter Forty

It was the week after Thanksgiving when Edward called again. He sounded sober, and made no mention of his middle-of-the-night call. He acted almost human as he asked when he could pick up the kids and take them to lunch; they agreed on a Saturday.

Elizabeth had asked Becca and Jimmy after Edward's last call if they wanted to see him, and they agreed that they would if he called again.

So, on the following Saturday, Becca and Jimmy sat out on the front porch waiting for their daddy. He said he'd be there at about eleven thirty or twelve o'clock. Twelve o'clock came and went, and no sign of Edward. At one o'clock, Elizabeth told them to change their clothes and go on out and play, that their daddy apparently wasn't going to show up. They didn't seem at all disappointed, more like relieved.

Soon it was Christmas again, and as was the custom, Elizabeth and the children spent it with her parents. Amy was now married to a partner in the law firm where she had worked for several years. His name was Carl Downey, a real nice man. He knew cute little jokes and riddles that he would tell Jimmy and Becca. And he played Go Fish and Old Maid with them.

John wasn't able to get home for Christmas; he and two of his long-time friends had saved their money for a year and were now traveling throughout Europe. If their money held out, they would be gone for three months. Of course Annette and Troy worried about him, but he was a grown man and could do whatever he chose. He sent them a post card now and then from different cities.

Tommy had been attending college and was at home for the holidays, the first time that Elizabeth, Becca and Jimmy had seen him in a while. He hadn't been able to get home at Thanksgiving, and was happy to make it there for Christmas. He was pretty sure that he would graduate in two more years.

The New Year began differently for Elizabeth than in years past, a nice change. She had a date to go to a New Year's Eve party. One of Dr. Parker's patients had asked her out. She'd been to lunch with him a couple of times, but never on a real date, so she was very excited. After she was all dressed up and ready to leave, Jimmy hugged her and said, "Mommy, you are so beautiful, and I love you. I hope you have the best time ever."

Elizabeth almost cried, but managed not to; she didn't want to mess up her makeup. She just said, "Thank you, Jimmy; that is such a nice thing for you to say. I love you, too, so very much, and I'm so glad you're my son."

He and Becca were staying at home with Louise. Elizabeth told them that they could stay up until midnight. And better yet, for Jimmy at least, she told him that he could call his girlfriend, Nell, and talk for a little while. The call was to be made long before midnight, though.

New Year's Day, 1959, was especially nice. Louise prepared a meal that is a tradition in the south: ham, black-eyed peas, collard greens and corn bread. Not only was it delicious, it was supposed to bring good luck for the year.

In the afternoon, the family played games. Jimmy's favorite game these days was Scrabble, and he was a good player. Becca wasn't too bad herself.

After the holidays, it was back to work and to school. Time was just flying by; in February, Jimmy turned fourteen years old. He was in high school now and was feeling very grown up. Becca would be twelve in May. When Elizabeth thought of her own age, thirty-one, it was hard to believe. She had been married almost half of her life. Even though it was still hard to accept the fact that her children would be adults in a few years, she knew that it was inevitable, and began to think of someday becoming a grandmother. She smiled to herself at the thought.

One day during the first week of April, Elizabeth noticed a red, sore-looking spot on Jimmy's cheek. It looked as if a bit of blood had crusted over. At first she thought it was a pimple he'd picked at, but decided that maybe he'd cut himself trying to shave.

He'd asked for a razor on his fourteenth birthday, and she'd bought one for him. He didn't really need it, had just a little fuzz on his face. But he was feeling mature, like an adult, and wanted to shave. When Elizabeth asked him about his face, he just shrugged and said, "It's nothing, Mommy, just a little cut."

A couple of days later, that "little cut" was looking much worse. The redness seemed to be spreading and his entire cheek felt warm. Jimmy insisted that it would be fine, that it looked worse than it actually was.

At work the following day, Elizabeth told Dr. Parker about the cut on Jimmy's face and asked if there was a topical medication to help in healing. He wrote a prescription for some kind of ointment, saying that should help. He also told her to watch the wound carefully for any signs of infection.

That afternoon, after Jimmy and Becca got home from school, Louise called Elizabeth at work. There was anxiety and concern in her voice. "Mrs. Johnson, maybe you should come home and take Jimmy to see a doctor. He has a fever and doesn't feel good, is kind of sick to his stomach. His face is also a little swollen."

"I'll be right there, Louise. It shouldn't take me more than thirty minutes. On second thought, it would be better for you to drive him to the hospital Emergency Room and I'll meet you there," Elizabeth said.

"That's what I'll do, then. I'll get him and Becca into the car and drive straight to the hospital. We'll leave right away."

Hearing that one of her children was sick put Elizabeth in a real panic, filled her with fear. She grabbed her coat and purse and headed for the door. Dr. Parker and his nurse Karen were with a patient, so she just told Wanda, the office manager, that she had to leave because her son was sick.

When Elizabeth arrived at the Emergency Room, there was no sign of Louise and the children. She asked about them, but they hadn't yet arrived. It was about five more minutes when she saw Louise, Becca and Jimmy coming through the door. She ran to Jimmy and could see that he was sick. He said his stomach hurt and that he was cold. When she felt his forehead, it was clear that he had a fever, and his heart was racing.

It wasn't long before a nurse took Jimmy into a little cubicle. Elizabeth followed, leaving Louise and Becca sitting in the waiting area. When the doctor saw Jimmy, he began asking questions: how did he cut himself, and when was that, was there a sudden onset of the fever and chills, had he been sick to his stomach, and on and on. Elizabeth was getting impatient; she wanted the doctor to do something.

Jimmy told the doctor that he had cut a pimple on his face when he was shaving, and that it had been a few days ago; he didn't remember exactly what day. And Elizabeth explained that it had been two days ago when she noticed the redness and irritated looking spot on his cheek.

The doctor took Jimmy's blood pressure and his pulse, took his temperature and listened to his heart. Then his demeanor seemed to change. Even though he tried to appear calm as he gave instructions to the nurse, clearly he was alarmed. He talked rapidly and Elizabeth didn't understand all the terminology, but caught a bit of it: something about blood cultures, intravenous antibiotics, need to stabilize his blood pressure, etcetera. Then he left, saying he'd be back shortly.

Now, Elizabeth was really frightened. She followed the attendant as he wheeled the gurney into a room. She was asked to stand back while they drew blood, but first she leaned down, hugged Jimmy and told him that she loved him and would stay right there with him.

Jimmy seemed a little disoriented, with his eyes flickering. His breathing was not normal, appeared much too fast and in short little spurts. He managed to say, "Oh, Mommy, I feel so sick."

"I know, sweetheart, but the doctor is going to help you. I'll be right here, okay? I love you so much, Jimmy." He tried to smile at his mother, but it wasn't his trademark smile, that big, sweet smile that lit up his entire face.

Elizabeth was crying as the doctor came back into the room. He took her arm and led her out into the hallway and said, "Mrs. Johnson, I believe that Jimmy has septicemia or what sometimes is called blood poisoning. If that's the case, it means that bacteria have gotten into Jimmy's bloodstream, and I'll be honest with you, Mrs. Johnson, that could be very dangerous. If there are bacteria, they will multiply rapidly and can be fatal. We'll perform some lab tests that will help us with a definitive diagnosis, and in the meantime, we're going to start him on intravenous antibiotics. That, hopefully, will stop the progression of any bacteria in the bloodstream."

Before the doctor could say anything more, Elizabeth began sobbing, trying to speak between sobs, "Oh, dear God, if only I'd gotten him to a doctor sooner. Why didn't I realize that the cut was infected? Oh, my poor Jimmy, just trying to shave like a little man, and cuts a pimple on his face. Now you tell me that he could die. Oh, doctor, please save my boy, please don't let him die. Dear Lord in Heaven, this is all my fault."

Elizabeth was practically hysterical at that point, and she suddenly went limp; the doctor caught her before she fell to the floor. He spoke to her softly, trying his best to calm her, "I can assure you, Mrs. Johnson, that we'll do everything in our power to save your son. And you shouldn't blame yourself. This is something that can happen very quickly, and it's no one's fault. Now, I'm going to have a nurse give you something to help you relax a little. When you're feeling better, we'll take you back into Jimmy's room. But you need to be strong and brave; I know it's hard, but you can't let Jimmy see you like this." Then he called for a nurse to help Elizabeth, and he went back into Jimmy's room.

The nurse gave Elizabeth a pill, and had her lie down on a bed in an unoccupied room. She asked if she could call anyone for her. Elizabeth gave her the telephone number of her parents. She also told the nurse that her daughter, Becca, and their housekeeper, Louise, were in the Waiting Room and should be told what was happening.

A little later Elizabeth woke with a start, realizing that she'd fallen asleep. She thought that pill the nurse gave her must have been very strong. She looked at her watch and felt sure that it had only been about an hour since she'd left Jimmy. She got up and walked hurriedly to his room. From the doorway, she saw a nurse there doing something at the side of Jimmy's bed. There were needles attached to his arms, as well as a blood pressure cuff. There were bottles of fluid dripping above him, and his eyes were closed. Elizabeth almost broke down, but managed to quietly ask the nurse, "Is he asleep now? Do you think he's going to be okay?" Tears rolled down her cheeks, and the nurse put her arms around her and held her for a minute.

"Mrs. Johnson, we just don't know much right now. Jimmy's asleep and there's nothing you can do here. Why don't you go back and try to rest? We'll come and get you if there's any change," the nurse told her.

"No, no, I don't want to rest. I want to stay here with Jimmy. I'll just sit here at the side of his bed."

The nurse told her to go ahead for now. Then she left the room and told Elizabeth that she'd be back shortly.

As she sat there, Elizabeth cried quietly and prayed unceasingly. Nurses were in and out. She had no idea how long she'd been there when her parents walked into the room. Elizabeth ran to them, motioned that they should go with her outside the room. Then she fell into her mother's arms, sobbing. Annette held her closely and said, "Oh, sweetie, it's gonna be all right, it's gonna be all right. Can you tell us what happened? The nurse who called just said Jimmy was very sick and that you'd asked her to call us. Troy and I came as fast as we could." She stood there holding Elizabeth in her arms, trying to give support to her daughter and not break down herself.

Finally, Elizabeth's crying let up a little, and she said, "They think that Jimmy has blood poisoning. The doctor said that's when bacteria gets into the blood, and that Jimmy could die from it. A few days ago he cut a pimple on his face while he was trying to shave. Bless his heart, he doesn't even have enough hair on his face to shave. I shouldn't have given him that razor. Oh, if only I hadn't given him that razor!" At that point, Elizabeth began weeping uncontrollably.

Now, as Annette tried to console Elizabeth, she couldn't hold back her own tears. Elizabeth's daddy had his arms around both of them, barely able to keep from going to pieces himself. He kept saying, over and over, "Jimbo's gonna be fine, he'll pull through. We need to keep praying, we just need to keep praying." The three of them seemed to be in a kind of daze, in disbelief at what was happening.

Eventually they went back into Jimmy's room. A couple of hours passed and one of the two doctors who had been working with Jimmy --- Elizabeth couldn't remember either of their names --- came into the room to check on him.

The family had been allowed to stay in Jimmy's room since there was no danger that the blood poisoning could be transmitted to anyone else. But one of the doctors had asked them not to touch Jimmy, and of course Elizabeth had protested. However, she became a bit more conciliatory when the doctor explained that there was a slight chance that something, even the cold virus, might be transmitted to Jimmy if they were up close, breathing on him. And of course they weren't about to take that risk. The staff wore masks and rubber gloves.

Now the doctor was back, examining Jimmy again, checking the chart where the nurse had been writing down his blood pressure, temperature and anything that changed. He asked Elizabeth to step out in the hall with him.

Clearly, the doctor was distressed and didn't like having to give the parent of a child bad news. He led Elizabeth to some chairs along the wall, and asked her to sit down for a minute. He began speaking softly, "Mrs. Johnson, there's little doubt that Jimmy has blood poisoning even though we don't yet have all of the lab results. I'm afraid his condition is worsening. I'm just so sorry to have to tell you this, but Dr. Townsend and your own family doctor, Dr. Jones, agree that Jimmy may be going into septic shock. His blood pressure continues to drop despite our efforts to try and stabilize it, and as you've seen, we now have him on a ventilator to help him breathe. He's lost consciousness, and his organs are starting to fail. I'm so sorry, but things look pretty bad right now."

Elizabeth was sobbing so uncontrollably that she seemed to have trouble breathing. She couldn't even speak, and the doctor leaned over and pulled her toward him. He just held her, saying soothing words that had little effect. He got the attention of a nurse and told her a kind of medicine that she should bring for Elizabeth. The nurse returned shortly with a hypodermic syringe. Elizabeth made no effort to resist as the doctor led her to the unoccupied room and gave her the injection.

He was still talking to her soothingly, and said the shot would help her. He told her he knew that nothing would alleviate the pain she was experiencing, that not even he, as a doctor, could understand and fully appreciate what she was going through. But he said that the medicine would help her body to relax a little and she needed that.

Elizabeth's daddy had walked down to the Waiting Room and brought Louise and Becca up to Jimmy's room. But Becca was crying so hard that Louise had to take her out again after just a couple of minutes. She had wanted to go to Jimmy, hug him and talk to him, but the nurse wouldn't allow it. That made her cry twice as hard. And tears were rolling down Louise's cheeks as she walked out with Becca. Annette went with them and tried her best to console Becca, her arms around her, rocking her back and forth, quietly talking to her. As they sat in chairs outside Jimmy's room,

Becca finally fell asleep. Louise walked around for a bit, trying to stretch her legs before she made the sad and lonely drive home.

The shot had knocked Elizabeth out. She was in the empty room the nurses had designated for the family. When Becca woke up, she and Annette went in to see about her and found that she was still sound asleep.

After having heard what the doctor said earlier, Annette was resigned to the fact that Jimmy might not pull through this, and it was almost more than she could bear. She had to think of Elizabeth and Becca, though, and try to help them get through it all. She could shed her tears and fall to pieces later, at least that's what she hoped, that she could hold off for a while before completely falling apart.

She had called Mary Ann to tell her about Jimmy, and bless her heart, she came to the hospital right away. She also had telephoned Edward, and was surprised when he showed up at the hospital a couple of hours after she had talked to him. It was obvious that he'd been drinking, but seemed coherent enough. After looking in on Jimmy for a few minutes and then talking to Becca for a little while, Edward left. He asked Annette to call him if there was anything that he could do. Annette thought it was a little late for that. Where was he for all those years when Jimmy really needed his daddy?

Elizabeth had slept for a little more than two hours after the shot, then got up and went directly to Jimmy's room. She begged a nurse who was there to let her touch Jimmy, just touch him and hold his hand for a minute; the nurse couldn't refuse.

Tears fell on the sheet as Elizabeth held Jimmy's hand and softly talked to him. "Oh, my precious baby, please come back to us. I love you so much, Jimmy, and you know how Becca loves you, and so do Big Mama and Papa."

The tears kept falling as she continued, "You are my special gift from God; please, please sweetheart, don't leave us!" Suddenly she gave a mournful sound and ran out of the room, where she collapsed right onto the floor in the hallway.

A nurse and an orderly picked her up and took her to the room where the rest of her family waited. Another nurse came in and held a little open bottle of something under Elizabeth's nose for a couple of seconds, pulled it away and then back again until she began to come around. She slowly opened her eyes, and the nurse told her that she was going to be fine. After a few minutes, she told Elizabeth that she needed something more to help her relax. She gave her a tiny pill and held a cup of water to her mouth. After so much medicine, surely she would sleep! Annette went to the bed and lay down beside her, whispering words no one else could hear. At last, Elizabeth stopped crying and was quiet.

Earlier, Becca had convinced Elizabeth to let her stay at the hospital. And before Louise left, they'd gone to the cafeteria, where she persuaded Becca to eat a few bites. When they returned, Becca was allowed to spend a few minutes in Jimmy's room. She stood alongside the bed and talked to him, "Jimmy, I hope you can hear me. I'm waiting for you to get all better. When you're well, we'll go fishing, and I know you can guess the first song I'll ask you to sing, the one I always do: *Skinnie Minnie Fish Tail*. You can't get through the whole thing before we burst out laughing. I think that's the silliest, funniest song that you know.

"I want us to sit out on the doorsteps, too, and look at the starry sky while you sing *Catch A Falling Star*. We almost always see a falling star, don't we, Jimmy? You can tell me more about those stars and planets. We'll get our jars from under the porch and catch some lightning bugs. Please, Jimmy, you have to get well. I love you! I'm gonna go now, but I'll be back to see you in the morning. I don't know if I ever told you that you're the best big brother in the whole wide world, but I'm telling you now, so don't you forget, okay? And don't you dare go anywhere, Jimmy, you hear?"

Becca hurried out of the room and into her grandmother's arms; Annette had been standing outside the doorway. She kissed Becca's cheek, and whispered, "Be brave, sweetheart, we have to try and be brave. And let's see if we can get some sleep now." She took Becca's hand in hers and they walked away.

Elizabeth woke up again in the middle of the night and went back to Jimmy's room. The ventilator was still going, and the IV tube was still in his arm. *Thank God, my baby's still alive. Maybe the doctors are wrong, maybe he'll pull through,* Elizabeth thought. Then she silently prayed, *Dear God, please don't take my boy; let him live. We need him here with us. He's so special, Lord, don't take him yet, please!*

After about an hour, she went back to the room where her parents, Mary Ann and Becca were sleeping. She lay down on the bed, but didn't cry. She just lay there for the rest of the night staring at the ceiling.

The next morning, Dr. Jones knocked on the door before entering. The whole family was awake, just sitting there in a daze. But Elizabeth knew the minute she saw Dr. Jones' face that Jimmy was gone. She began screaming, "No, no, oh, Dear God, no!"

The only words from Dr. Jones' mouth were, "I'm so sorry, so very, very sorry."

Elizabeth began running as fast as she could, straight to Jimmy's room, Becca right behind her. Jimmy was still lying there; the nurse was removing the tubes and bottles. Elizabeth lifted Jimmy's shoulders, hugging him, kissing him, mumbling something that wasn't audible to the nurse. Becca was hugging him too, weeping tears of such anguish that the nurse began crying, as well.

Suddenly, Elizabeth fell over on the bed, grabbing her stomach and crying out in pain, physical pain. The nurse gradually was able to determine from Elizabeth that she was having terrible pains in her stomach and side.

Becca appeared oblivious to her mother's state, and continued holding on to Jimmy, crying and talking to him.

The nurse told Elizabeth just to lie there on the bed, that she was going for a doctor and would be right back. Elizabeth was in excruciating pain, and wished that she would just pass out. Then she wouldn't have to deal with anything that was happening.

In a couple of minutes, a doctor appeared. He felt Elizabeth's forehead, took his stethoscope and listened to her heart. Then he pressed along her stomach and side. At one point, Elizabeth cried out in pain, saying, "Right there, that's where it hurts so badly."

"Mrs. Johnson, we're going to take care of you; just try to relax," the doctor said. "First, we need to get you to a room and do some lab tests. I can tell you now, though, that I think you have appendicitis. If it is your appendix, then we'll have to operate before they rupture; we don't want that to happen. I realize that you're in distress, grieving over your son's death, but this appears to be a medical emergency that we can't ignore."

"Oh, please, doctor, just give me something for the pain." Elizabeth was hysterical, her voice a piercing, frantic cry, "My son has just died, don't you understand that? I can't stay in here and have an operation. Please, I'm begging you, just give me something for pain and you can remove my appendix later."

"Mrs. Johnson, I'm so sorry about your son, and it's regrettable that this had to happen to you now, but if your appendix is inflamed it could be very dangerous to wait. That is a risk we shouldn't take. Now, unless you want to get a lot sicker, then you'll do as I'm suggesting. Are you willing to do that?"

For a minute Elizabeth was thinking that, if not for Becca she would want to die, too, then she'd be with Jimmy. At last, though, she told the doctor she guessed she had no choice but to do as he asked. The physical pain, combined with her agony over Jimmy's death, was almost unbearable.

An orderly came with a gurney and took Elizabeth away. Then, as the nurse was gently trying to pull Becca away from Jimmy, Annette walked into the room. She got the nurse's attention and after a tiny shake of her head, the nurse stepped back from the bed.

Becca was lying there beside Jimmy, her arms wrapped around him, murmuring and humming tunes. Annette couldn't hold back the tears as she said, "Come on, sweetie, we have to leave Jimmy here. Come on now, we have to go, okay?" The tears wouldn't stop, but she continued talking softly to Becca. "The doctors and nurses will be gentle; they'll take good care of him. Oh, sweetheart, try to accept that Jimmy will be fine -- he's in Heaven now."

At last, Becca raised up from the bed, appearing confused, her eyes red and irritated, the bed sheet wet with her tears. For a few seconds she just stood there, then bent down, kissed Jimmy's forehead and with heart-wrenching grief and anguish, said, "Bye, Jimmy, I love you so much and I miss you already."

She and Annette slowly walked toward the door. Abruptly, Becca stopped and looked back at Jimmy for a moment. Then she gave a little wave and continued walking to the door with her grandmother, both weeping, their hearts breaking.

It was a comfort, though, to know that someone, somewhere, was smiling and welcoming little Jimmy Johnson.

❀ ❀ ❀ ❀ ❀

♫ *Chapter Forty-One*

It was a story without a *happily ever after* ending, thought Becca; a reminder, though, of all the good times and the memories that she would cling to forever. Suddenly she was aware that her tears were gone, that she was no longer crying. She had shed at least a gallon, maybe more.

Becca looked at her grandmother and said, "I hope you're right, Big Mama, that it will get easier one of these days. Oh, how I hope it'll get easier!" She got up from the featherbed, adding, "Maybe we can go fix supper now; I bet Papa's getting hungry. It's likely he fell asleep watching television. He says he doesn't give a flip about that television set, but I think that's just talk, don't you?"

Annette chuckled and said, "I think you're right, Becca. He's just not ready to admit that he likes it. He probably is asleep now, just tired and worn out like the rest of us. We should get to bed early tonight. Maybe you can go riding tomorrow. Ol' Shorty will be glad to see you; that horse has missed you. We'll visit your mama, too. Just think, she'll be home in two days. Come on, sweetie, let's go wake up your Papa."

"Okay," said Becca. She was quiet for a minute, then, "Mommy will be coming home without her appendix. Jimmy told me one time that some scientists say our appendix has no particular function, and wondered why it was there. Then he gave me that amused look and said, 'you know what, Bec, they may not be essential now, but they must have been at one time or another, and tonsils, too. It makes sense that sometime during the evolutionary process they served a real purpose, and then were just left there'."

Becca smiled, the first time she'd done that in days, took her grandmother's hand, squeezed it, and said, "I'll always miss Jimmy, Big Mama. I know that he misses us, too. But I bet there's a twinkle in his eye and that special smile on his face as he plays his brand-new Baby Grand piano; he's playing it just for us."

✿ ✿ ✿ ✿ ✿

Elizabeth still works in Dr. Parker's office. She recovered just fine from the appendectomy, but she doesn't think she'll ever recover from Jimmy's death. At long last, though, she's begun to realize that life must go on. About eight months after Jimmy passed away she began dating Randall Evans. He works as an engineer at the Gillette Paper Mill. Elizabeth cares a great deal for Randall, but is not yet ready to seriously consider his marriage proposal. Becca likes Randall a lot, says Jimmy would like him, too.

Becca misses her brother so much. But she's anxious for high school, and after graduation wants to attend nursing school. She has a boyfriend, Paul, but she isn't yet old enough to date, so Elizabeth drives them to a picture show once in a while and picks them up afterward.

Edward was stabbed to death in a bar fight two weeks after Jimmy's death. None of the witnesses would come forward to say who did it, so it remains an unsolved murder in the town of Gillette. Becca, as Edward's only living relative, inherits the farm and all assets from Edward, who had inherited everything when his daddy died. Elizabeth and Becca have discussed the possibility of selling the farm.

Louise still works for Elizabeth. But she's more like a family member than an employee. Every Sunday afternoon she goes with Elizabeth and Becca to visit Jimmy. They usually take him a big bouquet of flowers.

Elizabeth's mother and daddy, Troy and Annette Bolin, still live on their little farm a few miles from Garden City, and seem to be quite content. They visit Jimmy at the cemetery as often as they can.

Amy, Elizabeth's younger sister, no longer works at the law firm. She and her husband, Carl, now have a baby daughter.

John, the older brother, is studying to become a Baptist minister. He finally married the girl he's dated since his early days in college.

Tommy, the younger brother, graduated from college and has started a rock n' roll band. He's pretty good on the guitar, but can't sing worth a darn. He carved a tiny wooden piano for Jimmy; it's the cutest thing, a little black and white piano in front of the headstone, anchored so it won't blow away.

Mary Ann has become a wealthy woman. Never in her wildest dreams did she think that one day her paintings would be selling like hot cakes. She's planning an extended trip to Ireland. Her maternal grandparents came from there.

Elizabeth's Aunt Naomi, Annette's older sister, finally moved to Garden City to be near Annette and her family. Elizabeth and Becca visit her often. They cherish the memory of that day long ago when she gave the piano to an angel named Jimmy.

CPSIA information can be obtained
at www.ICGtesting.com
Printed in the USA
FSOW02n0158100815
9768FS